CW01653950

## PRAISE FOR *THE VISIT*

'*The Visit* is an engrossing and tender portrait of a small town under pressure . . . Stark and elemental – at the heart of the novel is a sort of quiet yearning and a longing for love and for completion that makes Neil Tully's novel so brilliant and intriguing' – Colm Tóibín

'Compassionate but clear-eyed, brimming with insight and emotional intelligence, this is a novel whose characters will linger with you long after you've closed the pages' – Colin Walsh, author of *Kala*

'What a delight it is to read such a wonderful story, written so beautifully. Spare, authentic, effortlessly lyrical, it is a stunning novel, the work of a writer of the first order' – Donal Ryan

'Once in a while, you read a novel so accomplished that you want to read the author's backlist but, to your surprise, it turns out to be a début. That's how good Neil Tully's *The Visit* is. Combining great storytelling with lyrical writing, this deserves to be on everyone's must-read list for 2026' – John Boyne

'An exquisite and powerful debut novel from a compelling new voice in Irish fiction' – Joseph O'Connor

'An utterly absorbing and hugely readable novel, *The Visit* is a story that captures a transitional time in Irish history so incredibly well, that at times I felt I was watching it up close. Jim Field is a compelling protagonist, flawed, human and meticulously drawn. I was gripped from the start. The writing is so good' – Elaine Feeney, author *of How to Build a Boat*

'A strong debut that showcases both the viciousness and salvation of community' – Sheila Armstrong, author of *Falling Animals*

'Intrigue boils beneath the rural calm of this elegant novel; Neil Tully masterfully pulls the reader into a world where menace and the humdrum co-mingle uneasily. The prose is intelligent, gorgeous and empathic; the atmosphere subtly unsettling. *The Visit* is an accomplished, fully formed debut'
– Nuala O'Connor, author of *Seaborne* and *NORA*

'*The Visit* makes an incision into 1960s New Ross as Ireland readies to welcome President Kennedy, and defiant Patrick Hatten toils under the weight of his family's past – and the town's judgment. A portrait of an Ireland still rooted in tradition, yet hopeful for change, *The Visit* is an engrossing novel filled with rich prose, compassion and a tension that drives the narrative to the very last page' – Charleen Hurtubise, author of *The Polite Act of Drowning* and *Saoirse*

'Neil Tully is a deeply humane writer. There's great lyric beauty in *The Visit*, but there's real ballast here as well' – Seán Farrell, author of *Frogs For Watchdogs*

'Neil Tully's tremendous first novel has been, for me, the surprise of the summer. *The Visit* is a sheer delight, a considerable feat of the imagination, a proper story beautifully, delicately written and gripping from first page to last. Even in a country already popping at the seams with fine literature, this debut offering must be one of the year's standouts. It announces Neil as a writer of clearly considerable talent, and deserves to fly with critics and readers alike'
– Billy O'Callaghan, author of *My Coney Island Baby*

# THE VISIT

# THE VISIT

*Neil Tully*

eriu

First published in the UK in 2026 by Eriu
An imprint of Bonnier Books UK
5th Floor, HYLO, 105 Bunhill Row,
London, EC1Y 8LZ



A CIP catalogue record for this book is available from the British Library.

Hardback ISBN: 978-1-80444-199-2
Trade Paperback ISBN: 978-1-80444-200-5

*Also available as an ebook and an audiobook*

1 3 5 7 9 10 8 6 4 2

Typeset by IDSUK (Data Connection) Ltd
Printed and bound in Great Britain by CPI (UK) Ltd, Croydon CR0 4YY

FSC www.fsc.org
MIX
Paper | Supporting responsible forestry
FSC® C013604



The authorised representative in the EEA is
Bonnier Books UK (Ireland) Limited.
Registered office address: Floor 3, Block 3, Miesian Plaza,
Dublin 2, D02 Y754, Ireland
compliance@bonnierbooks.ie

www.bonnierbooks.co.uk

*For Sinéad*

*The crowd deepened. On the road and through fields, people were running. Schoolboys in white shirts and red ties, women racing barefoot through summer grass, their shoes in their hands. Young men balanced on gates and fenceposts, others fought for footing on limestone walls. Cheering rose from somewhere unseen, and tricolours and stars and stripes fluttered in the grey.*

*The first car rounded the bend and Patrick straightened on the thickest branch of the tall sycamore with a view of the road. He sighted the driver and the passengers. Guards and men in black suits. A nest of rooks squawked in the upper branches. The crowd drowned out the engine – a rope of people coiling, twisting, and knotting as they pushed to glimpse the passengers, warned back from the road by guards in freshly washed navy-blues. Patrick secured his balance against the trunk.*

*A roar came from beyond the bend, then the second car appeared. A black, open-topped sedan, flanked by motorcycles. The flags fluttered faster, the cheers soared, and every gaze landed on the tanned and shimmering figure – standing and smiling, one hand touching his tie and the other raised as if in benediction. Patrick's eyes filled. He imagined being down on the road, his father by his side, waving to this man who had stepped from television screens and newspaper pages. This man who seemed capable of slowing time. The car passed so close that he saw strands of brown hair through the rifle scope, moving in the breeze, lighter than it appeared in pictures. He watched with his breath drawn deeply, then exhaled the weight of every hurt and loss and sorrow he'd known, and a terrible immortality called to him.*

# New Ross, County Wexford

## June 1963

# 1

I heard them before they woke me. Engines that sounded like the town clearing its throat after a heavy night of fags and porter. I cursed my way from bed to the window and opened the curtain to a pair of new yellow tractors, turning from the belly of New Ross and straining against the incline of our terraced street. The glass trembled as they passed and I tried to see what sort of gobshite was taking them through town at six in the morning but couldn't make out the drivers from upstairs – only two pairs of hands gripping the steering wheels. They took a right at the top of the hill, leaving silence and a vapour trail of diesel behind.

'What in God's name is that?' Siobhán said, her eyes still closed.

'Somebody got new Masseys and wants to parade them.'

She sat up, drawing her red hair over one shoulder, her back to me. A shallow curve of sunburn marked the base of her neck, shaped by the summer dress she wore at the weekend.

The wire hangers in the wardrobe rattled when I stripped them of my uniform. 'What's the plan today?'

'I've to take Catriona to the dentist,' she said, on her way to examine her eyes in the mirror on the vanity table. She was up half the night, rubbing clove oil onto our little girl's gum. It took plenty of coaxing to get Catriona to tilt her head back so I could find the problem tooth. The first thing this world has damaged in her, with a little pink marble of infection grown up next to it. 'Will you hear anything about the Inspector exams?'

'Probably not yet.'

'I'm stuck with a sergeant a while longer.' She smiled in the mirror.

The promotion exam was tougher than expected – the same old arithmetic that used to trip me up in school catching up decades later to do the same again, while obscure clauses of the Road Traffic Act and licensing laws were like remembering my mother's name. The 27th will be the real exam anyway. Any mistakes and I might as well have turned in blank pages.

Siobhán started with her hair. There are intimacies only a married man is invited to share, and the day I tire of watching is the day I'll be fit for pasture. She brushed, plaited, and weaved the threads – her fingers working as if with delicate fabric, disguising pins and clips until it all hung perfectly – before carefully unravelling one strand so that it fell down the right side of her face. Both her mother and mine can't ever stop themselves from tucking it back behind her ear. She caught me looking and took a spare pin from between her teeth. 'I meant to ask you yesterday, are we short a few pounds this week?'

I turned to the mirror inside the wardrobe door, clocking my huge ears and my face a decade older than hers, then looked myself in the eye and lied to her. 'The car didn't sound right coming back from Cork, love, so I let John have a tinker. A couple of gaskets needed changing is all.'

She stood and started making the bed. 'Right, well you'll need to leave me some for the dentist.'

'Grand.' I put my hand in my left pocket and found it empty of more than coins, then checked the right and patted my chest.

'Did you see my handkerchief?'

She tutted and smoothed the blanket. 'Handkerchief. A rag is what it is.'

'Where is it?'

'I washed it. God knows it needed it.' She went to the wardrobe and reached to the top shelf then handed it over – its softness restored by whatever she'd done. The same small tear in the square of gauze-like netting at the centre, the edges decorated with a pattern of flowers, yellowed by the years.

'That thing is for the bin.' She brushed something from my lapels and in her eyes was the same distance I saw down in Cork at the weekend, visiting her parents for one last rest before this month's madness reaches its peak. 'I'll make breakfast. Don't wake herself on your way down, she had a bad night.'

When she was gone, I went back to the window. The sun flooded New Ross rooftops and warmed the Barrow beyond – the dark river flowing between the legs of fishermen standing in its shallow stretches, slicing the morning air with lines cast and recast. Continuing along the quay, where for the past week, men in shirt-sleeves with browned arms and faces have been building a platform for Kennedy – choosing every beam as if choosing a name for a child, measuring and nailing with such care it's as if it's Christ Himself who's going to come and stand on it.

I'll be on duty down in Dunganstown, close enough to smell his aftershave while he visits the farmyard his great-grandfather abandoned last century. The planning has me wrecked. From Mayor Minihan's men to chip van owners, headquarters and journalists, publicans and lorry drivers, ice-cream sellers and the US Secret Service. All with questions about licences and tickets and overtime and road closures and emergency routes. We're reminded by the higher ups that every shoe should shine, and that any guard with as much as an unclipped nostril hair risks embarrassing the force. It's why the tractors set me on edge – something military-like in their small and loud early morning convoy, as if they were on their way to cause trouble I could do without. Finishing up yesterday evening, it took two goes to get out of my chair, like my legs had given in to the tiredness and gone off to sleep before the rest of me. I sat on the bed and folded the handkerchief.

I wondered if Patrick Hatten cared a jot about Kennedy. The difference between the two about as great as the distance between the stars in the sky and the coffins in the earth. Maurice Kearney came to the station yesterday afternoon, a pencil tucked behind his ear like he'd come straight from his calculations to tell me that

Patrick owed three pounds and wouldn't be given as much as another grain of salt on credit until his account was settled. I paid Kearney from my own pocket, with the money Siobhán noticed missing, and reminded him to come to me if there's ever a problem. Siobhán doesn't want to hear another word about Patrick after the trouble he was involved in a couple of months back.

The lad is a bit like a stray dog. I keep an eye on him and throw him a few scraps. There are plenty of people in this town who'd just as soon drop him off in the wilderness and hope there's no scent to follow home. The problem is that Patrick could find his way out of any wilderness and they wouldn't like whatever starved thing came back. It's best to keep him where I can see him. I sorted the dole paperwork for him a few months ago, after his mother died. I'm not sure he even knew such a thing existed. I do call out to him the odd time. He let the place go to some state after burying Maura. She was a sort of ballast at least – like a prison warden, imposing some order on his days. A tidy house the day of her funeral was her legacy, like she knew in advance that she couldn't trust him to set up properly for visitors. He had knives and forks and glasses washed and dried and left on the table in case anybody came, but no food to feed them if they did. Imagine, setting a table for people and not thinking of what to put on the plates. Nobody came in any case, apart from myself, not touching the glass of murky water he put in front of me, ashamed by the feeling of unease that came over me just from sharing silence out on that lonely acre.

# 2

Patrick Hatten hung his best trousers over the washing line at the back of the house. They'd soaked in warm water and soap shavings overnight, and, in the sunshine, looked as clean as if he'd just bought them in Broderick's. They once belonged to his father. He closed his eyes and tilted his chin to the sky and imagined that he'd be proud, seeing his youngest son with work lined up at a time when work is hard found.

The high June sun baked his face, where a thick monobrow roofed narrow eyes and floored a forehead that stretched into short, dark curls. Oh, they'd swim in the Barrow and Booley Bay today, no doubt. They'd take picnics and bikes, cars, or packed buses. Women would pretend to be shy in their swimsuits, worn under loose skirts that they'd slip out of, then wade in water to their thighs, while men drank them in.

He slung a couple of shirts and pairs of socks and underpants over the line then wiped his wet hands along the back of his neck and his chest, his shirt open to his belly button. His skin had started to itch in recent weeks, any exertion or heat bringing on a bout of prickling that he could do little for only sit and scratch and wait for it to pass, watching little pieces of himself float away like dandelion seeds, as if he was slowly turning to dust.

The side of the house was a giant headstone of grey concrete mottled by lichen – the dead remembered in the flaking window-sills that his mother painted and the patchwork of slate roof that his father nailed. He crossed the neglected vegetable patch, where she had grown deformed heads of cauliflower and gnarled fingers of carrots. Where she dropped dead as surely as a magpie shot from the sky last December, so that when he found her – dirt on her hands and the morning light bringing a brightness to her eyes that he'd never seen in life – she was surrounded by loose vegetables, as if they'd rained down in fatal blows.

The radio droned through the window, competing with the buzz from the wasps' nest behind the toolshed. The gutters and windows needed a clean, the garden needed to be dug and weeded, and the sheds needed a whitewash and animals to shelter. A boundary of birch, ash and Scots pine stood to their ankles in summer grass, separating Patrick's patch of the world from the tainted land to the east – land that Peter Casey had all but swindled from his parents. To the west, the treetops of Lacken Fairy Woods, only a long puck away. The gate was rarely breached, unless Sergeant Field and his two huge ears came with some excuse to hear his business.

There was no trace of tyres or hooves that might have passed on the road during the night. His eye followed the line of electricity poles, staked endlessly across the county, their tops strung with wire, carrying the electric like some modern aqueduct. If you believed what people said, the source of a better life travelled those wires – more essential than water. All the talk in town and on the radio was of progress. Electric and indoor plumbing, cars for every home, televisions to rival radio. Lemass was said to be leading the country out of darkness and Patrick wouldn't be left behind. Some money coming in, and the land back in working order was all the progress he needed.

He went back inside and took a few coins from the top drawer of the dresser and counted what he hoped would be enough to buy some green and red wool, and a new bicycle seat in town, after stopping to visit Roche. He took his rifle from the corner in case he came across a rabbit that the old man would be glad of.

He went to the toolshed and knocked on the door but didn't open it. 'Goodbye, Cat,' he said. 'I'm off to see Roche and to get some two-ply. I'll be back later.' He took his bike from against the wall and before he pushed away, he was stilled by the sound of engines, and movement beneath his boots. Across the garden, birds scattered from branches. He walked to the tree line and looked between the trunks. Two yellow tractors were trundling down the slope of Casey's field – buckets lowered like snouts, backhoe attachments like raised tails and their riders made invisible by the glare of sunshine on their windscreens. They stopped their journey just short of his boundary wall and the drivers killed the engines as he climbed between the trees and stood on the limestone. Two men he didn't recognize climbed from the Masseys and shut the doors.

'What are ye doing here?' Patrick said, and the shorter of the men looked to him, shielding his eyes against the sun, then looked to his lanky colleague, whose wellingtons were far too big.

'Come on,' the small man said and started across the field towards Casey's, followed by the second, who looked over his shoulder every few strides.

'Hey,' Patrick shouted after them and they quickened their step, the tall man stumbling in his boots.

'What are these tractors for?'

His voice was carried beyond the men and lost in the countryside. Birds returned to the branches overhead. When he looked down, he saw that he was still holding the rifle in his left hand.

# 3

Town was as busy as every dole morning. I stood at the front door of the station and scanned the queue of men outside the Post Office across the road, waiting for Antoinette to open. Cyril Fay saluted from the middle of the line, and his son, Aidan, copied him – an apprentice in the family trade of dole collecting.

'Sergeant,' Cyril called, stepping from the queue, leaving Aidan to hold his place. He wore an overcoat and a homburg, despite the warm weather. I went to him and he stood with one dirty boot raised on the footpath and the other on the road, his thumbs hooked into his belt loops. He smelled of arnica oil and looked a rough decade older than his fifty-something years.

'Cyril, how's things?'

'Ah grand, Jim, grand.' Cyril looked up and down the road, for a sign of Antoinette and her head of tight blonde curls. 'I'd say you're hectic busy with Kennedy coming?'

'We're kept going, no doubt.' I eyed the other men, clad in shirts and knitted vests, hand-me-downs and patch-ups, standing with arms folded or hands pocketed, confessing the guilt of their unemployment to the town. If any were speculating about the new tractors, they were doing it too quietly for me to hear. 'Have you seen Patrick Hatten lately?'

Cyril tapped his teeth together and took off his hat, as if the sunshine might clear the fog of thoughts he was peering through. 'Hatten,' he said, doubtful. 'I haven't, the craythur. Has he been causing bother?'

'No, nothing like that.' I lowered my voice. 'Hasn't had his dole card signed is all.'

He glanced over his shoulder, then leaned a crusted ear towards me, inviting my confidence. 'Any inside news about the visit?'

I shook my head, tired of the question. 'The dole is Wednesday instead of Thursday that week, Cyril, don't forget. One time only.'

He laughed. 'It's one time only, that's for sure.'

'I better get in.' I patted his shoulder and the queue behind him stirred at the sound of a deadbolt opening.

He lifted his hat in a parting gesture, then rejoined Aidan while I searched the troop of men a final time. Every third mouth blew a plume of Woodbine or Player's smoke at the line of bicycles against the low wall across from them. A handful of children who'd come with their fathers were loose in the road, chasing and laughing with the lightness of those too young to understand their parents' struggle.

I'm hoping Patrick won't need the dole much longer. I talked Tom McCrann into putting up a job advertisement that I knew he'd see in the tackle shop. I promised Tom that if he took him on for the summer, I'd turn a blind eye to the dirty books, brought in by the case load with deliveries of angling equipment from Northumberland. Tom, with his tie and collar and *yessir* and *nossir* out front, and a hidden library of books in the back room that would have the censors building a bonfire. I told him to give Patrick the impression that he'd earned the job on merit. The sooner he starts, the better.

Colfer called *good morning* from the shade of the day room as I headed to my office. Flood was already on the beat. We've a quiet district. The odd stolen bike or animal, disputes over licences for pubs, cars, and dogs, Friday and Saturday night scuffles as a rule. More and more driving offences lately, and very rarely, the stuff no guard wants to see. Colfer's fresh out of the training college and wears the uniform like a boy playing dress up, his collar studs and tunic buttons shining as if dipped in chrome, always immaculately groomed. Flood has taken to him like a dog sharing a kennel with a new pup, barking orders and marking his scent with cigarettes while Colfer sits next to an open window, leaning his head towards it every time Flood lights up.

I dry-necked a couple of Disprin and hung my tunic over the back of my chair, then skimmed the post, knowing from the envelopes that none of them were the exam results and wondering if they were being held back until Kennedy had left. There was another stack of paperwork down from the depot. Postings for the big day, instructions on how to do everything but buckle our belts, all needing to be signed off as shared and understood. I spent the morning trawling through it, struggling in the humid air and glancing up at the sound of footsteps outside, to see if it was Patrick coming to have his card signed, my eye catching the framed words on the far wall each time. Kennedy's speech from Texas. I remember listening to it replayed on the radio, sitting forward when he said '*We choose to go to the moon.*' I recite parts of it sometimes – while thinking out a problem at work, or while shaving, or driving. Nights I'm struggling to sleep, I try to say it start to finish in my head. Siobhán had it printed and framed for me at Christmas. She looked at me from the picture on my desk and I leaned back, turning my wedding band around its finger, thinking of the lie I told her about the money, and the secrets I keep – wondering what she keeps from me.

We were walking her parents' farm at the weekend, far down the fields where she grew up. Being alone for the first time in a long time, we ended up lying down together, acting like teenagers at the edge of a small wood until we were disturbed by the footsteps of a herd of deer – not one bit spooked by us. The moment was lost and we sat up, her hand in mine. She looked back across the fields in the direction of the house as if she was looking as far back as her childhood and she asked me if I thought we were born a decade too early.

'How do you mean?' I asked, and she looked away and laughed and said she didn't know what she meant, then put her head on my shoulder until we decided we'd better head back.

By the time the midday bell sounded on St Michael's, the office had shrunk a few feet and even with the door open, felt hotter than a forge. I tugged at my collar and got to my door in time to see Flood pounding a path from the front door to the jacks. Colfer was pouring two cups of tea on the far side of the day room.

'Hatten's after missing his dole again.'

He looked at me and lost a mouthful from the cup in his left hand as he crossed the room, before giving it to me and shaking his head. He licked the spill from his hand.

'Maybe he's working someplace? Or gone off on the boat? He wouldn't be the first to head away without telling anyone.'

I shook my head. 'He'll never leave that house.'

Colfer drank. 'I can cycle out if you want? See if he's around.'

'No, you're grand. I'll spin out myself at some stage. You got your posting for the 27th?'

'I did. K-Day – that's what people are calling it now. It's your fortieth that day too, isn't it?'

'Jesus, don't remind me.'

Colfer put his cup on his desk. 'Crowd duty in town for myself, as expected. I won't be getting as close as you.'

The toilet flushed next door. Flood came in smelling of soap, his face and neck reddened by the morning sun and wearing a sheen of water from the tap, a wet patch darkening the rim of his collar.

'Did I hear talk of the Mad Hatter?' he said.

'He's missing again,' Colfer said.

'Thank Christ. We'll be seeing even less of the little gurrier when Peter Casey turfs him out.'

Flood's lips tightened as if they'd been run through a sewing machine. I put my cup next to Colfer's. 'How do you mean?'

He cleared his throat and went to his desk. 'Ah, Casey will own everything out that way someday, that's all. Did ye see those new machines of his this morning? Worth more than what the lot of us earn in a year.'

'I should have known they were Casey's with the show he made of them. There'll be nobody turfed out around here, as you put it.'

Flood rooted in a drawer, looking for something to say. 'I meant nothing by it, Jim, only that Casey will probably own half the county eventually. That's no secret.' He sat, pretending that something in the open notebook on his desk needed his full attention.

'Well, if you ever have more to say about it, Flood, my desk is right through there.' I pointed to my office, but he didn't look at it or me. I could hardly look at it myself, imagining the paperwork, and the dead heat, and the slick of sweat down my chair.

I headed home with an appetite for little more than fresh air. The house is only a stroll from the station, the last uphill stretch a struggle even on a good day. A family of sparrows moved into the roof gutter a few weeks back and their nest was spilling over. They'd been working hard on their new home, waking us every morning of summer with their chirping and scratching until Casey's tractors beat them to it today. The front door was open to a freshly scrubbed mosaic of tiles and the smell of white vinegar. The floor was wet all the way to the kitchen flagstones. Siobhán met me by the stairs with a kiss on the cheek and a double warning – to not dirty the floors, and to not wake Catriona.

'I'll do you some lunch,' she whispered. 'I wasn't expecting you.'

'Don't worry, love. I haven't much of an appetite. Have we any painkillers?'

'In the cupboard upstairs. What's wrong?'

'I've a headache building since that racket woke us. Peter Casey by the way.'

'Who else?'

I took the stairs lightly, avoiding the creaks I know well. We only have one neighbour, and poor Mrs Rattigan hasn't been upstairs since she tripped on her front step, so we have the benefit of quiet in the bedroom – no snorer or sleep-talker to have me banging on the wall. I've moved up in the world, from the damp quarters above the cells that I was in before we married. By the time we brought Catriona back from hospital a couple of years later, it felt like the first real home I'd ever had, after a childhood of four beds shared between nine, then the dorm at the training college, followed by the run of sorry shelters that a new guard could afford. It's nothing special – and much less than I promised Siobhán when I got down on one knee – but it's ours.

I splashed some water on my face and took another Disprin. Catriona was sleeping with her door open. A towel covered something in the corner of her room – whatever present Siobhán is helping her make for my 40th. She was on top of the covers, the same red hair as her mother strewn across her pillow. I watched for a few seconds, then left her dreaming. On the landing, I shut my eyes, and in the silence of the house I heard Siobhán's words from the weekend. Why did it take all the Kennedy excitement about town for me to realise how lonely her days might get?

Our bedroom gave no hint of how she'd spent her morning. I came home early a couple of weeks back and found the same letter on the vanity table, typed out several times over, next to envelopes addressed to *The Irish Independent*, *The Irish Times* and *Woman's Way*. It felt wrong to be reading it, as if I'd found her diary or tuned into her inner thoughts. The letter complained about the trouble a woman has in owning property of her own and asked what protection there is for women with children, whose husbands have deserted them for building sites in Kilburn, docks in Liverpool, and the roads and rail of every British town and city they could squeeze into. Women who could have their house sold from under them without any say on the matter. I see her check the papers some days, then put them aside when she sees her letters have found some editor's bin and not the printed page. I'd tell her to keep writing them only it must be something she feels the need to do alone.

She was in the kitchen when I came down and sat at the table.

'How was the morning?' she said, putting soda bread and salmon in front of me and sitting opposite, keeping her voice down.

'Grand, love. How did she get on with the dentist?'

'He pulled it. A baby tooth. She ran up to bed when we got in. All your talk about the tooth fairy. I told her she only comes at night but it hasn't stopped her trying.'

'Do you have pennies for her?'

'I do.' She poured two cups of tea. 'What's your afternoon like?'

'Ah, busy. Kennedy, Kennedy, Kennedy – what else. I've to drop out to Patrick Hatten this evening too, so might get in late.'

She didn't disguise her sigh.

'He forgot the dole again,' I said.

'He mustn't have much need for it.'

I pulled in my chair, while she cut a piece of salmon. I ate in silence, happy to let our sleeping daughter be the excuse to avoid ground that has caused us trouble in the past.

'Jim, there's been enough problems over that lad already. Valerie Casey still turns her nose up at me in town.'

'She turns her nose up at everyone.' I swallowed some tea and shook my head. 'Flood made a remark earlier about Patrick being put out and could hardly meet my eye when I pulled him on it.'

She looked at the ceiling, then put her hand on mine. 'How is it you're so quick to jump if Hatten's name comes up? You've plenty more you could be spending your time on.'

'I'm not going to him for the fun of it, love.'

She took her hand away and sat back. 'I know you want to do right by him. But he's not your son.'

The word might as well have been a door slamming. It jolted the air in the room and quietened us both. I opened my palm and her hand returned. She cleared her throat, and set her fork down, letting the ghost pass. 'Just be smart until you see what Inspector jobs come up. There's no sense in crossing Peter Casey without good reason.' She's asked more than once if a promotion to Dublin would be possible. I've seen her scan the job advertisements in the paper, with plenty more work available to a married woman in the capital. 'I suppose no good will come from me telling you this, but I saw Casey this morning, with some fellow in a smart suit. Outside the Royal.'

'Casey's usual territory.'

She tapped work-worn fingernails on the tablecloth as if making a calculation. 'Flood was with them.'

'Flood?'

'It could be as simple as a guard on the beat, stopping to say hello to Casey and his company.' She wrapped the salmon and I knew I'd see it again for dinner. I followed her to the sink and stood behind her, with my chin on her shoulder and my hands on her waist, the pair of us looking through the window at the concrete yard and the brushes and buckets piled in the corner.

She walked me to the door and kissed my face again.

'See you later,' I said and she smiled. 'You're okay, aren't you?'

She examined the floor's drying. 'I'm fine, pet.'

'But everything, I mean. Everything's okay?'

'Always.' She rubbed the back of her neck. 'Don't spend long out there this evening. If he wants his dole, he knows where it is.'

I took the long way back to the station and stopped at the quay, where I've seen Patrick sometimes, watching the boats come in. A man and his young son watched the same scene from a bench. I earned a few nods and tips of caps to go with the fresh air coming over the Barrow, a river that reminds me of Patrick's father – poor auld Sean, neither talker nor drinker. The world could do with more like him.

Sean went to work over at Albatross after they sold most of their land to Peter Casey. I'm not the only one who questions the sense in letting the land go, but I'm among the few who keeps my thoughts to myself. Maura was a woman who thought herself above farming. Above cattle and shit and muck and bovine TB and brucellosis. She wanted Sean in a shirt and tie job, even if it meant starting at the bottom, carrying shite across his shoulders at a fertiliser plant. Their eldest, Colm, jumped ship for England when no more than a boy. She sold the land, had a water tank and plumbing put in and for a while at least, could walk into the bank unashamed of their account balance. Then Sean failed her by not climbing the ladder she'd led him to.

He was never any trouble. Pink-faced from a life spent in fields, eyes that avoided you. The poor man went mad in his sleep one night. As if he had dreams so terrible that he woke up and brought some part of them with him. You'd be talking to him and feel as if he was looking at something on your shoulder or floating above your head. The eyes that once only found the floor started finding everything. His arms twitched and his fingers fluttered as if he was playing a melody on the air. He'd burst out laughing in mass for no reason, until Maura grew too mortified to keep bringing him along. It was a rotten thing, sending him off to Senan's the way they did. Prisons don't have a patch on these places where punishment is concerned. Patients rounded up without trial, souls consigned to asylums then only ever whispered about, if remembered at all.

I drove him there. I've told myself for a long time that I was just a guard – a man at his lowest, following my sergeant's orders to take Sean to Senan's by any means necessary.

The truth of it used to bring him to me in dreams. I'd wake in the middle of a silent shout, with Siobhán sitting up beside me, her hand on my chest as if to slow my heart. Slowing the patrol car alongside him, out near Corcoran's Cross. How he smiled that shy smile at me and trusted me when I told him I'd spin him to town. How when he realised where I was taking him, he kicked like a horse, cracking the back window with his work boots, roaring and protesting until a stray boot caught the back of my head and I pulled in on that empty road and rounded the car, drawing my baton, and beat him into silence. Every blow I landed filling me with shame, so that in the heat of it all it felt as if it was myself I was battering. I can look back and try convince myself that it was a different, younger man who did that awful thing. But it wasn't. I often wonder if I carry that violence in me still? What right had I to take him from his son the way I did, without as much as a goodbye?

The orderly at Senan's looked afraid of me when I dropped off poor Sean, thin and bloodied. I left the place with my heart punching against my ribcage and found Sean's bloodied handkerchief on the back seat, then sat in the car, holding it so tight that I tore a hole in the middle, crying until my throat was raw.

I visited him a few times and don't know if it was worse when he recognised me or when he didn't. When I asked him for forgiveness, they had him so dosed up that I may as well have been a stranger. He died with some untreated and festering wound on his arm, poisoning his blood and making him burn with fever the same as if I'd sent him to hell.

I remember calling to the house and Maura opening the door. She clutched her side like her appendix had burst, struggling for breath between sobs as if it wasn't herself that had talked to the doctors and my sergeant and somebody out in Senan's. Ticked the few boxes needed to take a man's freedom. I stood there, only just promoted, patting her on the shoulder with young Patrick sitting in front of the fire, staring into the flames as if everything he thought he knew or stood to know about the world was burning inside them.

# 4

The half door on Joseph Roche's cottage was open and Patrick saw the old man through the spy window, stooped to some task at the table. A sheaf of grey hair was spiked at the back of his head and his jumper was torn at the top of his bent spine. Patrick knocked and when Roche didn't turn, he called to him, the way his father did when he brought him here as a boy.

'Are ya well, Joe?'

Roche was a second cousin or some distant relative to his father, and Patrick called every few weeks, sometimes bringing something for Roche's ancient pot. Squirrel meat fell short of the flavour of rabbit, and rabbit was another hop behind the dark meat of a hare, but Roche took whatever he brought with the same grunt. He remembered stories his father told him as a boy, straddling the crossbar, listening to a different identity for Roche on the way to every visit. He was a rebel in hiding. An outlaw, wanted by the guards. A Frenchman who'd fought the Germans. A German man who'd fought the French. He was pro-treaty, he was anti-treaty, he was both at once. Whatever he was, he was a man who wanted to stay lost, and it seemed as if the Hattens were the only people who could find his stony hideaway, more cave than cottage.

Roche turned and eyed Patrick and his face didn't change, the dry skin lined like a tilled field. His head disappeared and Patrick knew he had taken a seat in his tattered old chair by way of welcome.

Inside, the door to the byre on the left was shut. Roche hadn't kept cattle in decades. Bluebottles and houseflies swarmed the central room. A single stem of honey-coloured flypaper hung from the ceiling, lined with the black buds of insects, moth wings peeling off like dying leaves. There was a pair of old boots on the table, a strip of tyre rubber next to them. Patrick could see that Roche was doing a poor job mending them. Not easy work for a man half-blind, with fingers stiffened and bent by arthritis. There was a pair of his father's boots under his parents' bed that might fit Roche. He'd tried to squeeze into them once himself, after soaking and stretching them but couldn't get them past his ankle.

Roche held a pipe between his gums and Patrick sat in the chair next to him, propping his rifle against the wall next to the fireplace, where nothing had burned in weeks. Roche was having enough trouble getting his pipe to start. Patrick felt the old eyes register his empty hands.

'No rabbit today, Joe, sorry. I'd say they're hiding from the heat. How are you keeping?'

The old man flicked his chin up and left it to Patrick to decide how he was. Patrick slipped into the role his father played on visits, stretching his legs and crossing his feet, clasping his hands and twirling his thumbs like a man who could only relax in a home that wasn't his own. Patrick would sit on the ground between the chairs, listening to the men talk about football and hurling and farming and the seasons and all the things he didn't understand about politics and war and the North. His father said more in an hour in Roche's than in a month outside it. When they started playing cards, Patrick was left to wander, with instructions to not go far in the wildness of Roche's unworkable land or to stray up the hillside of Carrickbyrne, where the rebels camped in 1798.

'See can you make sense of this, Joe,' Patrick said, leaning forward, tugging his sleeves past his elbows. 'Two men are after parking a pair of MF50s just over my wall, in Casey's field.' Roche looked at him. 'Turned off the engines, took the keys and walked back across the field. What do you think that's in aid of?'

Roche pushed his tongue inside his upper lip and looked away, shaking his head, like a man so disgusted by the answer that he couldn't say it out loud.

Patrick waited, and Roche brought his pipe to his lips again.

'What do you think?' Patrick said and Roche looked at him with vacant eyes, as if his grasp on the conversation came and went as easily as his pipe smoke. Patrick let his question go unanswered. Another smoke plume scattered the flies to the corners of the room.

'Well, I'll tell you one thing anyway, Joe, I'm flat out today. Flat out. McCrann is taking me on for the busy season.'

He'd take piles of money from tourists and day trippers, down from Dublin and not able to tell one end of a rod from another. Load them up with bait and lures, tackle boxes and waders. He let his imagination run into the future and a badge with his name on it, just like McCrann's. Patrick offered his hands to everything from farming to sweeping to butchering before he landed the job at the tackle shop. He'd gone to speak to Cullinane at the fertiliser plant, where his father spent years loading 10-10-20 onto trucks, but was turned away without as much as an excuse. He'd show them all in town that he needed no handouts. That he'd no longer have to go in for the privilege of Field signing his dole card, expected to thank the world just for letting him exist in it.

Roche showed more interest in a crack in the opposite wall than in Patrick's talk.

'I'm putting the land back to work. What's left of it.' He spoke as if his plans were a confession while Roche stared at the wall like a priest whose mind was on matters much more profound. 'I might bring you out some day to tell me where to start. We haven't kept anything other than chickens in years.'

Talk of the future brought Rose to mind – her curled hair and the smell of sweat and soap. Broad shoulders and fine thick arms, with big hands that looked made for footing turf. That she was Peter Casey's daughter was the cruellest joke the world had played on him. It was two months since he'd seen her huge frame crossing the field towards him, as awkward and heavy-footed as John Walsh's bull, her cheeks as red as the same bull's hide, her eyes struggling to meet his as she neared. Two months since Casey spread every sort of filthy lie in town after he found out that they'd been meeting and came to Patrick's door, promising to burn him out of his home.

Patrick wished Rose could see him now, with a job lined up and a start made on the house. For two months of Sundays, he'd made the pilgrimage to their meeting place, keeping a lonely vigil every time she didn't show. A few weeks back, he left a pincushion at the base of their tree – green velvet with a backing in the shape of a shell and the words 'A present from Brighton' written across it. He found it among his mother's things and guessed that it was gifted by one of his aunts, who visited once when he was a boy, and spoke with an English accent. When he returned the following week, the pincushion was gone and he could only hope it was Rose who found it.

Roche held his pipe away from his face and spat, adding to the sea of dirt on a floor that had never felt the soft touch of a mop.

'Have you been in town at all lately? The place is gone cracked for Kennedy.'

Roche looked at Patrick's rifle and finally spoke. 'That thing is banjaxed.'

Roche had eaten plenty of creatures, big and small, that the rifle had put to death, so Patrick knew he had a vested interest in the gun's accuracy.

Patrick looked at the slender barrel and walnut stock of his Winchester. The finger grooves on the stock meant it was made in '34 or '35, according to McCrann. The logo on the buttplate was tarnished and the barrel had a small curved scar on the underside since the days his father owned it. Leaning against the wall in another man's home it looked pitiful somehow, and Roche's words stirred the same defensive embarrassment that he felt when he heard a group of men laughing about his father outside mass, not long before he was taken away. He remembered their silence when his mother came out the door a few seconds later, her index finger and forehead damp with holy water, eyeing them while they looked at their shoes. How he wasn't a brave enough lad to tell those men that they didn't know his father. That he was a strong and smart man who knew that the loudest men had the least to say.

'That gun has never let me down, as you well know.' He lifted it and held it in both hands then took aim at the far wall. 'That tiny front sight. Trains you to be accurate.' He lowered it and returned it to the wall. 'Tom McCrann says that this is the last year they'll make that model.' He looked at the weapon, its reputation protected, then shook his head and clicked his tongue. 'A real shame.'

Roche flicked his chin again, then puffed his pipe and picked something from the corner of his eye. He brought up another pearl of phlegm and spat it across the room where it hit the floor with the sound of a solid object.

'The big house on the way into town, before the statues,' Roche said, still looking at the gun.

'Penrose's?'

'There'll be a proper gun for you there.'

Roche knew things about the surrounding land and its people without ever leaving his home, as if local wisdom was drawn to him like spring water to the surface.

'Maybe after a few months with McCrann. Other things will have to come first. I'm thinking Shorthorn?' Patrick remembered how once it had been Roche asking his father for help with land and animals, and now here he was, his father's son, no confidence in his instinct.

Roche turned to Patrick and his smile showed a single tooth in his top gum where on the last visit there had been four.

'I didn't say to buy it. If young Penrose is anything like his father was, then he won't even lock them up.' He put his head back and closed his eyes as if giving counsel had taken it out of him and Patrick wondered if there was much that could happen in the world that Roche hadn't seen.

'Have you any kittens?' Patrick said, sensing he hadn't long before Roche nodded off. 'My cat is getting lonely.'

Roche's chest rose and fell slowly, his quenched pipe on the chair between his thighs. As Patrick stood, Roche spoke from near sleep.

'Go out to the shed and see for yourself.'

Patrick took his rifle and looked down at Roche.

He got as far as the door when Roche called after him. He turned and looked at the dome of Roche's head over the back of the chair. 'Those tractors. Had they front loaders?'

'They did.' Patrick said. 'And a digging bucket on one.'

'There's only one reason Casey has them there so.'

'What's that?'

Roche's head dipped as if he'd fallen asleep.

'I'll bring a rabbit next time, Joe,' Patrick said and the flies sang him out.

There was an axing stump on the near side of the shed, with chunks of badly chopped wood next to it. The same way he could age the ash by counting the rings outwards from the centre, he could see Roche's ageing in the dents left in the stump – moving from a younger and stronger man's straight blows in the middle, to stray attempts that left shallow scars like whip marks close to the edges, where an older Roche hadn't the strength to keep swinging true. He thought of the empty stove and lifted the axe and inspected the blade. Butterknife blunt. He'd bring a stone to sharpen it next time.

He passed a pair of ancient bales so dry they'd turn to dust with a solid kick, his mind returning to the Masseys, hoping they'd be gone when he got home. In the corner of the shed, hiding behind a rusted trough of rainwater, a piebald cat looked up at him with wariness in her eyes and a litter of kittens inside her belly.

Bart Sinnott wheeled Patrick's bike to the back of his shop with a grunt and mumbled a few words, as inarticulate as a man whose tongue had been cut out. Patrick was sure he heard *come back around three* and looked at the clock on the wall to see he had a couple of hours to kill in town after getting the wool and calling on McCrann. He'd have happily spent them inside the four breeze-block walls of

Sinnott's Repair Garage with the radio on, the door tilted up to make a canopy over the footpath, shading a row of second-hand bikes for sale. His bike was a Rollfast, inherited from his father. Bought new after they sold the cart, its chain had turned for over a decade of uphill battles and pothole dodging.

He looked around the shop as he left, at the skeletons of bikes and spare handlebars like bullhorns, stray tyres and discarded seats. The workbench beneath the window, scattered with wrenches, pumps and tubing. Rims and spokes hanging on nails like parts of broken clocks. He imagined his hands, supple with oil and grease-blackened, his nostrils filled with the smell of Dunlop rubber after a day's work. Sinnott had been one of the many men to shake his head when Patrick was doing the rounds looking for a job and at least had the decency to give a reason. Two reasons – a son and a limping nephew he was training in, who were sitting on stools across the shop, facing away and talking in whispers about the bike on the bench in front of them, neither saying hello after they spotted Patrick over their shoulders. Sinnott wore glasses and a stained white coat that gave him the look of some back street doctor, and if his work cured the pain that stabbed at Patrick every time he sat on the bike, then maybe he was.

His rifle was stashed in a hollowed beech trunk near to his and Rose's secret meeting place. He kept hiding places in hedges, fields and ditches for several square miles. His father had shown him the beech. Traps and tools too heavy to carry back and forth were stored in places known only to himself and the wind. He walked Chapel Lane with his hands in his pockets and his tongue pushed into the space where he'd lost an upper canine to a fall at fourteen, the day he left school for the final time. Town was busy, the people of New Ross getting ahead of themselves with all their talk of Kennedy, as if it was them he was coming to see. Windows washed every morning, signs painted and repainted, the railings on the quays polished, manhole covers welded shut, roads freshly lined, flower baskets hung from anything that could take their weight, fishing boats and pleasure boats repaired and scrubbed good as new. Even the apples outside Coleman's had a spit-shined look, as if Kennedy might pop by unannounced. As if he wasn't off to Dublin, Cork and Galway too, with the sorry lot in all those places at the same carry on. Pope John threw a spanner in the works by floating off to heaven with his holy hands clutching a cancer-riddled stomach, and rumours that Kennedy might cancel his plans out of respect had fair wiped the shine off the apples.

He was passing the river when he spotted Sergeant Field coming down Bridge Street, his Garda cap held up by his ears. He went to his haunches behind a car, as still as something being hunted, to avoid having to listen to Field chatting as if he was an old family friend and not the same man who'd driven his father away to Senan's. He watched over the bonnet as Field went on towards the station.

At the side wall of McCrann's, he inspected his reflection in a car window. He tucked in his sweat-soaked shirt and pulled at the crotch of his trousers, then spat on his palm and dragged it across his hair before nosing each armpit. A pair of eyes watched him from the window above the drapery across the road, where Ann Nolan's interpretation of the American flag hung in the window display, missing some stars and stripes. He raised his hand and the eyes retreated to the shadows.

The bell above the door alerted McCrann to his arrival and the older man, who wore a collar, tie and nametag no matter the weather, looked up from behind the counter where he was tallying something in a notebook, then put his pencil behind his ear. The bell's tune made Patrick smile and he considered opening the door for an encore.

'Patrick,' McCrann said, returning to his notebook.

'Mr McCrann.' Patrick put his hands on his hips and the smell from under his arms was more potent in the confines of the shop. He dropped his hands to his sides to trap it. 'I was in town. Wicked heat,' he said and tugged at his collar.

McCrann shook his head. 'Too hot for me. Plenty of fishing though.'

'The salmon'll be boiled alive.'

Patrick put a hand in his pocket and looked around the shop. Single- and double-handed rods lined the wall to the left and cardboard containers hung behind the till, filled with hooks and lines, spoons and spinners. Tools and rifle cartridges were locked in a glass display. There were hats, jackets, boots and wellingtons near the window, bins filled with lugworms giving off their earthy stink, and a tank with countless goldfish stunned into stillness by the heat. Catalogues and magazines lined the countertop and a red setter named Moll slept in a basket in front of it.

He imagined evenings as master of the place, after McCrann headed away early. The bell above the door singing for his attention, greeting customers with a nod and a smile, then whistling home to his few animals and sitting in front of a warm fire, eating what he grew on his own land. He imagined having Rose for company, maybe waiting for him at the back of the shop, then thought it a dream too far.

'I'm in to check about starting. I'm ready for this weekend if that's still the plan.' He straightened, the way his mother told him to at mass whenever he angled away from the sound of the congregation communicating in their chorus of coughs, sneezes, cracking knees, groans, and whispered prayers. The wet, black umbrellas dropped under the pews like dead crows bleeding clear blood. Father Crowley's contempt for his flock and their heads bowing while he scolded them with his Latin tongue. Only the stained-glass windows and the rattling journey on the cart to and from the church made the ordeal worth it.

He rocked on his heels when McCrann didn't raise his head and in the part of his mind she moved into after dying, he heard his mother tell him to stop fidgeting like an eejit.

'My mother would come down to thank ya herself, if she was still around.'

McCrann put the notebook in a drawer under the counter and rooted around for something that didn't want to be found, then shut the drawer with a sigh.

'Listen, Patrick. I'm not taking you on.' He met Patrick's eye and planted his palms on his countertop like a doctor giving a terminal diagnosis.

Patrick took his hand from his pocket. A car passed outside. Moll stirred in her basket. For a few seconds, he forgot to breathe.

'I'm not busy enough is all. I thought things would pick up.'

Patrick pushed his tongue into the gap in his teeth. He turned and looked out the window, at the blue sky that McCrann had just admitted was reeling plenty to the water. McCrann rounded the counter.

'Casey's been on to you. Is that it?'

McCrann raised his palms and shook his head. 'I'd have taken you on, Patrick. I had great time for your father, God rest him. Whatever goes on between you and Casey is yere business alone.'

'Casey's a liar,' Patrick said, feeling the same as when he was cornered by teachers and priests back in school, beaten into confessing to sins that weren't his. 'Mr McCrann, I need this job. Need it something awful.'

McCrann planted his feet and raised his chin. 'There's nothing more to say, Patrick. It's not happening. I don't want any trouble, do you hear me?'

He looked into the older man's eye and saw that he wasn't for turning, then looked around the shop like a person leaving their home for the final time and turned for the door under Moll's uninterested gaze. He lifted a copper lure from a box on the shelf next to the door and put it in his pocket.

'I'm keeping this,' he said, his back to McCrann, who didn't answer.

He opened the door and stepped outside, the bell's song in his ears, reworked as a sorry lament.

Down on the quay, a school band was practising 'The Boys of Wexford'. A teacher from after Patrick's time stood in front of them, arms moving like a puppet, conducting the troop of boys in their Christian Brothers uniforms, the sound of their whistles and drums and young voices lost on the breeze.

# 5

Colfer dropped in a list of names and vehicles, stamped with approval for licences that allowed them to be on the road on the 27th. Even when a President visits, a town needs its milkman and postman out in the morning. Garda vehicles, ambulances, a few journalists and private cars – all approved to share the roads with the motorcade.

His hair was parted more left of centre than usual, as if he'd over-thought it, and it gave him a slightly lopsided look. He wore enough aftershave to make him a fire hazard. He left a second list on my desk after I finished scanning the first.

'These applications are still pending, Sergeant.'

'Colfer, you've been here long enough to know to call me Jim.' I lifted the second page. 'Now, let's see who thinks they're roadworthy.'

I wasn't surprised to see Peter Casey's name among the applicants. It wouldn't be enough for him to simply witness Kennedy's visit, he'd have to be part of it for him to care at all. He's one of a carful of locals from different groups and associations – the golf club, the bridge club, the rotary, the co-op – staking a claim to be among the crowd when Kennedy goes to Dunganstown.

'Most of these will be disappointed.'

I put the list aside and Colfer didn't turn to leave.

'Get out with it,' I said and he looked like a schoolboy, asking for permission to go to the jacks.

'Sergeant. Jim. Would it be alright if I leave early this evening?'

His cheeks reddened and the hair wax made sense. 'We'll cope, I'm sure. Though the lucky woman might not, if you don't wipe a layer of that musk off. Still, I'm glad to see you're getting to know the locals.' I remembered my nerves before early meetings with Siobhán, worrying over how a woman like her could be interested in a man with ears this big.

'Thanks, Jim. Did you find Hatten?'

'He'll turn up. He always does. Listen,' I said and he straightened. 'Come to me if Flood says anything like he did earlier. About Hatten or Casey.'

Flood had explained away meeting Casey this morning as a chance encounter on the beat. He said the suit was a man over from England discussing thoroughbreds, and that he didn't even get his name.

Colfer shut the door on his way out, sniffing his wrist. I rubbed my temples at the thought of how much worse my headache would get if Peter Casey didn't get permission to move in Kennedy's orbit. I'm just about recovered from the hounding he gave me about Patrick a couple of months back.

Casey fancies himself as some sort of unelected statesman. From generations of Wexford blood, with a big dairy farm and one hand in everything that's going on, the other extended for anyone he thinks might be of use to him – bankers, TDs, solicitors and Gardaí. He has the size and posture of a retired heavyweight and can talk for fifteen rounds about his success and his standing in places far bigger than New Ross, hiding his bulk in tailored suits and behind a thick belt that holds his gut back like a dam holding back water. If you listened to him, he'd convince you it was himself who talked Kennedy into coming, and that the Taoiseach is as good as his errand boy.

He's building a stud out where his land is swallowing Hatten's. Stables like cathedrals is what he'll tell you, happy to spread the notion that he's Wexford's version of the Aga Khan. He came back from the Grand National in March with stories of Vincent O'Brien, letting on he was his great friend and soon-to-be rival. Finiskil is what he's calling the place. A Brit-friendly way of saying *finscéal*, our own word for legend. The Hatten house sits on the southern bend of Casey's planned training track, and Casey thinks of it like a stain on a good suit, something to be scrubbed away, to make room for the offspring he wants from his new thoroughbred. The horse might as well have wings for the way people go on about it.

Rose is his youngest – sixteen and shaped like a great big bell. So quiet it's like the clapper has been taken out of her. There are two lads and three more girls who work like his five fingers to keep this town and county in his grip. Then poor auld Rose, like a second thumb, everybody wondering would it not be best to just cut her off.

Hatten and Rose must have come across each other on the road one day and taken a shine to each other. Bell and the beast. What they talked about is anybody's guess, but I doubt it'd interest the Secret Service lads much. Noreen Deasy saw them sitting under a tree out by Corcoran's Cross. Noreen, being Noreen, went straight to town to tell anybody with a pair of ears about it and gossip spread like headlice in a classroom. By the time some bastardised version reached Casey, Rose was as good as defiled. Even Noreen tried to quell that type of talk, saying she'd seen nothing of the sort. Casey dragged Rose to Doc Murphy all the same, who told him Rose was as untouched as the moon. Then the story was that Hatten tried to force himself on Rose and that his brave girl fought him off. With the size of her, nobody doubted it. Casey came in, demanding I do something and even Rose was moved to words and told us that they'd never done a thing but talk. That they were friends. I told him I can't charge somebody with being friends. Casey still hasn't forgiven me for not jumping fences and responding to his whip.

That sort of small talk is what makes small towns. It's why I keep my distance – friendly, but not a friend. Not a sergeant who'll come in for a few pints and stay for a lock-in. If I get too close, my business becomes the town's business, and I'll have every man and woman asking me to bend the rules just a bit and just the once. Until the next time. I've seen it happen.

I know jokes and nicknames. I've heard them all since I was a boy. Sam Maguire, Liam McCarthy, FA Cup – if it's a trophy with handles, I've been called it, on account of these ears. They say New

Ross is the only town in Ireland where you don't have to call the Guards, only cup your hand and shout and Sergeant Field will hear you if you're within five miles. They wonder how a woman like Siobhán could end up married to a man with lugs like mine. It took me so long to get her to marry me – took her saying goodbye once before she came back – that maybe she wondered herself.

I asked her if they bothered her one time in the early days. I'd spent half of my pay packet to meet her in the Metropole in Cork, our early love spanning counties after I was transferred from Anglesey Street to New Ross. She crossed the hotel room to where I was looking at my reflection in the window, the Lee passing outside in the night, and she took my ears in her fingers and kissed them, then whispered into the left one that she knows that when she says she loves me, I can hear her from anywhere.

I went into Kearney's after work, to see about my copy of *Conquest*. I tell Maurice it's for my nephew and he orders it in special. You can't go in these days without him hovering next to you, whispering about the *foreign invasion* of British supermarkets and how it'll mean the end for shops like his. He has a sign in the window, rallying people to shop with the small store as if he's recruiting an army. He told me that *Conquest* would take another few days and I stopped myself from telling him I'd get it quicker if I went round-trip on the ferry to get it in a British supermarket. The magazine comes every few weeks with little stainless-steel stove-enamelled parts of a rocket. The models are simple enough, about eighteen inches tall. You collect the parts, clip them together, and away you go. My hands weren't blessed the way my brothers' were, so I can't build my own. Still, I'm competent enough to design and cut the finer details from sheets of balsa wood with a Stanley blade – the feed and filler tubes, the combustion chamber and bulkhead bracing. Sand them in the light of a long-armed jeweller's lamp at my workbench, then paint them and glue them in place, so my finished models end up looking like all that's stopping them from flying is a lack of jet fuel.

I don't know if Kearney believes me about the nephew or not, but it lessens the chances of stories going around that Sergeant Field spends his evenings at home building rockets meant for young lads. It wouldn't take long before the stories grew chapters, that have me in a spacesuit in the living room, insisting Siobhán calls me Commander. Is it any stranger than sitting down with a crossword or shouting at the radio about a game of football?

I had an interest from an early age – in the stars and the galaxy and what might be beyond them. Lofty thoughts for a lad from Wexford. Then came girls and the Gardaí, and it all lay dormant until Sputnik went into orbit in '57. All that excitement was relaunched. I took out library books and trawled the newspapers, looking for any update about two nations racing for some invisible finish line in the sky. I'd whisper it around these parts, but hurling doesn't have a patch on that sort of competition. I remember sitting in the waiting room while Catriona was taking her time being born, and I saw a young lad with a copy of *Conquest*, opening the parts of a rocket. I went and sat next to him and asked if I could see what he was working on. I was fidgeting with the pieces when a nurse came to tell me I was a father to a healthy girl. It's about as close as I'll ever come to knowing how an astronaut feels – about to be launched at known and unknown dangers, knowing that it could all be lost in an instant.

Siobhán teases me when I get carried away with it all, but it's so incredible that it's hard to think people talk about anything else. Imagine a V-2, blasting off from a dusty pad in New Mexico. Tearing through sky and cloud for 60 miles of upward flight, and while it's up there, just about touching heaven, sending a photograph back to Earth – our first glimpse of ourselves from outer space, as good a view as God himself. My mother was born the same year a plane managed to shudder along for 900 feet at about the same speed as a brisk walk. Now we send rockets up, hitting eighteen thousand miles an hour, lined with solar cells that draw power from the sun. Imagine the discoveries we'll make, the same as those men who boarded ships hundreds of years ago and set off for the edge of the world.

See, this is when Siobhán would be laughing at me, bringing me back down to earth and the likes of Peter Casey and Patrick Hatten and the feeling that the temperature is rising in their cold war. I went in to Antoinette to collect Patrick's dole, and she treated the transaction as if I was after nuclear codes. I decided to leave him wait another night, wanting to see Catriona before she went to bed.

I leaned against the railing above the river on my way home, watching small boats being unloaded, groups of fishermen sunburnt and smiling. I spotted Colfer, next to the reason for his early finish. Claire O'Gorman, the youngest daughter of our local TD. They were walking close, though not yet arm in arm. The moon was pale, as if waiting behind a curtain for its black stage to be set. I watched people making their way home. Men in suits, men with dirty hands and faces. Women carrying files and folders, others trekking home from factories. Old men with rolled sleeves and stooped shoulders, shopkeepers sweeping footpaths and closing shutters, schoolchildren with a summer of long evenings ahead, mothers weighed down by shopping bags and pushing prams. It was hard to imagine that in just over a couple of weeks, eyes from every corner of the world would see a man looking back at New Ross from all but the same spot.

# 6

Patrick sat on an upturned wooden crate at the centre of the room. A plate lay on the floor next to him, stained by the drag marks of tough bread through Batchelor's beans. The only light came from a weak turf fire. The chimney was due a clean and he imagined the smoky air settling in his lungs like a dark fog. The front door was open to the silver-black silhouette of trees by the road and the shrapnel of stars around a bullet hole moon. The diggers were sleeping over the wall when he got back from town and he leaned against a trunk of ash and watched them until near dark.

He rubbed his thumbs and index fingers together in slow circles, swallowing the urge to talk out loud, a habit he was trying to break – formed in the weeks after his mother died, just to hear a voice in the house. He thought about McCrann avoiding his eye and speaking to him as if he was a simple child, and imagined Casey twisting McCrann's arm with lies and badness. He should have fought harder. Argued for one week to prove his worth. His mother always told him that if he had nothing useful to say then to say nothing at all and all that practised silence was working against him now. She followed up sometimes, saying that if he lived by the rule then she might never have to hear his voice, reminding her of what a disappointment he was.

'You should've made your case, Patrick,' he said, then covered his mouth like he was protecting a cough.

He circled his palms against the coarse wooden slats on the crate and thought of Rose and her fine quiet way, and how they'd sit together saying little – and how little was plenty. He loved to hear whatever few words she had about the tough teachers and tougher nuns. How she reddened when asked about her lessons, as if how little she learned embarrassed her, and how she smiled when he told her he could never follow most of it. The memory of being next to her was enough to fill the house at its loneliest. He started speaking to her imagined incarnation not long after he started talking out loud, playing out scenes while he cooked his dinner or fed the cat or sat next to the fire, telling her about his day. He once set two plates and rationed out a portion of stewed rabbit to his invisible guest, then felt embarrassed – even without witnesses, and never did it again.

Turf shifted in the fire.

The most she'd ever spoke about was horses. She told him that she renamed her father's horses and found ways to visit them despite Casey forbidding it. She stole stable keys and convinced workmen to let her in while Casey was away. Patrick told her about Bullet, the horse they once owned – and the strong and coarse tongue licking his palm clean of strawberries claimed from the garden, the breath warm and sweet, perfumed by whatever he ate. He told her that Bullet was afraid of storms and that he'd leave his bed at night and go to the shed, rubbing the horse's neck, watching jagged blades of lightning slice the sky into pieces, then cupping his hands around those long, funnelled ears and humming, any made up tune that drowned out the sound of earth and sky doing battle. He told her that when he talked to Bullet it was as if the horse wasn't just hearing him, but listening to him, and how it felt as if he could tell it anything, something in the depths of those wise eyes that made Patrick sure Bullet understood. He told her about the man and his two sons who came one wet morning, and his father helping them to load the last Hatten cattle into a trailer with Kilkenny plates. How his protests were ignored as Bullet was loaded into another. He shared everything he could remember about that morning and she didn't say anything when he finished, just sat with him for a long silence.

He felt closest to Rose in all they didn't say. How they'd looked skyward at the same moment to watch the arrowed formation of swallows in April. How at the sound of any engine on the road they crouched tight against the wall, without ever admitting why. And how when his arm accidentally touched hers, they'd both redden and look away, until their eyes met again and they were both smiling.

Rose stirred him out of the daze he was in after his mother died. She sat with him as if she could sit all day, and made him believe that they could have more than their Sunday meetings, and made him ask questions of himself and how he could go about getting it. Money seemed to be the answer to every question.

'You should've made your case to McCrann, Patrick,' he said, louder this time. 'Isn't that right, cat,' he called out the open door.

He looked to a resurgent flame in the fire and it reminded him of Jim Field calling to the house years back and how he knew, before the sergeant said a word, that his father was dead. His gentle father, who'd rub his head and take him walking along the river in sunshine or rain, showing how the river dressed for the weather just the same as people did. How on a fine day it wore something light enough to see to near the bottom, and how rain and storms sent it rushing for heavy black robes. He could close his eyes and still see him, a couple of paces ahead, back bent from farming fields before swapping it for carrying fertiliser day in day out. He took everything he knew about the land six feet beneath it, wrapped forever in Wexford's soil of silt and slate.

A breeze tapped the door against the wall in a slow and quiet rhythm, reminding Patrick of the schoolboys and their instruments down on the quay. He thought of Kennedy sitting and listening to their racket, smiling for the cameras, having to pretend their music was something worth crossing the Atlantic for.

He tapped the crate in time with the door, increasing the tempo, then let his voice well up in protest against his mother, and McCrann, and all those old priests and boys from school, and the sneers in town, and Peter Casey, Peter Casey, Peter Casey – hovering above everything like an eternal curse that took the land and his job and took Rose – coming to the house teeth-clenched and shining with sweat to warn him away from her, threatening to burn him out of his home. A stream of ragged sounds flooded from his gut, up his windpipe and burst out like some ancient sea-shanty as he pounded his makeshift drum louder and faster and his song escaped through the open door and crossed a great ocean of darkness.

He woke shivering next to a fireplace of ash. The front door was open and he tuned into the sound of early birds and wondered which of them he'd put a bullet in before summer was through. Say what they might in town, they couldn't deny his shot. He could perch on a wall above the beach at Duncannon Fort and shoot the flake from a 99 from fifty yards. He stood and unfolded his body like a penknife in need of oil, his lower back rigid after a night in the chair. He turned on the radio and remembered his chant from the night before. The presenters had more talk of the Good Pope and his funeral and the crowds still hanging on in St Peter's Square, crying enough tears to fill the fountains of Rome.

He remembered waking to the sound of the hammer on the mouse trap snapping shut during the night. He knelt next to the cupboard. The mouse's luck had run out at last, the trap crushing the four chambers of its clover-sized heart. He slid the trap out and opened it, then put the mouse in his pocket – about the weight of a roll of coins – and the bloodied trap back in the bottom drawer.

It was six months since his mother died. He'd aimed to mark each month with some prayer or remembrance, but had already forgotten three of them, the days and dates rolling into one shapeless season of loneliness, with nothing to build his hours around. The framed picture on the wall was the only one of a full family and the only picture Patrick had, beyond the handful of wedding pictures in a fake-leather-bound album in a bottom drawer in their bedroom – his father shy and rarely looking at the camera.

The radio was one of the extravagances his mother bought to prove that she wasn't another struggling widow surviving on a pittance. She'd return from town, carrying these luxuries to her bedroom, out of his reach. A fine pair of leather shoes that she changed into near the church, stepping off the road to where she wouldn't be seen. An umbrella with a carved wooden handle. A tailored coat that meant two weeks' worth of meals of whatever she pulled from the garden. After she died, he went to the room like an explorer finding a cave full of treasure, and took the radio to the kitchen.

In the picture, her faded head wore the same short hair he'd always known. She was younger, softened by being captured outside on a bright enough day to wear a squint. Her hands were on his young shoulders, and Colm stood next to his father, arms folded across his chest, giving the impression of a boy who took photographs very seriously. He doubted that any of them, standing at the side of the house that sunny morning, would have imagined how quickly four would become one. He thought about others he'd lost. Rose. Dermot Dempsey and Barry Rossiter, a couple of lads from school who never minded stopping for a chat, until they joined the ranks that left for foreign shores. How many people were enough to protect against ending up alone?

The tractors watched him walk to where he'd found her. He crouched and put a palm against the soil, where her head rested for the final time, then turned and lay on his back and moved his body into the shape she'd been in, the left arm off to the side, the right-hand palm up, fingers curled as if holding some invisible fruit. Her legs parted slightly. He lay there, sinking into her shape, and watched some rags of cloud, as slow and peaceful as leaves crossing a pond, and thought that it wasn't a bad way to die at all.

'Not a bad way to die at all,' he said to the sky.

He lay long enough for the clouds to clear the scene, then stood and went to the tool shed. He opened the corrugated door the few inches he needed to slide in sideways, then shut it behind him. The orange cat was in the corner, avoiding his eye. How easy it had been to coax it into its prison, trading freedom for a few saucers of milk.

'Good morning, Cat. Sorry I didn't come last night. I think we're in a bit of bother.' The cat blinked. 'I brought you something,' Patrick said, walking slowly towards it.

It made no move to escape, probably remembering what happened last time it tried. He squatted and smiled, his blackened fingernails angling towards the shaded earth. He pulled the mouse from his pocket and held it in his palm, where it fit snugly, getting a feel of the rubbery musculature. If he curled his fingers around it and squeezed tight, he'd crush it. He imagined killing a live one one-handed, getting a measure of exactly when a thing was dead. Did it know it was dead before its end came? Did his mother know as she sucked that last drag of morning air? Or his father, as his breaths wound down to nothing? She'd probably turned in her grave to show her back to her husband, just as she had in life.

He tossed the mouse to the cat, who gave it a glance, not trusting it.

'You like that, I know you do.' He smiled his gap-toothed smile. He put out his hand and made a summoning sound but the cat didn't move.

'Are you excited about Kennedy? You are, you are, you are.'

The cat stayed still and Patrick laughed.

'Ah, you're only lonely. I still haven't found you a friend. Listen, leave it with me.'

He stood and backed to the door and squeezed out, never taking his eyes off the cat. At the side of the shed, he put his eye against a gap in the stone, in time to see the cat nose the carcass, then sink a claw in.

# 7

The sparrows were back on duty this morning, chirping and scratching in their nest above the window. There's peace in that quiet, with Siobhán breathing next to me. Before the calls of car horns, and workers chatting in doorways, and mothers shouting after children, adding their voices to the small-town choir. A wet patch had spread another inch across the ceiling, dampening my hope that a dry summer would take care of it. I reached above the headboard and thumbed a piece of curling wallpaper back to the wall, thinking about an Inspector's extra hundred pounds a year and the difference promotion would make – if the right post came up. No point trapping my girls off in some Atlantic-battered stretch of Mayo or Donegal.

I turned to her. There was a book face down on her nightstand, next to a brass carriage clock, one of her few simple luxuries that were mostly wedding presents. I put an arm around her and kissed her cheek and she put her hand on top of mine, her eyes still closed, while I whispered in her ear.

'Did I ever tell you about the Cork woman who was a famous astronomer?'

She exaggerated a snore and I put my hand inside her nightdress and walked my fingers across her ribs. She smiled, but didn't open her eyes.

'Go on so, tell me about her. What woman doesn't love astronomy first thing in the morning?'

'Agnes Mary Clerke. Born not far from your neck of the woods. Home-schooled in the arse end of Ireland and became one of the most respected astronomers in the world.'

'Jim, if you get me any more excited, you'll be late for work,' she said and I nudged her with my hip.

'Well, I'll keep going in that case. She spoke German. Italian. Greek. French.' I counted the languages out with my fingers on her freckled shoulder. 'Travelled the world.'

'And which of our great institutions did she make her name at? It wasn't in Cork or I'd have heard of her.'

'She moved to Florence at twenty-five. Then London.'

She opened her eyes. 'Of course she did. If she'd stayed here, she'd have been speaking her four extra languages to her four walls.'

I kissed her neck, then turned from bed.

'Have you thought any more about going back to work?'

'I have. I want to. I'd love it if O'Gorman was hiring, even if it was just a bit of typing to start.'

'To start,' I said and smiled at her. Her father, Con, ran as an Independent in '44 and '48. There was some talk of running in the South-East constituency a couple of years back but I think his heart was gone from it, but is beating away in Siobhán. She works with the church, helping the same widowed and abandoned women she writes her letters about. She tells me that since the church is half the problem, she'll squeeze as much charity as she can from it. And still, for all her private dissent, she'll be at mass every Sunday or praying every other night, working through a life of compromise.

'I saw Colfer with O'Gorman's youngest yesterday evening.'

'Young love. Remember that?' she teased.

I pulled the blanket off and she shrieked and brought her knees to her chin, and her nightdress rode up to show her legs from thigh to foot, tempting me back to bed. She watched me looking at her, then smiled and stretched out again while I took my shirt from a chair and put it on.

'I could have a word with O'Gorman.' I threw the blanket over her. 'A TD always likes to keep the Guards on side.' I went to the wardrobe for my uniform. 'With Catriona in school, you'd be well able for it.'

'You know what they'll say around the place.'

I knotted my tie in the mirror. 'They'll say that you're a holy show of a woman, not staying at home looking after your child and husband.'

'And about you.' She turned from bed, smoothing her hair from her face.

'They'll say that I'm a holy show of a man, not able to provide enough for my wife and daughter.'

She met me by the door, still wearing the warm smell of sleep.

'But that'll only be some of them. Most of them are just tipping along with too much on their own plates to care about what's on ours. And more important, I don't think you really care. You know you could do anything.'

She smiled, but just about. 'It's all daydreaming anyway. He wouldn't take me on even if there was work going.'

'He wouldn't take you on for fear you'd take his job. Come on. Let's wake the poor creature. See did the tooth fairy come.'

I took her hand and we tiptoed across the hall to Catriona's room, where she was asleep on her back, her hands above her head on the pillow, as if she was lifting an invisible trophy in her sleep.

I told Tom McCrann that I'd never known him to be a man to go back on his word. I went in hoping to see Patrick behind the counter, getting a feel for how the place operates. When I asked Tom when he was starting, he only stared out his window, his mackerel breath swimming through the air and catching on the stink of warm bait and damp setter. I knew Casey had talked him out of taking Hatten on, and that McCrann weighed me and Casey like two salmon pulled from the Barrow and settled on the bigger fish. Sound enough logic, to his credit. I can think of a thousand ways I'd sooner spend a Saturday than standing in water to my thighs waiting for a fish to bite, so he wasn't even losing a customer.

I could only shake my head the way my father used to when I let him down and hope that McCrann might feel a fraction of the shame that look used stir in my gut. I didn't lower myself to acting on the so-called dirty books. As far as I'm concerned, if a man is sitting reading a book it means he isn't out causing hassle, even if Edna O'Brien's *Country Girls* terrify the censors. Siobhán tells me she can't see what the fuss is about. I'll store the leverage all the same – there's a time for tossing something back in the water and a time for whacking it across the head.

I went back to the station, far too busy to go job hunting for Patrick Hatten. More guidelines were down from Dublin, about how to keep the Secret Service lads happy. They came down back in May, part of an advance group, led by men with names like Salinger and Duke, making sure New Ross was fit for their man and not harbouring any head-the-ball pretend communist or student sympathetic to South Africa that was likely to blow him up. Straight-backed serious types in tailored suits and polished shoes. You'd get more chat from a headstone. They sniffed around the station as if they were looking for the source of a bad smell. Laid out maps and tracked routes to the hospital. Asked what locals own guns, trawled through files of recent crimes. One humourless Nordic-looking man mountain came straight out and asked me if there'd been any threats. I made a bad joke that from all the giddy talk I've heard it might be the women who want to get Kennedy alone and he took out a notebook and asked me to write down their names.

I was on my way out for lunch when Flood came into the office and shut the door behind him, leaving us standing face to face, like men who'd waited far too long to sort out their differences.

'This must be very serious, Flood.'

'You might be right there, Jim,' he said. 'Eamon Doran was in Ryan's last night and the poor man was hardly over the shock. He had men pouring whiskey into him, trying to get him right.'

'Out with it, Flood, I've things to do.'

'Eamon and Matty Whelan were doing good honest work for Casey yesterday morning, moving those tractors to where Casey told them to, nothing more. Next thing Patrick Hatten is on the wall next to Peter's field, aiming a rifle at the lads like he's John Wayne. Poor Eamon could do nothing but run. Matty saw the whole thing and ran after him, the pair of them expecting a bullet.'

'Aiming a rifle at him?'

'Aiming a rifle at him.' His tone suggested that he'd proven some point or won some argument I didn't know we were having. 'That's the way they told it. You told me to come to you, so here I am.'

'I've heard enough stories in my time to know you need to hear more than one version. Saves you racing into things half-cocked.'

Flood shook his head. 'If you ask me, there's only one way to deal with that lad before somebody ends up hurt.'

'I'll go out to him today,' I said, and Flood pushed his chest out as if I'd just agreed to his order. Like myself, he was waiting on promotion exam results. I looked back at him as I left, standing in the sergeant's office with his hands on his hips, looking all too comfortable.

I went to Gerry Foley for a trim, half-expecting him to spot the cause of the headache while he combed and snipped – a crack right down the middle of my skull maybe. A razorblade, trapped in a fissure. The tight cut of a guard does my ears no favours.

'You'll be busy before the 27th, Gerry. Everybody will want to look their best,' I said, while he worked, wet eyes examining my hair through a thick pair of bifocals. He eyed me in the mirror, then went to the counter and turned up his radio. Gerry is the only man in Wexford who won't talk about Kennedy, as a rule. Some grievance he has against America since a brother of his went over to chase a dream and found only hardship and the shelter of some Boston doorway to die in. Gerry doesn't even know where he's buried.

'Sergeant's discount,' Gerry said, finishing up and heading to his till. I left the money on the counter.

'You hardly need a lad to sweep up the hair, Gerry?'

He took his broom from behind the counter and gripped it, as if testing its weight. 'No. I can still manage.'

'Fair enough.'

Through the window, I spotted Casey on his way into the Royal, a big hand on the back of a younger man in a suit.

'Thanks, Gerry, see you soon,' I said, turning from the counter and hurrying out, through the cloud of Pinaud powder still colouring the air. Casey clocked me and I quickened my step, then got held up by a traffic jam of two crawling cars. He must have known that I'd ask him why he'd bother taking a few hours' work away from Patrick, because he nearly shoved the suit up the steps and through the doors. When I got there, I looked across an empty lobby, wondering where I'd seen the other man's face before, like trying to remember a dream that moves further away with every waking blink.

# 8

Patrick was coming from the river, three eels in a canvas bag over his shoulder. His preferred stretch of water was full of the things, pulsing along the riverbed. He'd used ten droppers on the night-line, set earlier in the week, and probably caught more than three but left them there long enough to wriggle free. He didn't like their oily meat and the butcher, Pheilim Riley, told him that he'd never be interested, scratching at those sore and red eyelids so that little flakes of skin fell on the meat counter like unwanted seasoning. The cat liked them boiled, so Patrick carried on setting his lines and pulling the muscled ropes of them from the water – ugly creatures shamed into the dark long before man walked the earth.

A blue car was parked close to the ditch just beyond Ballyrue Cross. ZI plates for Dublin city. Next to it, a man in shirt sleeves and a waistcoat was perched on a wooden stool, behind a large easel with paper clipped to it. The man's coat was slung over the stone wall behind him, next to a jar of cabbage-green water with three wooden brush handles rising from it. The black hair of the bristles, flattened at the murky bottom reminded Patrick of the eels. The man didn't hear his footsteps.

Patrick studied the painting, a close enough likeness to the land and low hills beyond the easel, though the painter had misjudged the spread of the triangle of evergreens in the distance. The sky was a shade of turquoise blue never seen in Ireland and the fields were being put to different use.

'Why are you putting sheep in tillage fields?' Patrick said.

The man set his brush down before turning on the stool, taking a cloth from his left shoulder, where it left a damp stain on his light blue shirt. He wiped his hands then tossed the cloth to the low wall. His hat shaded a face tanned a shade darker than any Irishman and his smile showed a set of teeth as white as quicklime.

'Artistic licence,' the man said.

'You're American.' Patrick had never heard the accent when it wasn't coming from a cinema screen or radio speaker.

'I am. Well, I'm Irish-American. George O'Malley, if you can believe it. What's your name, son?'

'Patrick.'

The man grinned. 'I might have guessed.'

Patrick stepped closer and looked at the painting, then beyond it, then back to the painter.

'Why is the sky so bright?'

'It's a mystery.' The man tossed his hands, shaking his head at the limits of his talent.

'What is? The sky, or why you painted it that colour?'

'You can decide the answer to that one.'

'Why are you painting that anyway?' Patrick considered the painting from another angle.

The man glanced back at his work-in-progress. 'Oh, I do this for fun. Relaxes my mind, I suppose. I'm afraid I'm not much good. I don't think it'll be in a gallery any time soon.'

'But why here?' The chemical smell of watercolours brushed the air between them.

The man thought for a few seconds. 'I was just driving. This is my first time in Ireland. It's a damn sight poorer than I thought it'd be, but it's about as beautiful as I expected. I think you could stop just about anywhere and see something worth painting.' The man looked east as if to prove his point and Patrick followed his eye along the same road he'd walked since he was a boy.

'Is that why you're here? To paint Ireland?'

'No, I'm a newspaper man with a little time on his hands. I'm here to cover the homecoming.'

'Kennedy?'

'Who else? His great-grandfather left this country about the same time as my own. People like stories like that. Full circle – where the beginning and the end are the same, but also very different.'

'It's hardly a homecoming. Unless you can tell me which house is his.'

The man laughed. 'You're not as excited as everybody else? Seems as though 'most every person I meet is a third or fourth cousin.'

Patrick rounded the car. 'They're cousins the same way you're Irish.'

The man laughed again, louder this time. 'I like you, son. You just don't give a damn, do you? You see me in town sometime, you let me buy you a drink. You're old enough to drink, aren't you?'

Patrick scratched his nose.

The man looked at the bag, hanging alongside Patrick's dirty and patched trouser leg.

'What have you got there?'

'Eels. Three of them.'

'I've never tried eel. They any good?'

'The finest.'

'You know, if I took them back to Miss Flynn, I think she'd use them for my supper.' The man stood and reached into his pocket, then took out a black leather wallet. 'How much for two?'

Patrick needed the money. By his count he'd need to save every penny of months' worth of dole to buy a single Shorthorn. He looked at the bag, then the man.

'I'll trade you. The lot of them for that painting.'

The man looked at the painting. 'That thing isn't even finished, son. Between you and me, it's just about worthless. Are you sure you wouldn't prefer the cash?'

'Three for the painting.' Patrick lifted the bag towards the man.

'Well, alright.'

The man took the clamps off his board and held the painting in front of him, appraising it one last time, before handing it to Patrick. They completed the trade and the man lifted the bag up and down a couple of times.

'I look forward to these. I hope you have some pretty Irish girl to give that painting to.'

Patrick thought about Rose, then rolled the paper into a tube then held it to his eye like a telescope, eyeing the man through it. He lowered it when the man cautioned him that the paint was still wet.

'I'm going to hang it in the house.'

'Well, I'm honoured, even if it probably looks even worse now you've rolled it. You know, you Irish are funny people.'

'How are we funny?'

'I met a man a couple of days back. I was way out west, where my ancestors are from.' He wagged two fingers vaguely towards the Atlantic and shook his head. 'There are parts of this country that are from another time. I was driving, no place in particular. I came to this old cottage and the man who lived there had come to his door, at the sound of the car, I suppose. He came out to the road and ran his hand over the hood as if he'd never seen a car before and same as you, noticed my accent. I told him where I was from and he asked me if I'd ever spent time in Boston. I told him I had, and this poor old guy. Shit.' The man laughed and shook his head. 'He asked me if I knew his son. Said he hadn't seen him since he left. He gave me a name and description, as if Boston is just the same as his little village.' The man looked to Patrick.

'And did you?'

'Did I what?'

'Did you know his son?'

The man looked more closely, as if he was studying him. 'No, son. I didn't.'

'Well, now you know to look out for him. Tell him his aul fella was asking after him if you ever meet him.'

Patrick raised the painting to say goodbye and walked to the centre of the road. When he got to the bend, he looked back without stopping and the man took his hand from his pocket and waved. Patrick didn't wave back, just continued into the shadows cast by a line of silver birch.

*

He unrolled the painting after dinner and walked the ground floor, holding it in front of him. He went upstairs to his bedroom, trying it in different positions. Above the dresser, next to the wardrobe, above his bed. He settled on the bare wall across the room, so it would be the first thing he saw when he woke.

He hammered a small nail through each corner of the painting, and stood back and looked at it, moving a step to the left, then the right, then back.

'That's a grand job,' he said, then said it twice again, emphasising different words.

He sat next to the stove, copying his mother's evening routine of knitting, with her leather suitcase open on the floor. The case was another extravagance, and its only journey had been the trip from town. She used it to store her knitting materials – wool and cotton, tacks and pins, scissors and measuring tape, a darning egg, thimbles and stitch holders and her collection of newspaper and magazine clippings of patterns and designs that remained far beyond his competence. Rags of sheep's wool lay in the corners of the case like small dead animals. He remembered collecting the wool from fences and hedges at her request, to use as rustproof stuffing for pincushions.

He picked up the needles for the first time in spring and filled empty hours practising slip-knots and casting on and knit and purl stitches. He wore calluses on his index fingers despite not having knitted anything to completion. A planned pair of gloves became ill-fitting mittens when fingertips proved beyond his reach. The beginnings of a hat were sewn into a torn jumper when he couldn't wrap his head around the crown. Rectangular patches of wool were scattered around the house and he'd forgotten what most of them were the beginnings of.

He pushed his tongue into the gap in his teeth, trying to understand what he was doing wrong and what the book meant by *varying tension*. Whatever it meant, it seemed to explain why things he made often turned out too loose and came apart easily. He knitted a few rows then set it aside and wondered who taught his mother.

She could knit anything, and took on a deeper intensity when making lace, as if an invisible judge was over her shoulder and the quality of her work determined something of immeasurable significance. He couldn't learn by words alone. He needed somebody to show him how to do a thing right, so he could see it in real time. The way his father taught him about farming or swimming or cycling.

He walked the room with his hands in his pockets. He touched a few tools on the table, brushed some sawdust to the floor, then stood on the doorstep. Clouds huddled in patches, preparing for an advance on the sun. Through the gap in the wall in the tool shed, he saw the cat walking soundlessly back and forth, nosing buckets and cans and its empty saucer. Patrick wondered if they were both in need of a good drink. He'd heard men say it. *What I need is a good drink*, or *Come on and we'll have a good drink*. The American had said he'd buy him one if he saw him.

Like his father, he had no taste for the stuff and hated seeing men with too much taken, slobbering and bleary-eyed, talking rubbish and expecting everybody to listen. Belting out-of-tune scraps of songs and getting thick when nobody joined in. Stumbling around town ready to fight the world, with all sorts of sorrow and sadness on display. He hated how he felt the next morning, his skin and mouth dry as sandpaper, a whisper coming from somewhere in the fog of his mind, telling him that he'd done something wrong or some way shamed himself, even after he only had a couple.

One of the priests at Christian's used to speak in seanfhocail and warned plenty of classrooms of boys away from drink. *Nuair a bhíonn an deoch istigh, bíonn an chiall amuigh – When the drink is in, the sense is out.*

He cycled to town through a countryside evening too perfect for loneliness, with an endless span of sky that makes the heart want for something it can't explain. He avoided Ryan's, where he might see Peter Casey or Flood, and stood his bike outside Gallagher's – a dark hovel at the end of town, with a small shop where drunk bachelors bought the few bits of food that sustained them.

The place smelled of turf smoke and decades' worth of tarry Woodbine. A man named Flannery was drinking with two others at a table to the left. Patrick avoided his eye and cursed his luck. Was there no place he could go without inviting stares? He'd bought five chicks from Flannery at the market at the turn of the year, with a promise that they came from a long line of productive hens. By early summer, Patrick hadn't collected a single egg and realised that Flannery had sold him cocks. He killed all five in a rage of feathers and squawking after the sound of their clucking reminded him one time too many that he was the butt of another man's joke. He regretted it while his knife was still wet with blood and his chest was still rising and falling in a fever of anger. If nothing else, it was a waste of good meat, with too much to eat before it turned. Pheilim Riley took most of it for a pittance.

He went to the bar with his head down and Gallagher stood from a tall stool, leaving a knotted blackthorn walking stick against the wall and scratching one of several large brown spots on the dome of his bald head. There was a picture of Kennedy behind the bar, next to a small trophy awarded to Gallagher's granddaughter for singing at the Feis two decades back – the only thing in the pub still shining. 'Don't ask me for work again,' Gallagher said, grabbing a tap to steady himself. 'What are you having?'

Patrick eyed the taps and the trio of optics. 'Smithwick's,' he said, having seen the name on the side of delivery trucks plenty of times.

'That's Kilkenny drinking,' Gallagher said, but took a glass and filled it all the same.

Two old men sat at either end of the bar, like lifelong rivals under a vow of silence, separated by twelve feet of countertop. One looked into a pint of water and made no sound at all, not even when he returned the glass to the countertop. The feeling of being watched warmed Patrick's blood and he fought the urge to scratch his chest and back or to turn around and look at whatever eyes were fixed on him, wanting to be nothing more than another nameless drinker, just for an hour. Why was it that he longed to sit among company when facing another night alone, then longed for his chair by the fire once he was among other men?

He carried the pint to a corner table, and the men across the room erupted with laughter at something Flannery said.

He struggled to swallow the first malty mouthful. He could think of no quicker way to waste money – at least burning it would give a bit of warmth. The door opened and the light that came in cast Gallagher's in a miserable glow, dust motes scattering through it like rats after a barn door opening. A man entered, raising nods from the drinkers by the window. Patrick watched as Gallagher filled a glass without taking an order.

When the man took his pint, he turned and eyed the room, then raised a hand in Patrick's direction. Patrick didn't place him until he came and sat on the opposite stool.

'Mr Rossiter,' he said, recognising his old schoolmate's father, broad and dark-haired, with huge brick-laying hands. He wore his shirt tucked in, his face and arms were clean and his shoes were polished.

'Patrick,' Rossiter said. 'I hope you're not taking up bad habits.'

Patrick looked at his drink. 'Where's Barry these days?'

The man drank then exhaled with satisfaction, as if he'd walked twenty miles for that first mouthful. 'Dublin, for now. But there's a crowd over in Birmingham, all lads you were in school with. They might tempt him across. How are you keeping yourself?'

'Grand.'

'How long is your mother gone now?'

'Six months,' Patrick said and took another mouthful, no better than the first.

Rossiter shook his head. 'Jesus but it was sudden. Are you keeping busy?'

'Trying to. I'm going to put that land back to work now that she's gone.' He heard his voice take on new inflections, trying to talk with the ease of men he heard at mass and markets.

Rossiter looked doubtful. 'She didn't leave you with much of it. It was a grand farm once upon a time.'

'I don't need much.' They drank in silence. 'Peter Casey is after parking two Masseys next to my wall.'

'He's doing a fair amount of work out at the stud, so maybe that's all it is. I did some work with the lights. Christ, have you seen that horse of his?'

'Yeah,' Patrick said, 'once. From a distance though.' The thought of the horse stirred the same pang of jealousy and longing he felt when he saw young men walking with their wives.

'How long have they been down your direction?'

'Since yesterday morning. Just sitting there.'

'Hold tight a bit longer. Don't give him the satisfaction of a reaction.'

Rossiter drank and looked to be about to make a suggestion when his head was turned by one of the men at the window letting out a loud *Cock-a-doodle-do*, followed by three machine-gun blasts of laughter. Rossiter didn't laugh, but the look on his face told Patrick that he understood the joke.

Patrick took his glass in both hands. The man let out the sound again, and his grip tightened. Flannery and the other man laughed in harmony.

'Don't mind them,' Rossiter said. 'The same men will be getting carried out of here by their youngsters in a few hours.'

They were interrupted by the joker coming to the table, his hair shaved close to his head like a schoolboy ravaged by lice, his feet scuffing against the floor as he walked, reaching into his pocket and taking out some coins. He smelled of sweat and his left arm was branded with some unknowable symbol – something resembling an eye, printed on his skin in dark blue ink. He burped and put his left hand on Rossiter's shoulder as if to let him in on the joke, then looked at Patrick with a lop-sided grin. 'C'mere to me.' He turned to the men at the window, then back to Patrick and raised his voice. 'Would you happen to have any eggs for sale?' he said, extending a palm full of coins then bending with a peal of laughter that sounded like a donkey's bray. The other men laughed and Rossiter took a drink.

'That'll do, John,' Rossiter said over his shoulder, eyeing Patrick, whose jaw muscles were pulsing. He tapped his foot against the floor and put his left hand in his pocket.

The man straightened and stepped nearer to the table, examining Patrick as if he was trying to read some fine print across his forehead. 'How is it that two brothers can look so different?' he said and Patrick looked at Rossiter, wondering if the man thought they were brothers. 'Your parents were no oil paintings, but all the same,' he went on, looking to the other men for encouragement. He finished what was in his glass. 'You look about as mad as your father did in the finish.'

The legs of the table screeched along the floor, and drink spilled over the rim of the glasses as Patrick stood, pulling his knife from his pocket. Before he could free the blade, Rossiter was standing, grabbing Patrick's wrist with his left hand and the drunk's collar with his right, yanking him forward so the man's head rested on Rossiter's shoulder and his glass fell to the ground and broke into two large parts. Rossiter bent his head and spoke through gritted teeth. 'That's enough, I said.' He pushed the man away then turned to Patrick and released his hand. 'Put that back in your pocket. Now. Right fucking now.'

Patrick did as he was told and returned the knife with a shaking hand. Gallagher came to them, bent over his walking stick.

'Out,' he whispered, looking at Patrick. Even the men at the bar looked on.

'I was minding my business,' Patrick protested.

'Out,' Gallagher repeated, raising his black stick and tapping the rubber-capped bottom against Patrick's pocket. Gallagher turned in a slow arc and Rossiter looked to Patrick. He wanted to tell the old man that he was only trying to scare the drunk back to his table.

'Go on, Patrick. It's not worth the trouble.' Rossiter looked towards the door.

Patrick looked around the pub and felt eyes all over him and wondered how all those eyes could see anything but an injustice. 'Not one of ye man enough to say something,' he said and nobody answered. He rounded the table and left without word, two-thirds of his pint untouched.

Rage propelled his cycle home, the muscles in his legs fuming against every incline, his skin itching and so warm that he wanted to tear it off like a jumper. He fixed his gaze forwards and his eyes watered in the wind as he cursed the town and whatever it was the place wanted from him. He stayed hidden away and they called him idle and a shame to his parents. He tried to work and they wouldn't let him. He tried to drink alone, the same as every low man in the country and even that was put against him.

He tired beside Loughlin's field, where a blue Fordson circled the hay. He stood in the sweet air, thinking of the nesting birds scrambling to escape the mower, ending up sliced as easily as the grass. He walked on, pushing the bike, the chain whirring.

A black car with Dublin plates was parked outside his wall. A tall man in a hat and long coat came through the gate and looked Patrick's way as he rounded the front of the car.

'Hey,' Patrick shouted, pushing off and cycling hard with the last of his energy, while the man climbed in and shut the door. He caught up as the car pulled away and slapped the back window with his palm. 'Go on, fuck off away from here,' he roared after it, then watched it round the bend, leaving him in the smoke of dust it kicked up from the road, the house as empty as he'd left it.

He was dragging the tip of his pocket knife through the dark halos of dirt beneath his fingernails when he heard an engine die and a car door open and shut. He leaned to the window, wondering if the man in the suit had returned, then dried his hands on his shirt at the sight of Sergeant Field coming through the gate. Patrick decided against asking if Field knew the man. His big ears had probably already caught wind of what happened in Gallagher's. He moved a pot of three potatoes off the heat and opened the front door before the sergeant could knock.

'Patrick,' Field said, planting his feet. 'Fine bright evening.'

Patrick shut one eye, took in the last of the light then scratched his chest through open top buttons.

'Tom McCrann told me he had to pull the job from under you?'

He looked to the sheds. 'That's his business.'

'Well, I was sorry to hear it, Patrick. Can't beat a day's work. And a few bob extra is always welcome.' Field put his hands on his hips. 'Though it looks like you keep busy.' He looked over the results of Patrick's morning exertion – the vegetable garden, weeded and raked. A zinc bucket at the corner of the house, overflowing with dirt and grass, and a wooden ladder against the wall, beneath a newly cleaned gutter.

A wren broke the silence with a string of whistles.

'I forget how quiet it gets out here. I could get used to it.' Field looked in the direction of the Masseys beyond the wall. 'They spoil the scenery a bit, don't they?' He smiled and Patrick didn't. 'Any idea why they're there?'

'What am I supposed to have done wrong this time?' Patrick straightened.

'Ah.' Field put one hand in his pocket, tugged on an earlobe and turned east, looking through the trees and over the maze of limestone walls and pasture land. 'You met the men driving those tractors yesterday morning?'

'I broke no law.'

Field smirked. 'Indeed you didn't. But you know better than anyone that stories don't have to be true to be told. There's people saying you aimed your gun at the pair of them.'

Patrick pressed his thumb into a splinter on the door frame. 'I was heading out hunting and had the gun with me. I never even raised it.'

Field met his eye. 'You need to remember that people don't care what's true, Patrick. Just whatever story suits them best.' He took the dole envelope from his inside pocket and handed it to Patrick. 'And you need to remember to collect this. I won't bring it out again.'

Patrick pocketed it and said nothing.

'I'll leave you to it so. If you ever need anything, you know where I am.'

Field was halfway to the gate when Patrick called after him. 'You can tell whoever was out here checking on me to stay away from my land.'

Field turned. 'Who's that?'

'Some fella in a suit and shiny car. Tell them keep away from here and they won't need to worry about me. Same goes for anybody else looking for a reason to come to this door.'

Field ignored the insinuation. 'When was this?'

'Only a couple of hours ago.'

'Nothing to do with me, Patrick.'

Patrick watched him drive away, surprised that he wouldn't have minded him staying a bit longer, even if it was just chatting shite about the quiet and the sky.

# 9

Siobhán had her arm around Catriona, reading to her on the couch, when I got in. She glanced up but kept reading, sounding out big words, tiredness in her voice while she turned a strand of Catriona's hair in her fingers.

'How are my girls?' I said, and Catriona looked up and jumped from the couch.

'Daddy!' she said, wrapping her arms around my waist. 'We looked at the bird's nest from a ladder!'

'The bird's nest? The one outside? Where did you get a ladder?'

I looked at Siobhán. She closed the book and put it to the side then looked at the clock on the mantelpiece to tell me I was late. 'There was men fixing the Kielys' roof.'

I saw in her face that she was in no mood for being pressed on taking Catriona up a ladder. 'Why don't you go read something for grown-ups, while me and the little missus find something to do?'

'I've dinner to make. How's your head?'

'Oh, fine. Fine.' The pain blinked somewhere behind my eye, reminding me that it hadn't gone away.

She stood and put her hand on Catriona's head and left the room without a word.

I crouched to one knee and ran a knuckle across Catriona's soft cheekbone and she tucked her elbows in and laughed, recharged by my arrival and ready to wear me out.

'Was it scary on the ladder?'

'A little bit. Mammy was holding me.'

I heard Siobhán chopping in the kitchen, the hiss of gas, the clatter of a saucepan, the window opened to let out the steam.

'Do you know how to build a rocket?' I said to Catriona.

Her cheeks reddened and she brought her thumbs together, picking at her nails and looking towards the empty doorway, before shaking her head, as if she was trying to keep a secret.

'Let's go make one.'

I tapped her on the end of her nose and it was like pushing a button to make her smile. She ran to the kitchen to tell Siobhán, while I found an empty roll of cardboard. I took one of Siobhán's old magazines from the rack in the sitting room, and an envelope fell from between the pages. Addressed to Siobhán in neat handwriting, with a fresh post-mark and no letter inside. I put it back where I found it, then went to the kitchen and took a scissors and some tape from the drawer. Siobhán smiled at me, the way a stranger might, while she squeezed past on the way to the sink. She had the radio on low, some sad piano piece that seemed to never end and I sat at the table with Catriona, who brought her crayons and sat dangling her little legs over her seat, while we made a basic craft out of cardboard and the pages of *Woman's Way*. She picked colours she liked, then we cut them up in the shape of stars to stick on the side while Siobhán worked between the counter and the cooker, stealing a few looks through clouds of steam.

'Now, we need to put a flag on it. Will we do Ireland's colours?'

'Green, white and gold,' she said, sliding green and orange crayons from her set and looking at me.

'You do it, love,' I said and she smiled and coloured a warped rectangle somewhere around where the cargo bay would be. When it was finished, it stood on the table between us, slanting to one side, and I asked Catriona, 'Do you think it can fly?'

And of course, she did.

Siobhán turned her light off early, her book untouched. I kissed her shoulder and said goodnight.

'Night, love,' she said and pulled the blanket to her chin, lying on her side and facing away. I thought about asking her about the letter. It could have been a reply from a paper, or an old friend, or a book club, or might concern any number of things that aren't of concern to me. All the same, it's never easy to be reminded that even in a marriage as close as ours, there are parts of a person that can't be understood. I sat with my back against the headboard, looking into the near-darkness, the curtains open to a badly bruised sky.

I remember the first nights we shared a bed, weekends in whatever Cork hotel I could afford, pretending to be a married couple to escape the judgement of strangers, people we'd never see again and who we worried would bear witness to our great unmarried sin. Not able to stay in the house Siobhán shared with two rosary-beaded secretaries from Limerick. Checking in as Mister and Missus Field, the little charge of pride I felt whenever I said it to a receptionist, with Siobhán's arm linked in mine, one of her cheap dress rings moved to the appropriate finger to add to the deception. We'd lie awake, not wanting to sleep away the luxury of time together. Some nights I'd sit on the floor next to the bath, my head resting on the porcelain while Siobhán soaked for long spells in the warm water before I led her, towelled and soft and pink-skinned, to the bed. Nights of heaven after days so alive, walking the city hand in hand, neither of us wanting to let go. Buying oranges in Cudmore's, coffee roasted in the windows of Woodford's and parcelled-up roast chicken straight from a spit on Bridge Street, pretending these luxuries were how we'd live if we were always together. The shy silence when we passed the wedding rings in Egan's window display. Setting up picnics on benches near the Lee or the Shandon Bells, waiting for night and the quiet corners of hotel bars.

I wouldn't have guessed that years later we'd be sharing a bed, with Siobhán asleep or pretending to be, while I sit up, giving an audience to all the worries of night. No love has been lost, there's been no hardening of hearts. There's no place I'd rather be than next to her. Time has passed, that's all. Life has landed a few clean hits of loss, and reality, and promises she made to herself in youth have gone unkept. Is it any wonder she thinks about being born a decade too early? We met when she had youth and time whispering in her ear, telling her she had a plentiful supply of both.

I remember finding her waiting outside the station one evening, and my heart jumping to the lovestruck conclusion that she couldn't bear the distance anymore. That all our talk about our future and marriage had resulted in her deciding to join me in Wexford. I can remember how still she was when I held her, how my kiss was given but not returned. A delayed smile, eyes that shied away. Her coat buttoned to her chin, her bag clutched in front of her like a woman in a hurry, then the tears when she told me that she'd come to end things. Putting her hand on my face and asking me to not ask her to explain something that she couldn't explain to herself. Her kiss and tears wet on my cheek when she told me she'd travelled with a friend and her husband, who were waiting in a car to carry her on to Dublin. Walking away while I was still calling after her.

Almost a year later, I met her brother at a Garda dance in Cork. The do was in the Metropole, where we'd once visited, and I could see the ghost of her in the lobby and by the bar, putting her head back and laughing to the chandeliers. Con told me that she was bound for America, that he thought I'd want to know. I couldn't bring myself to try to talk her out of it. Her life was her own. I remember coming back from that wedding, the lowest point of that lonely time, and my sergeant telling me on Monday morning that there was a man I had to pick up and drive to Senan's, no matter what it took. Poor old Sean Hatten.

I stared at the cloud of damp on our ceiling and battled the memories with what came after. Two years without her, carrying Sean Hatten's handkerchief in my pocket, reminding me to never sink so low again. Two years that started with Tony Coughlan – the undertaker – encouraging me to take his daughter, Bernadette, to the pictures, until I eventually relented and took her for walks along the river and around Tintern Abbey and Dunmore East. Those walks and months led to Tony hinting at marriage, telling me I'd have his blessing. I only allowed myself to think of Siobhán for a few moments before I slept, imagining her next to me. I remember meeting Tony in town one wet Saturday, when he summoned me to a doorway as the rain fell harder. Tony told me that in his eyes – eyes matched by a sky-blue shirt – any man in Ireland would be lucky to marry his daughter and that he knew I thought a lot of her too. He said that in my hesitancy to bend a knee, he saw that somebody else had my heart wrapped up and he advised me, with his hand on my shoulder in some fatherly gesture, that if whoever it was ever came back to my life, to never let her go.

Then one evening, in the gentle flow of the simple, steady life I'd built, I stood watching the dark Barrow pass and heard her voice behind me. I turned to her, exactly as I'd known her and altogether different, smiling the way she smiled when I used to visit her in Cork. There are a few moments in life that you know you'll never forget, even while they're still playing out. She told me that night in my quarters above the station that she'd never left. That all the things that were driving her from Ireland were things that she wanted to try to fix in whatever way she could.

I turned to her and she was certainly asleep. I wanted to tell her that none of her effort was in vain, that because people like her stayed, our little girl will reach our age with a new millennium in touching distance, in a world altogether different from this one. That her efforts are like a quiet storm, missed by those who shut their eyes to it. That she'll keep going and keep leaving her mark wherever she strikes and eventually people will have no choice but to take notice. I put my arm around her and did my best to drift off, pain storming through my head and spreading to the temples, while I lay awake thinking about Patrick, and Peter Casey's machines over his wall – aimed at the house like a pair of Soviet missiles.

I found him in his doorway when I called out this evening. Harming nobody. He cut a sorry figure. Needle thin, like the sole survivor of a shipwreck after months alone on an island. I suppose that's almost what he is out on that land. He had the same aul shirt on him, itching away as usual. I went out once, not long after Maura died, with a parcel of old clothes of mine. I haven't seen them since, as if wearing them would be some sort of admission that he'd needed the help.

I was chatting away, trying to see would any word stick and a quiet came over the place that made it feel as if we were the last two men in Ireland. Sometimes I get the feeling that he's sizing me up, like a dog over a dinner plate, wondering can he trust what's in front of him. He always backs away, deciding that he's better off going hungry. It's as if there's something he wants to talk about. Or maybe he just wants to lean against his door and chat with a visitor, like any other man on a fine evening. Then I'll be saying something, thinking he's listening, and I'll see he's smiling at his finger, bent in the doorframe, lost to this world a few seconds at a time.

He told me somebody had been out to the house earlier. Sounded like the same suit I saw walking to the Royal with Casey. It stayed with me, the vague outline of the face I saw, and it gnawed at me long into the dark hours. I heard noises on the landing right in the depth of that no man's land between night and morning and I moved close to Siobhán, listening to her breathing. I sat up at a creak on the floorboard outside our door. Everything is different in those hours. You start to believe things that daylight makes a mockery of. I stood and crossed the room, certain that I'd find Patrick Hatten there in the hallway, and what's worse, part of me was glad of it, thinking he'd come to me for help. I opened the bedroom door and the cat was looking up at me in the dark, one paw raised.

I brought her downstairs and sat at the table, knowing there was no point going up to try and sleep. I poured her some milk and poured myself some tea and sat in the dark drinking with a couple more painkillers. I went in to work on the V-2 but couldn't concentrate, knowing that if I kept at it the thruster or stabilising fin would go on arseways. It's precision work, not meant for a man who should be in his bed or with a mind on Masseys and men in suits and the feeling that Patrick Hatten's world was a cage closing in on him.

It came to me then, while I sat looking at the near-finished model on its start table. All the little parts of that face I saw outside the Royal. The angled jaw, the nose flat in side profile, the eyes set a little too shallow in their sockets. The curls of brown hair that I could see around the hat he had on. It reminded me of Patrick himself, and then it came ringing through my head as clear as an air-raid siren. It's his brother, Colm. Colm Hatten back from England and meeting Peter Casey in the Royal Hotel could only really mean one thing. He was home to sell the land. I sat in the armchair in the corner of the room, trying to think of any other reason, but try as I might, I couldn't come up with anything that would be good news for Patrick.

# 10

He woke facing the opposite wall to the painting and when he turned over, it disappointed him. Without the benefit of sunlight or lamplight or the backdrop of the easel, it looked blotted and unfinished, as the man had warned. He stood in front of it and considered it in its new light and thought that maybe the man was a poor painter, then thought that the same man probably didn't care the least bit whether he was good or not – sitting with his easel in the quiet of a foreign country, painting for no other reason than the pleasure of it. He could probably set fire to every landscape as soon as he added finishing touches and have lost nothing at all.

He ate a bowl of porridge and left some almost-turned milk for the cat, which managed to hide in its small confines, then stood outside the door of the toolshed and spat, looking through the trees at the tractors. He left for the woods off east, kicking away the tyre tracks left by the car the previous evening as if by doing so he could rid his land of its memory. He was armed with a spear-thrower as long as his forearm and a dart as long as himself, the faces of the men in the pub still grinning in his mind. Both were carved from carefully chosen pine – the best darts coming from the lower branches of mature trees. Anything too light would be as unstable as a kite at the top of the Blackstairs. Anything too heavy meant needing to get too close to easily spooked prey. He didn't take his gun. The challenge was to make a perfect shot with a single dart. To kill his prey the way man did it before man could speak.

The road was busy with hauliers and vans on their way to the creamery, overtaking and leaving a trail of 2-Star fumes for him to near-suffocate on. Some passed so close he almost ended up in the ditch. Cans and bottles rattled on the back of a cart driven by a pair of old women, taking near every drop of milk they'd drawn to sell for pennies. When he reached the river, he followed its journey south, his short shadow cast on the surface like something for the flies to feed on. His feet began to prickle as if he was walking over thorns and he closed his eyes and breathed slowly, willing the sensation away.

He crouched on the bank and scooped a handful of water over his head, then opened the buttons of his shirt and splashed his chest. He took off his boots and sank his feet into the water and the prickling eased as if it had never been there. Voices came from downstream and he leaned forward to watch the distant shapes of men pulling sparkling cobwebs of net from the water, catching fish like flies, and drowned the thought of being the one who sold them the kit they needed.

He kept his feet in the water until they felt like frozen trout, and he imagined the crowds down at Arthurstown, sweating and queuing for ice-cream and chips, kicking ball and swimming, burning in deck chairs. He stood and walked on barefoot, his boots hooked on his fingers. He hoped he might see Rose, walking the road or sitting against a tree in one of Casey's fields, and more than once, his mind tricked him into believing that he had.

He'd been in the forest an hour and ignored a group of fallow that were too easy to pick off. Puncturing one of them with his dart presented no challenge. He needed a kill that called for patience, planning and skill. A kill that focused the mind.

He walked slowly, sometimes shutting his eyes to see if he could make his footsteps completely silent. In one of these closed-lidded moments, he heard a rustling to his left and opened his eyes to a young stag angling through a clearing, its antlers mutated and curled, its head stooped and shaking, milky bands of spit hanging from its mouth. Patrick had seen the affliction before and what the deer needed more than air was a dart through its flank. He whistled through his gap and something took flight overhead. The stag looked at him and didn't bother running, just aimed a sad, black eye like a plea.

He pressed a finger to one nostril and released a pellet of snot from the other. He let the animal stagger on a few paces and every step seemed to hurt it.

'You poor bastard.'

He spat and placed his dart in the thrower, knowing that a poor shot would mean a slow and painful death, without the option of a mercy bullet. He held the weapon horizontally behind his ear and steadied his breath, watching his target's head gripped by the shakes like some drunk on a windowsill waiting for the pub to open. After a slow exhalation, he put his weight on his front foot, snapped his throwing arm forward and watched the dart hurtle through space and into the broadside of the deer. It fell sideways to a grave of leaves, both lungs punctured.

Patrick walked to it and pulled out the dart and watched the blood seep from the wound.

'It's okay,' he said, crouching and putting a hand on the deer's head. He looked into the eye, like a fine and rare black glass that reflected the world. He saw his own shape backlit by the sky and imagined the deer begging him to ease its pain while blood filled its lungs. He took its ear between his thumb and index finger and circled it gently, making shushing sounds while it died.

He sat next to it for a few minutes, turning his bow-knife in his hand and eyeing the forest, unable to spot the herd that had abandoned it.

# 11

Siobhán came into the kitchen, bringing morning with her. She kept her voice down while she scolded me for not sleeping in our bed. I didn't mention my worries about us, and the empty envelope and how it reminded me of when she left me all those years back, plans suddenly revealed and strangers waiting in a car to take her away. I told her I was up thinking about Patrick.

'Why are you fixated on him? What is it that's worth you looking so run-down?' she asked, putting a pot of tea in front of me, Catriona still sound asleep and the cat moving between mine and the table's legs.

'I'm not fixated on him.'

'Didn't you talk the ear off me yesterday evening. About his dole and his house and the quiet of the place. I prefer when you're going on about rockets and Kennedy.'

'I'll hold you to that,' I said, but she didn't smile. 'Stop worrying, love, I can manage plenty of things at once.'

'You can, yeah – when you're going through Disprin at the rate you are and only eating half of what you normally do.' She shook her head and leaned to open the window, letting the stuffy air escape to the yard.

'Once Kennedy has been and gone things will settle back down. I can't help that Hatten's name keeps coming up.' I poured two cups of tea. Siobhán adds enough sugar to make a paste and thinks she's married to the strangest man in Wexford because I take mine black. I shook my head and said nothing more, only put the lid back on the sugar bowl, drawing a look from her. I've explained it all to her before. That I drove the lad's father to Senan's and stood next to him the day he was made an orphan, watching his mother's body being plucked from the garden and loaded into a van the same as a sack of vegetables.

'You don't have to go running every time, as if he's the most important thing on your plate.'

'The man you saw Casey with, love. Outside the Royal.' She looked at me from over the rim of her cup. 'I'm near-certain it's Colm Hatten.'

She put her cup down and her eyes did some calculating. 'The lad who went off to England?'

'The eldest son home like magic after both parents are gone. We both know how that goes.'

She hesitated, her shoulders softening her posture to something like concern. 'But he'd hardly throw his brother out. His own brother.'

'Who knows? But it looks like Casey already has him hooked.'

She put an elbow on the table and her forehead against her hand. 'What a mess. Do they understand that the boy won't leave his home without trouble?'

'Well, they couldn't have timed it worse.'

'Promise me you'll be smart, Jim, we can do without being in Peter Casey's firing line.'

'I will. But if Casey wants that place, it will be done properly.'

She gave a nod of weary acceptance. 'All I'm saying,' she said, standing at the sound of Catriona's waking calls, 'is that getting on Casey's bad side will be more trouble than it's worth. It doesn't matter what side of Patrick Hatten you're on, he's liable to do anything. I don't want your goodness to blind you into thinking he cares one bit what effort you go to for him.' She put her hand on my shoulder as her final word on the matter. 'It'll be a hot one today,' she said, and left the kitchen.

When she talks about me like that, about my supposed goodness, I swallow the guilt like poison. Can a man ever be good after what I did?

I heard her singing to Catriona while they got ready for the day. They came back to the kitchen, the warmth of her bed still on Catriona when I wrapped my arms around her. Siobhán put a cardboard box in front of me, filled with homemade jam, butter, bread, Fairy Liquid and baking soda, paraffin oil and candles.

'Now, since you're doing home visits these days, you can drop that down to Rita after work.'

I gripped the cup with my weak hand, squeezing it so tight I thought it might break, then drained my tea and stood, lifting the box and kissing Siobhán on the ear, thinking that it looked as if I had a day of strength ahead of me and that I'd better make the most of it. What was it Kennedy said, about fixing the roof while the sun is shining?

The place was lively when I got in, everybody up to their eyeballs and in bright and early to make sure they got out on time for dinner and the long, warm evening that was promised. The countdown well and truly on. Revising plans and contingency plans and every man and his brother coming with a question or asking for a favour. There's no leave allowed while Kennedy's touring our little island. Even though it's not my say-so, I've lads coming in complaining about needing the leave and wives torturing them over trips that were promised. Any guards that don't have the new uniform are to be posted beyond Kennedy's orbit, so some of our own will be standing off route, staring into fields instead of getting a look at the man who stopped us from blowing ourselves out of existence.

When he walks by in Dunganstown, it will take all my strength to keep my hands by my side and not offer one to him. It takes vision to see the possibilities of space. And vision is only half the battle. Having the guts to follow through is the other, when so many will tell him it's a fine way to waste money better spent for what's needed here on Earth. I've heard fellas saying that the visit is nothing but a politician's move, to shore up Irish votes or to charm us into NATO. I'm not one of them. I'm among the countless others, unashamedly under the spell of the suits and sunglasses and speeches. The eyes that stared down the Soviets and didn't blink. I look at Kennedy – a man born only a few years before the Free State – and see Ireland's full potential, some version of the future that we'd be better off hurrying up and arriving at.

I heard Casey before I saw him. Laughing with Flood outside my door, ashamed at him for all but bending the knee and asking how the stables were coming along. I'd found him early, eating breakfast in Croake's with an egg-stained plate in front of him and a newspaper folded open on the racing pages. I asked him to come in for a word when it suited, to see could I get out of him what he wanted with Colm Hatten. I could have talked to him there and then, but I like to think that even a man as sure-footed as Casey feels at least a bit off balance inside the walls of a station.

He knocked as he walked in – no chance he'd wait to be called – then lowered himself into the chair, putting his hat on his knee.

'Jim,' he said. 'You want to talk to me, and as it happens, I want to talk to you.'

I rubbed my eyes, in no humour for his performance. 'I see you've brought Colm Hatten back from the dead.'

'Oh, that boy was far from dead. Quite the opposite. That's the sort of Irishman we should be sending into the world, not the shower that give us all a bad name. Chancers, beggars, brawlers and half-wits.' He joined his hands on top of his stomach. A fold of pink skin spilled over a shirt collar so tight that I imagined the top button gnawing his Adam's apple every time he swallowed. His dark hair was combed to one side, comet tails of grey streaking through it.

I wiped some crumbs from the desktop and let on I knew all about Colm Hatten's ventures in England.

'I assume it's his land you're after?'

Casey smiled. 'Exactly right, Jim. The last piece of the puzzle.'

I put my hand on a notebook on my desk. A ploy I use, to hint to whoever is across from me that there are things written inside that he doesn't know about. 'It could be a bigger problem than you think.'

'How's that?' He trapped his top lip with the bottom one, and glanced from side to side as if some person might have come in bearing new information. 'I see a straightforward deal. Aside from the trouble I had tracking Colm down. He's selling, I'm buying.'

A phone rang in the next room. Flood passed the door holding a cup of tea and for a second I thought he might bring it in and put in front of Casey, like a waiter desperate for a tip. I thought of Siobhán warning me to tread carefully.

'What about Patrick?' I raised my hand before he could interrupt. 'I've no place telling you what you can and can't buy, but humour me a minute. Like it or not, that's his home and it's been his home a lot longer than his brother's. He's just a lad about the same age as one of your own boys, Peter. You know as well as me that he won't find it easy if you take it from him.'

He traced his finger around the dark rim of his hat.

'Jim, there's finer lads than him leaving every day. Maybe it's best he joins them. Even better if he hops off halfway across the Atlantic. Or Colm can sort him out, but that's family business. I'm creating jobs at the stud that mean some of those lads might be able to stay.'

'So why not give a job to Patrick Hatten? Sweeping the yard, cleaning the stables, shovelling horseshit. You could soften his landing at least.' I shook my head. 'This is personal, Peter. Why else would you have those tractors looking over his wall?'

He showed his hands as if there was no other way to see it. 'This is business, Jim. If you want charity, take him to the church. Have Siobhán sort him out. The tractors were upsetting my horses so I moved them down the field. Nothing more than that.'

'With a front-loader all but resting on his wall, Peter.'

'Come off it, Jim, this isn't the border in Berlin. There's land bought and sold every day in this county. His mother certainly had no problem taking my money. If she squandered it, I suppose that's my fault too?' He leaned forward. 'If I'm to compete with the likes of Ballydoyle or that shower over in Newmarket, I need more space. More space means cutting through the hovel he calls his home.

I held back while Maura was still there, out of respect. But my respect doesn't extend to that dirty divil. I'll not bring up what he did to my youngest. Now that, I'll grant you, was personal.'

'We've been over that plenty. None of it helped his standing any.'

'He didn't help his own standing did he, doing what he did?'

'What you said he did.'

'Said he did?' He set his jaw in defiance. 'Watch your step, Jim, and don't play the fool. A lad like that has all the sense of an animal. Gets a sniff and thinks a girl is ready to lie down for him because she was stupid enough to give him the time of day. I won't risk her being so stupid again.'

I raised my hand. 'Enough.' He settled back and moved his hat to the other hand. 'You could move the whole operation thirty yards east and not know any difference.'

He shook his head and smiled like a headmaster in response to a pupil's naivety and I knew I was going to lose, playing out a few desperate moves and running out of board.

'Not according to the engineers. And even if I could, Patrick Hatten would be haunting the place and too close to Rose.' He laughed at the absurdity of the thought. 'Owners and syndicates down to see their thoroughbreds and their investment. Demanding a place worth big money, and that lad skulking around. Animals worth a fortune within his reach.' He shook his head. 'Shouldering that gun every time I see him. Looking at me like he wants to blow me away. If we sent the fucker to the moon, he'd still be too close.'

He shifted his gaze to the far wall, where some dark premonition was taking shape and for a second, I could see it myself, and understood the root of Casey's scorn.

'I don't know how I didn't see it until now.'

He turned back to me. 'See what?'

'You're afraid of him.'

'Ah, Christ, now I've heard it all.' He laughed, playing to an invisible audience, but he couldn't hide it. 'I warned you once to watch your step.' He pointed a finger at me. 'You're getting two chances only because of the office you're in.'

I put my elbows on my desk and clasped my hands. 'Peter, I can manage Patrick where he is, I've done it long enough. Whatever trouble you think he is now will be much worse if you chase him out of sight. And let's say the law says he has a claim to the place? What then?'

The pointed finger turned into a raised palm. 'On that front, I have no worries.' His hat changed hands again. He seemed to stop breathing while he decided if he should carry on, but couldn't resist the chance to show that he'd thought of everything. 'Colm Hatten – as well as almost everybody in town – understands that his brother isn't the full shilling. He told me he drove out the other evening and saw his brother on his bike and was shocked by the cut of him. Like something haunting the place. He wondered if it wouldn't be best to send him the same way his father was sent. For his own good, of course.'

'Senan's?' I saw the pieces fall into place. Colm gets the money and a ticket back to England, telling himself he's done the right thing. Casey gets the land and rid of Patrick. Patrick gets the same sorry treatment his father did. I stood and Casey rose with me, uncomfortable at being looked down on for even a second. 'I'm sure you had nothing to do with that idea?'

'That family had a rough shake of things, that much is true.' He tapped his hat against his chest and looked at some memory on the ground. 'But lookit, it might not go that far. If he packs up and leaves quietly, maybe Colm will hold fire.'

I rounded my desk and went face to face with him, as if up close I might be able to see what it was that made him capable of sending a young man away to a place that's a hospital in name alone. His intention was to use me as messenger, to deliver his ultimatum to Patrick.

He smiled the smile of a man about to make a winning move. 'You know for all this talk, Jim, you haven't asked me what it was I wanted to talk to you about?'

'Well, I'm all ears.' I sensed him holding his tongue from making a smart reply and felt my face redden and my ears all but twitch.

'Do you know what one of my men found on his Massey this morning? A bloody stag's head dumped on the bonnet. Crows taking turns picking at it. I suppose you'll still tell me that this is a youngfella that's right in the head?'

I cursed Patrick for not heeding my advice. 'The days of rounding people up like strays are on their way out, Peter. It won't happen on my watch.'

'Terrible what we used to do to them. Wasn't it yourself who drove poor old Sean to Senan's? God rest him.' He looked at me as if he knew things about me that I didn't know myself.

'If you've said your piece, Peter, I've work to do.'

I looked at my desk, a man in checkmate, reduced to sweeping an arm across the board, letting Siobhán's note of caution be a poor excuse for saying nothing more. He put on his hat and saluted by raising two fingers from the brim. 'Give my best to Siobhán and that lovely little girl of yours.' He walked through the station, laughing and joking with the men under his spell while a weakness came over me as if he'd cast some other spell to rob me of my strength.

The land wore a fevered look all the way down to Rita's. Every living thing in need of a day's rain. Cattle and horses were stilled in fields, loitering close to troughs of water. Birds flew low in search of worms that wouldn't be found in dry earth. Patches of pale-yellow rash streaked the grass, and the river moved through it all in an endless sweat.

I drove with the windows down and left them open when I pulled in outside the concrete farmhouse beyond Ballybough. You could stand at the end of the field behind Rita's and boot a football across the Barrow into Kilkenny.

I took the box from the back seat and walked to the front door, the same as a few years back, after Siobhán told me about this bruised woman she'd seen in town and got talking to. I knocked louder and

Rita appeared from the side of the house, sleeves rolled, drying her hands on a brown dress.

'Ah, Jim. I heard you knocking. I was round the back.'

'Rita. How are you keeping?'

'Grand.' I handed over the box and she took it with arms like thin, strong ropes, her eyes registering what had been brought. She'd long gone past embarrassment about accepting it. 'From Siobhán, I suppose. She's very good. Tell her I was asking for her.'

'I will. That's been a warm week.'

She looked at the sky and shielded her eyes, the box balanced between her opposite hip and elbow. 'I'll be glad of some rain when it comes. Still, we should enjoy it.'

'How are the children?'

She smiled. 'I had a letter from Eileen earlier in the week. She's getting along fine. She's living in Salford now.'

'Will she be home to see you soon?'

'She won't. You know it's nearly a year since she left. Time does what it wants.'

'What about the lads?'

She tossed her head. 'The lads. I'd be lucky to hear from them if they were living next door. Eileen said she wrote to them in London but heard nothing back. Will you come in for a cup of tea?'

The place was sparse and clean. There was a head of cabbage on the countertop. I sat and she turned the kettle over the fire. I ran my fingertips over the tablecloth. Imagined her cleaning it for nobody but herself. Dusting the empty house. Climbing the stairs to bed. Waking in the morning to do it all again.

She sat next to me and put her hands on her thighs, then smiled what might have been the saddest smile I'd ever seen, while waiting for the kettle to boil.

'I suppose ye're fierce busy ahead of the visit?'

'We're kept going, no doubt. What about yourself? You're not getting lazy on me?'

'Ah. There's always something for doing.'

'Will you be in town for Kennedy?'

'Oh God, I will.' She looked like a woman trying to remember what excitement was supposed to look like. 'Where will you be sent?'

'Nearby. Dunganstown.'

'Oh, won't it be great to see him without the crowds?' She went to the kettle, then took two cups from the cupboard and brought them to the table. 'I don't have any biscuits to go with it, Jim, sorry. You take yours black, don't you?' she said, pouring.

We sat in silence and she didn't touch her tea. It was hard to imagine the same house once filled with children and an air of threat and violence hanging like heavy gas, waiting for a spark. A little kingdom of fear, ruled by the small man of country muscle who'd opened the door to me that first time I called. John Kirwan. Who balled his fists when I told him I was here to talk to his wife and looked at the few things Siobhán had sent down and told me he didn't need charity. His eyes set on Rita when she came to the door, her smile swollen in one corner, assuring me that there must have been a mix-up before inviting me in for tea. He might as well have been a ventriloquist, his lips tight, but his words coming from his wife's mouth.

He was gone one morning when she woke. A couple of shirts and trousers, his only jacket, toolbelt and hat gone with him. A harmonica that she hadn't heard him play since their first year of marriage, taken from the drawer next to the bed. The meagre things he judged essential for starting a new life, or abandoning the old one at least. Rita was left with four children, who eventually reached leaving age too, so she ended up alone in a house that John still owned. A married woman, so not even able to draw the dole. From whatever corner of the world he fled to, he kept a grip on his wife's throat.

'No word from John?'

She drank at last. 'No. God forgive me, but there are evenings when I hope to see a guard in the driveway, coming to tell me he's after dying someplace.' She shook her head. 'If he walks in that door, there's nothing I can do only let him.'

I shook my head. I had little comfort to offer. 'I can't imagine he'll be back, Rita. Six years is a long time.'

'Thirty years with him was a long time.' Her eyes were wet and she looked at her tea, both hands wrapped around the cup. They betrayed her age and hard life, in their deep lines and thin skin and swollen joints. I wondered if Rita could remember a time when her body hadn't been damaged by another, when her cheekbones, ribs, and gut had never met fists and boots.

'How's your little one?' she said, trying to pretend the glaze of a tear was a sparkle at the thought of Catriona.

'She's flying it. Chattier by the day.'

'Ye're blessed.'

I swallowed another mouthful. 'We must spin her down sometime.'

'I'd love to see her. If ye ever need someone to keep an eye on her.'

'You're very good, Rita. Is there anything you need done around the place?'

'Not a thing. Tell me, what's Siobhán up to these days? There's too much in her head to be in the house all day. You don't need me to tell you that.'

'She's keen to go back to work. Just waiting for school to start again.'

'Tell her not to wait too long. She could do anything, that woman.'

She stood with me and we went to her doorstep and looked across the field at the river, halfway between the port and the estuary.

'Are you away home for the evening?'

'Not yet, Rita. I've one more call to make.'

'No rest. Tell Siobhán to come and see me.'

'I will indeed. Mind yourself.'

She touched my arm then went back inside and closed the door.

The sound of my engine sent a few birds circling overhead. I turned the car away from the river and took the long route, avoiding town, cutting past the workers in summer fields, the evening sun stalking me. I thought about Rita and what she would do for the rest of the evening and how slow the time might go.

If you told me I'd get thirty more years with Siobhán it would sound like far too little, but her thirty years with John Kirwan felt like eternity. I thought of busy work days that slip away, days that don't seem to have enough hours and how we have no control over time at all. How it passes through us. How we're just oxygen for it, telling its old stories and predicting its future. How it uses us up and when it's finished with us and we're gone, with all our love and hurt and memories gone with us, time will be there still, breathing through every soul, the only thing that knows no end.

I felt Sean Hatten's handkerchief in my pocket as I drove to see his son. It was Rita who unlocked some fragment of the mystery of why a man like Sean carried this delicate thing from farm to fertiliser plant. I was sitting where I sat this evening, listening to her cry, not long after John had left. I took it from my pocket and offered it to her. Before she dried her eyes, she looked at it, then looked at me and handed it back and said her tears weren't worth Mount Carmel lace. She spread it on the table and traced a finger over the pattern and told me about the Carmelite nuns and an industrial school opened before the famine, where girls were taught needlework by way of employment and how by the turn of the century those girls and women's fingers had made some of the most sought-after lace in the world.

The past is no different to lace. Mostly holes and dark spaces of lost memories, with some strands and patterns linking together to make something we carry with us. The most we can hope for as time passes is a recollection of some bright moments from some bright hours. My mother, kissing my arms where thorns scratched them while I picked blackberries. My brother Declan's hair blowing in my face while he straddled my crossbar, freewheeling down Shanahan's hill. Siobhán, walking towards me while the organ filled every inch of that church in Clonakilty. The first night I went to Catriona's cot on my own, holding her while she howled into my shoulder, pink and helpless. And that morning with Rita, a battered, broken woman, with children to raise and no money to do it, the rest of her life uncertain, unwilling to wipe her tears with a piece of fabric because she judged it much too beautiful.

# 12

Patrick waded from the safety of the bank, through a green scum of duckweed, and the itch drowned in cool, silken water. His father told him that duckweed travelled on the feet of birds and spread as fast as wings could flutter, and that everything in nature has a way of finding its place. He turned onto his back and laughed and wondered if that included the head of the deer he killed. A heron stood on the bank downstream, its neck stretched out and the yellow blade of its bill angled to the surface. He closed his eyes to the sun and remembered his father's strong hands, softened by the river and gripping his torso while he taught him to swim, never angry if he failed and resurfaced in a fit of coughing. The dark of the water scared him into thinking that something was reaching from the bottom, trying to pull him down, or worse – that there was no bottom. Only his father's voice could calm him. The way he said his name so gently. *Patrick, it's fine. Let's try again.*

He imagined all the unwanted kittens and pups that the river must have swallowed – squirming in cloth-sack coffins – and looked at the sky and imagined Kennedy's helicopter, its blades slicing clouds and the sound of it like a hundred tractor engines on its way to land over at O'Kennedy Park. He heard a couple of men in town, complaining that Jackie wasn't coming, while they mixed cement to refix slabs that the President would never see, let alone walk on.

When he was finished, he lay on a flat rock and drew the last warmth from it and felt a perfect communion with everything around him. The water to clean him, the sun to dry him, the ground to feed him, the birds to sing to him. He wondered how his father would deal with the tractors. He'd probably go hat in hand to Casey and take any explanation given no matter how unreasonable. He was stirred by the voices of two men in the next field talking about beef prices and he lay as still as the heron until they were gone, then stood and dressed.

He picked his way through John Walsh's field, sidestepping fresh and stale discs of cow shite. He carried wet clothes under his arm, just washed in the river. '*Patrick, it's fine. Let's try again,*' he repeated to himself as he walked, calming as he neared home with his body cleansed, any cuts and scrapes rubbed with dock leaf. He parted the cloud of the job that was taken from him, the sun lighting his thoughts, imagining walking with Rose after a morning together by the river. Her voice that spring morning, when her words were trying to catch up with her brain while she spoke about horses and Casey's prized thoroughbred – Altar, or Arthur, or Antler – he couldn't remember. She said it was the finest animal in Ireland and people in town said the same. He'd only seen it once from distance, and tried to convince himself that the horse's reputation was just another thing bought and paid for by Casey's money. He wondered if Rose liked the pincushion and if she'd keep it hidden somewhere in her bedroom, a secret to remind her of him.

He hopped the final stone wall and slipped at the sight of Field at his doorstep, in the stance of a man delivering news of a death. He dropped one of the washed shirts and left it, not wanting to be seen pawing in the dirt.

'Two days in a row,' Patrick said. 'Town must be quiet.'

Field turned. 'Patrick. Can we go inside?'

Sweat glistened on Field's skin and Patrick imagined that the sergeant had a tough night of sunburn ahead. He looked older when he squinted, lines from the corners of his eyes like tendrils, roots spreading in search of water on his parched face, ears like an old man's – so big he could probably hear the grass growing and the flight of the white butterflies through the wildflowers. Patrick remembered walking Main Street at his father's hip, admiring the much younger Field's uniform while he saluted the pair of them.

He passed without word, glancing to the sun-browned bloodstain on the Massey, before going through the open door to the shade of the house, glad to have done some tidying, as the sergeant followed him in.

# 13

I tried to let on I wasn't desperate to sit down, wishing I could have gone straight home from Rita's. It was as if the sun was focusing a beam on me all day, burning itself out trying to melt me into a puddle. Blazing away all the early-morning optimism about my health, and any confidence that I had enough in me to deal with Kennedy and Casey and Rita and Patrick.

Patrick made no move to stop me, as if he'd forgotten I was there as soon as he turned his back. He was standing in the middle of the floor, like he didn't know what to do with himself, uneasy to have somebody beyond the front step, then he put a pile of wet clothes on top of a cold stove.

I tried to see the place through his eyes. A dark museum that told the story of his life. Of what had been and might have been. Of what would be no more, once Peter Casey had his way. The collection of things that told of a time when the Hatten family wasn't fully doomed to failure – the chrome-plated stove that Maura had likely taken a martyr's pride in, the radio that she'd deemed more useful than the land she sold to pay for it. The jaundiced faces of Christ and his apostles in the pictures on the walls, and the huge dresser with its stacks of unused saucers and plates like a shrine to the dead woman of the house. A pair of knitting needles on an armchair as if she'd just gone out to the shed. A trace of her in the sewing machine with a broken balance wheel at the end of the table.

Then all the evidence that she's gone from the place. The gun in the corner, next to bamboo fishing poles and lobster pots. Her once spotless kitchen table, lined with hunting knives and unidentifiable wooden works in progress, sawdust on the floor swept into a pile. A fistful of wildflowers in a far too small glass on the sill above the sink.

What came over him one morning, this strange and quiet lad, that made him want to pick some flowers and put them in water? I looked at him and he wiped his nose and shifted his feet, as likely to swing a punch as he was to offer a seat. How does an unknowable creature like Patrick Hatten come to be?

When he sat, I joined him at the table.

'Listen, Patrick. I'll get right to it. You're in proper bother.'

He folded his arms and flicked his chin up and a turn of his eyes said *When am I not*?

'I don't mean with me. You need to listen to me.' I tapped the tabletop and he met my eye for as long as a blink. My finger came away powdered by sawdust. 'This isn't about some aul one complaining about you taking a shortcut through her field. Peter Casey has done a deal with your brother, Patrick.' This time he held my gaze and didn't blink. 'Colm is back from England. That's who you saw here yesterday.'

Patrick shook his head, rattling it like a money box to see if what he needed would fall out. 'That wasn't Colm. Why would Colm drive away when he saw me?'

'There's a good chance that he's a very different man to the boy you knew. I have brothers I haven't seen in years. I don't expect them to be the same if we ever meet again.'

He shook his head again, still short-changed by what I was telling him. 'This isn't even Colm's house to sell. That's my father's land. My father built those sheds and roofed this house. His grandfather built the walls outside. He farmed that land before Colm was born.' He pointed out the door. 'I'm the one who's held on to what's left.'

'Your mother left it all to your brother, Patrick.' It struck me that he and Rita shared the problem of living in a home that a piece of paper said wasn't their own.

He scratched his chest as if a tide of insects was crawling over him. The other hand went to his back and he stood, and sank his hands into the bundle of wet clothes, then took them away and wiped his forehead and neck. 'How is it I was never told this before?'

'I don't know. I know that there are men who can talk to solicitors and make wills appear and find brothers in England that didn't want to be found.' He looked at me and I knew he was listening as much as he ever would. 'Casey wants this land and he told me that there's no loyalty on Colm's part. So, hear this if you hear nothing else. If you do anything at all, other than pack your bags with a smile and a thank-you, he'll try have you sent to Senan's. I've seen it done.'

The mention of the place brought an end to his itching and he looked at me but through me at the same time. I blinked the sweat from my eyes and as he came closer, I stood to meet him.

'Don't mention that place to me.' He pointed a finger at my chest. 'You of all people.'

I swallowed my shame, knowing that it would do him no good. The shame was all mine, not to be shared – or at least that was my excuse for never getting on my knees and telling Patrick, or anybody, what I did to his father. 'Are you listening to me? Do you think you helped yourself by leaving that stag's head on Casey's tractor? Didn't I bloody warn you? You might as well have wrapped it up and gifted it to him.'

'It makes no difference whether I did it or didn't do it. Do you not understand that?'

I said nothing and he didn't come any further. His breathing slowed and he went to the dresser and put his head down.

'Talk to your brother, Patrick. If he's selling this place then you need to get a fair cut. You could get away from here and the likes of Casey with enough money.'

He righted a cup so its handle faced the same way as the others.

'Talk to Colm, and do it soon. There'll be no business done over the weekend, so if you'd like, I'll go with you Monday morning. We could even try and meet him with the solicitor.'

He turned and stared over my shoulder and his vacant face reminded me of Sean after the sense had gone from him. I turned to the wall, to see what he'd been looking at. A family of four Hattens stared back, close to smiling, the young Patrick with his mother's hands on his shoulders, Colm next to Sean and already nearly as tall as him. You could have given that family a million guesses and not once would they have landed on how it all turned out. I put a palm on the table, feeling as if I'd stood too quickly, then felt myself fall.

I was on my back when I returned from the faint. Patrick was crouching over me, splashing lukewarm water on my face, flicking it from his fingers like a priest offering a blessing. He pulled back when he saw me looking at him, then stood with his hand extended and I took it and he pulled me to my feet. I almost reached for the handkerchief but stopped myself, thinking he might recognise it.

'You're sick,' he said.

'It was just a faint. The heat.' I brushed myself down and wiped my head with my hand. 'Take my advice, Patrick.'

I paused at the threshold of the door like a man afraid of the light. He looked at me as if it was me that needed his help and not the other way around, and maybe he's right – maybe I need his forgiveness as much as he needs anything thing from me. 'Your father was a good man, Patrick. I'll keep Casey at bay as long as I can. But it will be like holding back the tide.'

On my way to the car, I noticed things I hadn't on my way in. A rectangle of soil, freshly raked and tidy as a newly filled grave. The screech in the gate, oiled into silence. The tubs of lime in the shed. He was a man cleaning the decks on a sinking ship.

Something lay in the dirt by the wall across the road. I recognised it as soon as I picked it up. One of my old shirts, freshly washed and freshly dirtied. I put it on the fence and looked at it in the rear-view as I drove towards town, drooping like the flag of some defeated army. I rolled down the windows and floored the accelerator, hoping the breeze would work like smelling salts.

# 14

He sat at the table for a long time after Field left, staring at the chipped and dented wooden surface, the burn marks of pots and pans through the years, the stray cuts of knives, the damage done by errant chisels and hammers. He went outside with a saucer of milk and the sky was red, as if the sun had died a bloody death and a gauze of pink clouds was soaking up the spill.

The door of the tool shed screeched a warning to the cat, some loose stones dragging along the concrete. He put the saucer down and sat against the wall, the milk halfway between his toes and the cat. A small pile of dirt, dust and dried cat shit was gathered against the far wall, swept in the morning's flurry of work, like his mother and her duster – going from yard to barn to shed with the brush the same way she went room to room, clearing every surface of the day's worth of dust, just in time for the arrival of more.

He rubbed the thumb of one hand against his middle finger and patted the ground with the other. The cat stopped short of him, then nosed the bowl and started drinking. 'Well, Cat, Colm is after coming home to us. I'll talk to him. That's all that's needed.'

It was nothing more than the latest case of the Hattens being judged in the harshest light. Running off to England was one thing, but abandoning a brother and selling off the family's place in the world was another. It was Colm's home too. Field was just another man who couldn't be trusted.

'Field is in a bad state, Cat. On his back like a dead man he was.' He thought about what Field said about taking his share of money. More than he'd ever had in his pocket or might ever have again.

Enough to take to England or America and do what with it? Fall in with crowds of drinkers, telling sad stories and singing about all they left behind, hiding in dark pockets of cities that didn't want them. Sitting on trains or buses and seeing finely dressed women who they can dream about back in some boarding house of men snoring through the same dreams and waking to the same regrets. Christmas in some sad hall with priests and nuns doing their duty and feeding them whatever passed for food, soaked with watery gravy while they celebrated like it was Christ's funeral. Every one of them, to a man, wishing they were back in front of their simple fire, with a candle burning in the window for nobody in particular.

The cat didn't finish the milk. It looked to Patrick, bearded and wet-whiskered. Patrick smiled and pulled a head of rainbow trout from his inside pocket, wrapped in newspaper. He'd pulled as many bones from it as he could manage and eaten the rest for dinner, chopping it an inch further from the head than usual, thinking the cat would be glad of extra.

He spread the paper and tapped it. 'Only caught yesterday. Sorry for not finding you a friend. I'm still looking.'

The cat came close, its paws rustling the newspaper. It leaned to the meat and Patrick smiled at the thought of it reading the headlines. The cat turned its head to the side, little blades of white fangs flashing while it worked on the fish with its back teeth.

He reached out and rubbed the animal from neck to tail in long, slow strokes. The cat didn't shrink to Patrick's touch and he put his head against the stone wall and decided that he'd face his brother after lunchtime tomorrow, reasoning that every living thing was more agreeable on a full stomach.

# 15

I came home to an empty house and went to the sitting room after hanging my tunic up and opening my shirt buttons. I opened the windows and sat in front of the television but didn't turn it on. I bought it as an anniversary present last year. The gift for six years is supposed to be iron. It was second-hand, but came with Seamus Fortune's word that it was good as new, though he changed the subject when I asked why it had been returned to him and why he was selling it so cheap. He's opened it up three or four times since, examining the circuitry, tracing his thin fingers along green and yellow and red wires, moving an ear close while tinkering with resistors and capacitators with fine needles of tools pulled from his apron without looking, the whole complex assemblage looking like a bomb that could blow ourselves and Mrs Rattigan off the map. There's surely some iron in there somewhere. We watch the news and turn it up whenever there's music on and slap the side of it when the picture gets spotted with little black and white squares like an empty crossword. I should have known it didn't stand a chance against Siobhán's beloved books.

I heard her key in the door and Catriona's voice repeating some words that were new to her. *Sunset. Magazine.* I met them in the hall and Siobhán's face dropped when she saw me. Catriona wrapped her arms around my thigh.

'Jim, you look like you were dragged through a hedge.'

'Were you dragged through a hedge, Daddy?' Catriona echoed the words into my stomach.

I put my hands on her shoulders and smiled at Siobhán, who came to me with a brown paper bag in her hand. She looked me up and down, then brushed the back of my trousers clean of the dust they'd lifted from Patrick's floor. She softened, maybe sensing something of how glad I was to see the pair of them.

'For your nephew,' she teased, and I opened the bag to the latest issue of *Conquest*.

We ate dinner together, boiled potatoes and salmon, while Catriona fussed with her bit of mash and peas. Siobhán asked about Rita, and we decided to visit her after the big day.

We took tea and biscuits to the sitting room and then I was on my back again. Only this time as a man renewed, with Catriona held above me, moving her back and forth like she was floating or flying. It didn't matter that my arms were so tired, I'd have held her there all night if she liked. How many years until she gets too heavy to lift? Siobhán was reading on the couch behind us and I looked at her upside down, stealing glances over the top of her book.

When it was time for Catriona's bed, Siobhán knelt and kissed my forehead, her loose strand of hair tickling my cheek.

'Go on away and play with your toy. I'll bring her up.'

She's right of course. It's only a toy, with the new parts labelled – fuel tank, igniter, engine. I carved out ground plug connections, oxygen vent pipes and steam exhausts, and the genius it takes to design these things, let alone get them up in space, made me feel like a very simple man. The plan is to bring the rockets to the school after summer. They might give the children the same amount of wonder and hope as last October gave them fear. Youngsters not sleeping at night, afraid of Armageddon. Even myself and Siobhán lay awake, talking about it and putting our hopes in Kennedy's hands. People in town blessed themselves when they said the word – nuclear – and summoned the memory of the innocent bombed down in Campile during the war, to caution against thinking we were immune from fallout. Harmless creamery workers blown up in broad daylight by the Luftwaffe.

Siobhán had carried on her reading in bed. I decided not to tell her about the faint.

'Did I tell you the good news?' I settled next to her.

She smiled and put the book face down. 'Go on?'

'We're heading for a drive with her ladyship tomorrow. There's one more day of fine weather promised.'

She put the book on the nightstand and turned off her light, then kissed me in the dark and pulled me closer and I felt that there's nothing wrong at all with being a simple man.

# 16

Patrick walked into Gerry Foley's, wearing his father's only suit and a few drops of his mother's old perfume. It had stood untouched on a shelf inside the front door since she died, next to a bottle of holy water brought back from Lourdes by some uncured pilgrim years ago, gifted with the direction to dab it on her husband's failing head. She'd wet herself with the perfume before opening the door, the neck and both wrists for a rare visitor of merit. Nothing at all for a tinker or farmer.

Two bald men who had no business in a barbershop looked him up and down. He shut the door to the mid-morning sounds of the town. Foley was smoking while cutting a man's grey hair. He glanced at Patrick, then to an empty chair next to a coat stand. Only after Patrick sat did the two bald men sitting next to the window nod by way of acknowledgement, before turning to one another and sharing a look of unspoken incomprehension over the new arrival.

'I hear Kennedy's going to be pucking with the Rackard brothers after he lands,' said the older of the men after a silence, his hands clasped on the top of a walking stick between his thighs.

'Someone's pulling your leg.' The younger man scratched his moustache.

'I'm only saying what I've been told.' The man rearranged his hands on his walking stick.

'I'll tell you something that I shouldn't,' the moustached man said, straightening and raising his voice for the benefit of his audience. 'He's landing over in O'Kennedy Park, by helicopter if you don't mind. Then driving down to the quay. After that, it's straight to

Dunganstown. If you see him at O'Kennedy, they hold you there after he leaves. If you see him at the quay, you'll be like sheep at a mart. And if you want to see him at Dunganstown, you've to be invited, or you'll be looking over the wall while he has tea with the relatives.'

The older man repeated the words *tea with the relatives,* shaking his head as if the American President drinking tea on a farm in Dunganstown was some portent of the end.

Foley stopped cutting, and stood with his scissors dangling by his side and a cigarette hanging from his lips. 'Not another word about it in here. I'm sick to death of it. If he comes in here, he'll pay the same price as every man. It'd be more in Billy Rackard's line to be out training.'

'Has Rackard another season in him, Gerry?' the man in the chair asked.

Foley exhaled smoke through his nostrils, into the face of his customer, and shook his head, straightening as if they had at last moved on to serious matters. Patrick listened to the men's back and forth, studying their turns of phrase and mannerisms for some appropriate gesture or posture to adopt when meeting Colm.

'Jesus, he better,' Foley said. 'Because he was carrying the rest of that shower last Sunday.' He put his scissors in his shirt pocket and took a brush from the shelf by the mirror. He swept his customer's forehead and neckline then patted his shoulder. 'Now, Sir. That'll keep you going.'

'Grand job,' the man said, brushing something unseen from his shoulders and trousers, then standing as if he didn't quite trust his spine, taking a handkerchief from his back pocket and wiping his nostrils which would also have benefited from a trim. From where he sat, Patrick could see the spindly lengths of nose hairs, dangling like flies' legs from each dark hole.

He watched the transaction, having never had his hair cut by a barber, confirming that the exchange worked the same as in any shop. A figure quoted, a till opened, money transferred.

'I'd say Rackard's won his last All Ireland,' the freshly trimmed customer ventured, as Foley handed him his change.

'You might be right,' Foley said and the man saluted the older men as he left, passing Patrick as if he wasn't there. Patrick had half-listened to the match on the radio and struggled to raise much concern that Wexford fell short of the Leinster final. He played in school, wielding his hurley like a weapon, bruising shins, being knocked around the pitch by bigger shoulders, learning early that it wasn't the game for him.

'Now, Sir,' Foley said, brushing the chair clean. 'What can I do with the thatch?'

Patrick stood and the bald men eyed his dirty shoes and short trousers, the hem of one leg caught in the back of a thick and darned sock. He nodded at Foley on his way to the chair, then sat with his elbows on the armrests, smiling.

'I'm on my way to a meeting.'

'Not a scalping so,' Foley said, pulling a scissors from blue water beneath the mirror. 'It must be an important meeting if you're in to get the hair cut special.'

'The biggest yet,' Patrick said. 'The biggest yet.' He pointed at a black and white Brylcreem poster on the wall, where a man in a suit wore a side parting, slicked back with smooth lines left by the sharp teeth of a comb. 'Like that.'

He turned to the mirror and was repulsed by the sight of his reflection – skin freckled like the trout he shared with the cat, black spaces between yellowed teeth, and a suit as loose fitting as the cloak Foley draped over him, littered with grey blades of the previous customer's hair. He imagined what his brother would think and pulled his elbows close to his body, regretting that he hadn't waited for Field. He looked away from the mirror.

Foley dragged a comb through Patrick's hair and shook his head. He took a cigarette from his top pocket and lit it, then pointed the comb at the picture on the wall.

'You've hair like a wire brush, son. I can't do that for you.' Patrick kept his eyes on the picture. 'Not to worry,' Foley said, exhaling a cloud of smoke. 'I'll tidy things up all the same. You'll look like a fine businessman,' he said and winked in the mirror.

Patrick looked at his knees while Foley wordlessly sprayed and chopped and ran a blade around the edges of the back and sides, glad he'd been judged to be a customer not likely to make small talk. The radio was on low in the corner, and after falling quiet at first, watching on to see what Foley could make of his subject, the men resumed their chat, satisfied that Foley had things under control. They spoke in the whispered voices of schoolboys at the back of a classroom, about Dunganstown, speculating that Mary Ryan's cottage had been plumbed and roofed using the state's purse. Even a toilet was put inside in case Kennedy got caught short.

Patrick watched his hair fall to the cloak and floor and thought of the matted fur of a mangy dog. Foley misted the freshly cut edges with something that burned. Patrick felt a shiver of pleasure at the touch of a badger brush. The fresh scent from a cloud of white powder was then replaced with a stink of warm white smoke from Foley's nose.

'Now,' Foley said, pulling away the cloak like a magician revealing the animal underneath. 'That's as good as it gets.'

Patrick examined himself, nodding his head at the marginal improvement, knowing that Foley was right, and that for all the smoke and mirrors, this was as good as he'd ever get. He smiled and clapped his hands once, as the previous customer had.

'That's a grand job.' He followed Foley to the till, shuffling a handful of coins, a couple of them sticking together as though something had melted in his pocket. 'What do I owe you?'

'Ah, call it two bob for a trim.' Foley stubbed in his cigarette in the ashtray on the counter, adding it to the burial mound of butts.

Patrick straightened at what sounded like sympathy in Foley's voice.

'Is that what Kennedy would pay? The same as any man?'

Foley sighed and flicked his hand towel over his shoulder. 'I can charge you more if you want. But it's two bob for a trim.'

Patrick searched the shrapnel for what he needed, glancing to the watchful faces of the men in the window seat. The older man raised a finger.

'I have you now,' he said, wagging the crooked bone at Patrick. 'You're Sean Hatten's young lad.'

The sound of his father's name got Patrick's attention the same as Brother Byrne's belt, slapped against his wooden desktop during Irish lessons.

'God rest him,' the man said and Patrick's eyes flicked between the trio of men as if some unspoken secret was being shared.

'I don't need charity,' he said and put three shillings on the counter top. Foley put the coins in the till. The men searched him for some likeness to his father as he left.

Outside, he wiped his forehead and looked at his fingers, decorated with trimmings of freshly cut hair. He felt the men's eyes on him, imagined the stories they'd told and would tell, the rumours they'd give breath to, and he walked on, wondering if a man would be forever judged by the place and the people he came from. He rounded the corner and leaned in the shade against the side of the building, steadying his breath, and reasoning with his skin. His brother was a couple of hundred yards away and he thought of Field again, and wished that he'd taken his offer to help him through a conversation he didn't know how to have.

The breeze coming off the river on his way to the Royal made a ditch of the neat parting Foley had fashioned and curls like wild hedgerow reached across from either side. He spat in his hands and tried to fix it in the wing mirror of a car parked outside, until the driver moved him on. He'd walked by the hotel every time he visited town for as long as he could remember. He'd seen well-dressed people skip down the steps, heard music coming up from the Cellar Bar, seen newly married couples pose outside for photographs and often wondered why they hadn't managed to come to the place just once – even for a cup of tea – when his parents were alive and well.

He climbed the six granite steps, then dodged the eyes of a pair of receptionists, tracking him like sniper rifles as he crossed the lobby. In the dining room, cloth-covered tables were spread evenly, in a way that his mother would have appreciated. A group of men with American accents laughed in song, while their forks and knives tapped along against plates of beef sliced thick as bread. Other diners talked, stirring ice in glasses – young families on their holidays and a handsome couple, probably on honeymoon, who grinned at each other across the table. He knew that these shining people were the reason they'd never come when his parents were still around. His mother would have been ashamed to be dragging him in after her, with his father holding his cap down at his side while she imagined whispers about her eldest who'd run off to London. She could have sold every inch of land and had the bank balance going up to calculator numbers and still she'd never fit in.

He couldn't see Colm. A solitary man across the room lowered his newspaper to reveal a tanned, leathery face, like something pulled from a bog. A waistcoated man in a white shirt strode towards him as if he was fire that needed to be put out.

'Can I help you, Sir?' the waistcoat said.

'I'm here to see Colm Hatten. My brother.' Hearing the name out loud made it feel like a dream. The man told him to follow, then led him on a winding course between the tables, to the window in the far corner, where Colm sat with a newspaper folded next to him, drinking tea and looking across the town square like a man who owned everything he saw. He looked nothing and everything like the person Patrick had known. He was boy and man, brother and stranger. Patrick put his hands in his pockets to hide their shaking and his mouth held his breath like something he could neither swallow nor spit out. He thought he was crying, but felt no tears.

'Mr Hatten,' the waiter said, and Colm raised his head, then shifted his eyes to Patrick and put his teacup on the table. He ran eyes of disgust and pity up and down and Patrick felt like a beggar, dressed by charitable nuns and brought inside for a hot meal.

'Will I bring a menu, Sir?' the waiter said to Patrick.

'Bring him the beef,' Colm said, eyes fixed on Patrick. 'He needs it.'

'Very good,' the waiter said and walked away, while Colm gestured to the empty seat. He didn't stand. Patrick sat and looked at his brother's suit and clean fingernails, his hair parted like one of the pictures on Gerry Foley's wall. He pulled his chair in tight and noticed that his brother's eyes were small, like a stoat's, and wondered if they'd shrunk. The silence lasted a few seconds, as if both were trying to find words worthy of the moment.

Patrick wagged a finger, smiling as if he'd just been let in on some private joke, whose punchline was the cutlery and the little portions of butter and jam and the empty plates tiered inside what looked like a bird cage with the bars removed, then slapped the table lightly. Colm looked at the cloth as if he might see the black and red remnant of a fly.

'My brother. Ten years.'

Colm took a draw from his tea, watching over the rim of his cup.

Patrick straightened, putting his palms against his thighs and presenting himself for appraisal.

Colm swallowed and put his cup down. 'You don't look well, Patrick,' he said, an English-sounding syllable somewhere. 'Neither does the house.'

Patrick reddened, his confidence rattled like a dog given a belt of a newspaper across the nose. 'It was you in that fine car?'

'It was.'

'The house took a while to get going after Mam died is all. She had the place so set in her ways. It's getting there.' He smiled, then stopped when Colm raised a hand.

'I'm selling the house, Patrick. I take it that's why you're here. It's not what I ever thought I'd tell you when we met again, but here we are.' He moved his cup to the side and straightened an invisible crease in the tablecloth with his fingertips. 'You've had half a year to show that you can make something of it. If you were an apprentice in my garage, you'd have been shown the door long ago.'

Patrick smiled. 'That's what I'm here to tell you. I won't stop until that land is working the way our father had it.' He leaned over the table and lowered his voice. 'The one thing that Casey wants but can't have. Because we own it.' He checked his shoulders. 'You know he's threatening to send me off to where they sent our father if I don't leave? I was told you'd let him.'

'Nothing has changed around here then.' Colm tugged an earlobe. 'This place has always been full of talk. I'll tell you what *is* true, Patrick. You're not well. I can see that just from looking at you.'

Patrick brushed down the parting in his hair.

'The house is a mess. Dogs would move to the shed if you tried to put them in it,' Colm went on. 'I'm selling it. And unless somebody offers more, I'm selling to Peter Casey. Now, here's my offer to you, and it's more than fair. You'll get your cut. A damn sight more money than I had when I climbed on a boat with nothing in my pocket. You can try to stand your ground, and some people would agree that you have a right to. But let me promise you this – I'm too busy to stay around fighting your corner if Casey tries to make things go another way. The smart move, Patrick, is to listen to me. As your brother. Take the money that's on the table and move on.'

Patrick looked at the man opposite him, and any trace of the brother he knew evaporated. He saw a stranger, with a strange accent. A man desperate to fit in, wishing he was an Englishman, and Patrick could see his mother's son. If he looked hard enough, he could see their father in the slant on Colm's nose and in the narrow chin and he made a final attempt to see if any of their father's blood was carried in Colm's veins.

'Do you remember killing the pig?'

Colm's eyes widened to near human size. One of Patrick's few memories where Colm was clearly present. The pair of them, with Joseph Roche and their father, catching and pinning the animal. Its hooves tied with rope, battling as a foursome against its thrashing bulk, its squeals filling the shed, where a huge vat of boiling water was giving off steam. The unholy weight of it, dragged and hoisted to a bench where it was held on its back. Patrick kneeling beneath the head with a wide pan, the animal going out heroically, never surrendering even though its fate was sealed. Roche dragging a blade across its neck and blood pouring like gravy, the pig's screams reaching heaven and hell, until it was dropped into the boiling water where it softened and died, before it was shaved and strung up again, the carcass stripped of everything of use, the chunks of meat salted for weeks. Patrick remembered it all. The house busy with his mother and her sisters, married in other parts of the island, to men who didn't embarrass them the way his father did. All hands chopping and preparing the meat as he brought it to them, fingers covered with flour and breadcrumbs and porridge oats, willing to help in return for their pound of flesh. The taste of blood in his mouth, the stains where it spurted on the floor of the shed.

A plate of beef and vegetables was placed in front of him. 'They were great days,' he said, his nostrils responding to the gravy, his mouth filling. 'Do you remember the meal we'd have after?' He looked at the plate. 'Even better than that.'

'Barbarism,' Colm said, looking out the window, shaking his head. 'I used to dread the day, the weeks building up to it, seeing the salt ready in the kitchen. You know I left the gate open one year hoping the bastard thing would just run away? Woke the next morning to it lying in its filth. I hated every second of it, Patrick. Do you understand what I'm saying? These memories you have are just inventions. These happy times that we were a family. They never existed. There was never any *us*. Just two unhappy people for grey years on this grey island, who decided to live under one roof and ended up with two sons for company.'

'Is that why you left? You were too soft for it?'

'Soft,' Colm said, his top lip curling. 'Only around here is a man thought soft because he doesn't want to slaughter animals to put food on the table, or dig in fields for a pittance. Soft,' he said, repeating the word with scorn. 'When I was fourteen, I fell in love with an older woman. You were only six or seven.' He smiled. 'Maureen Glynn, you hardly remember her? She worked in the shop on Saturday mornings. Smart. Built for a world beyond here. She went to London to become a nurse and my young heart was broken. Of course, I know now that it was just silly, a boy's love – turned to a puddle by a fine-looking woman. She probably didn't know I existed. But I was a boy smart enough to take stock of what was around me. Do you know what I saw?'

Patrick looked at the food steaming in front of him.

'I saw nothing, Patrick. Nothing. A farm of land that our mother was happy to sell off because she knew our father was failing and knew that I wanted nothing to do with it. Knew she couldn't trust you with it. Our father, losing his mind and bound to join the lunatics up the road. Letting Casey near steal it from them for the price he got.' He laughed, a little chuckle of triumph. 'At least he'll pay properly this time. You think I should have stayed for a life of butchering and shooting and scraping by? A life out there with the pair of ye? Maybe a wife down the line to squeeze in next to *us*?'

Patrick tugged at his collar and looked to see if any windows were open, then scratched the warm pocket behind his knee, and itched one foot with the other.

'You don't get to feel sorry for yourself in this world, Patrick.' Colm gestured to the folded newspaper as evidence of a rotten, unfair world. 'You had more in that house and land than I did when I went out on my own. I own two pubs in Kilburn now. And a garage in Acton. I've a wife and a house. I have a son and a daughter. You think it was just given to me? Soft. No, brother. I did it the hard way.' He shook his head. 'Stay shackled to our parents and you'll end up the same as them. Christ, I see some of him in the way you're looking at me now, Patrick. Like a simpleton.'

'Don't talk about him like that,' Patrick said, smiling still, rage boiling in his chest. Wanting to ask about his niece and nephew, and wanting to slap his brother's face at the same time.

'He was a weak man to let her bully him the way she did. A simple man from simple times. If Peter Casey makes something of what they squandered, then it's a damn better use than giving you a place to lie idle.'

Patrick's anger rose, so strong that it could part an ocean. He imagined sweeping the table with his hand, sending a wave of food and plates onto the floor.

'Weak and simple? That's what you call our father after not even coming home to bury him.'

'It wasn't him you buried. Just some broken version.'

Patrick stood and leaned over the table. The tip of his tie dipped into the gravy boat like a sharp tongue.

Colm leaned back and looked around the room. 'Sit down, Patrick. People are staring.'

Patrick dipped a finger in the sauce, then freed his tie. 'Do you know what I'll do if I see you out at my house again?' he said, trapping his brother in his gaze. Patrick pushed his tongue between his teeth, his nostrils flaring like a dog at the start of a hunt. He felt eyes from other tables on him. 'I'll tell ya what I'll do. I'll put a hole right there.' He reached over the table and pressed his finger into the middle of his brother's forehead, where it left a dripping brown print.

He opened his top shirt buttons as he walked through town, his tie dragging a stain across his shirt like a dog's dirty tail. A car stopped and beeped and heads turned in doorways as he crossed the road to the station.

The public office was grey and empty, with one of two bulbs on the ceiling not working. His head was spinning and he clenched and unclenched his fingers then knocked on the frosted hatch. He had no plan of what to say but knew that he needed to see Field to tell him that reasoning with Colm hadn't worked. A hazy silhouette moved behind the glass then the hatch slid open and a look of disgust formed on Flood's face.

'The cut of you, Hatten. I wouldn't bury my worst enemy in that suit.'

'I want to see Sergeant Field,' Patrick said, looking over his shoulder as if somebody might have followed him from the hotel. His breathing and heartbeat were ragged.

'That's a fine way to behave, not even a hello. Will you not say hello to me, Mad Hatter?'

'Field,' Patrick said, scratching his neck and then his chest. He pulled his shirt from his trousers and Flood curled a lip. 'I want to see Field,' he shouted, and dropped the gavel of his fist on the countertop. Flood drew back and wrapped a hand around his baton.

'Oh, you cheeky fucker, coming in here shouting at me. Field isn't here, but when I'm done with you, you'll wish he was.'

Flood shouted after him as he ran, some instinct dragging his body to his bike, in the shade behind Gerry Foley's, where he sat against the wall and let his heartbeat slow, and cursed Field, and his foolishness for believing that the sergeant would help him when he needed it. He couldn't remember a single promise he'd been given that had been kept.

# 17

I went into Dr Murphy this morning, after telling Siobhán to pack for a surprise. I told her to bring a swimsuit and some sandwiches, with Cullenstown in mind, then left her with another lie, telling her I was heading to the station and wouldn't be long.

There can't be a doctor in the country that's a worse advertisement for health. Gut pouring beyond his beltline, ruddy-faced, with his teeth and fingertips stained by the wire-thin cigarettes he rolls and chain smokes. His little surgery a sauna of sweat, smoke and sickness. A place I try my best to stay away from, but the Disprin wasn't even close to loosening the vice-grips around my head.

I've good reason to be suspect of a headache. I woke during the night, head throbbing and the blanket pushed aside, my eyes rolling back as if to try and see where the pain was coming from. Lying in a sweat, worrying myself into a terminal diagnosis, remembering how we lost Declan. Every blessing I was given as a boy felt like the result of some miscalculation, some uneven distribution of health between brothers. As if I'd somehow stolen Declan's strength, so he couldn't race the other boys at school, couldn't play ball or cycle fast enough to keep up, and couldn't fight off the invisible army that set on his brain and took him from us at thirteen, vomiting and howling on a children's ward in the general, with my mother at the head of the bed, rubbing his cheek, and my father at the foot of it, staring at the fevered length of his youngest, knowing he was lost. The nurses couldn't even lie and tell us he went peacefully.

'Sergeant,' Murphy said, splashing some water on his hands then patting the back of his neck. 'A morning like that would make a man thirsty.'

I spotted him glancing at the clock, knowing his mind was already sitting on a stool over in Ryan's. His opening hours are dictated by his thirst and I sensed an early finish. John Ryan lets him drink for free when he plays the accordion. You haven't seen music come alive until you've seen Murphy bouncing the instrument on his huge knee like a baby, filling its lungs and conducting its cries, his thick fingers nimble as mayflies. People flood down from hills and up from valleys when they hear Murphy is on a long session.

'How's the little one? Kate, isn't it?' He spoke without looking at me and continued signing papers on his desk.

'Catriona. She's grand now, thanks. Had a tooth pulled.'

He winced. 'Cotter? The man has the precision of a lump hammer. I'd say it's about time ye're having another.' He dropped his pen and turned to me, smiling. 'A boy, if you can manage it. Or soon we'll have nobody to line out with O'Hanrahan's. I met a man recently who told me there are local clubs struggling to get the fifteen lads needed for a team.'

He knows nothing of our loss, or why there'll be no more – boy or girl. Waking next to Siobhán in the spare bedroom while we were visiting her parents, a couple of months before our second was due. The coolness of the blood on my legs, the fear on Siobhán's face when I turned on the light to the red sheets, with Catriona crying in a cot across the room. The doctor in Cork telling us that one is all we'd ever have. The long, grey days that followed while I held her hand on silent walks, waiting for her to be ready to share words about that unnamed boy. I was going to suggest naming him Declan. It's as if my twin wasn't meant for another minute in this world no matter the incarnation. When I think of him, lost to my parents, and our boy lost to us, I wonder if there is a family anywhere untouched by tragedy and since there likely isn't, how is that people treat each other with anything but kindness?

'One is plenty for now.'

'Ah, indeed,' he said, deciding against any small talk that would keep him longer than necessary. 'What brings you in?'

'There's a circular saw working against a knot in my skull. On and off for a few days.' I tapped the top of my head.

'Isn't that lovely wife looking after you at all?' he smiled, making light of it. 'You're probably flat out with work these days? If you don't mind my saying so, you're looking a bit ropey.'

'It's busy, I suppose. But busy is good.'

'I'm sure, with Kennedy coming. Are you sleeping?'

'In patches,' I said, while he stood and indicated for me to roll up my shirt, before strapping a blood pressure monitor around my upper arm and pumping it. He contemplated the figures.

'Any dizzy spells? Or fainting?'

'Well. I've come close to it.' I held back, thinking of the rumours that might spread.

'You need a break, Jim. I can tell that just from looking at you. Once Kennedy is gone, you should follow him out the road and not come back for a few days. Head off to the coast, or over to Galway.'

I tossed a hand. 'Ah, I've been tired for most of my life. We were only away in Cork last weekend and we're off for a spin today. Did I tell you I lost a brother to meningitis?'

'He might as well have been trampled by a heifer, Jim, because meningitis doesn't run in families.'

'Something isn't right.'

He sat again and leaned back, reddening further and his nostrils flaring, too used to worried mothers and frail pensioners taking his word as gospel. All of them too timid to ask a question when he puts their problems down to women's maladies. Siobhán won't see the man and it's no wonder. She says that if she's ever struck down I'm to call the vet before I call Murphy.

'Well, there's not much more I can do for you here and now. Especially if you don't want to listen to me. I could send you off for a scan if that's what you want. For some prodding and probing. But I'm telling you now, I've been seeing you ten years. You're running on fumes.' He dragged a key towards him with his index finger and unlocked the middle drawer of his desk, then took out two little unmarked brown bottles of tablets. 'Take these for the pain.' He handed me one bottle, then lifted the other. 'Take these because I said so. If you're not right after a break, come back into me. And don't tell a sinner you got those direct from me.'

'Thanks, doc.'

He softened. 'Will I see you across in Ryan's this evening?' he asked, standing, as my hand turned the door handle.

'I'm afraid not.'

'Back to the women in your life.' He tucked his shirt tightly inside his trousers.

'That's right,' I smiled and stood. 'I'll see how I get on with these, and we'll take a few days soon, myself and the women in my life.'

'Margaret will settle up with you another time,' he called to my back as I passed through the empty reception.

I pulled in a few miles outside town and told Siobhán that it was her turn to drive. She's as excited behind the wheel now as she was the first time, the summer we married, making bits of my father's front field while she got to know the pedals and gearstick. Once she had the hang of it, I got used to being the passenger. We'd spin off to the beach or the mountains any weekend we could, newly wed and invincible.

'So, where are we going?'

'As far as Nuala's.' I left the engine running and opened my door and Siobhán hesitated and examined herself in the rearview.

'Nuala's? Didn't you tell me to bring a swimsuit? You should have told me, Jim.'

'We might stop on the way. Cool off and have those sandwiches.' I swallowed the ulterior motive that explained my change of plans.

'What about Nuala, what will she think when we land on her door just before dinner?'

It was a symbolic protest. She was saying this as she rounded the car, dying to be on the road with a long drive ahead of her and

Catriona in the back, watching on. I climbed over to the passenger side as she got in and shut the door.

'Nuala will only be delighted to see her favourite sister-in-law. And her little niece.' I turned to Catriona and grabbed the toe of her shoe. It was a day for Wexford strawberries, heat humming, the horizon trembling like a plucked guitar string. Murphy's tablets had won their first round with the headache, and I put my worries about Patrick to the side, reasoning that nothing would happen in the half-day I was away. Sitting in a car in short sleeves, with an arm out the window and a woman like Siobhán starting the engine is one of life's great pleasures, lost on too many men who wouldn't be caught dead with their wife driving them around.

Siobhán checked her seat belt then revved loud and long as she always does, her regular joke that pre-empts me telling her to drive carefully. She pulled onto the road and her smile widened, her protest forgotten, as the speedometer moved steadily clockwise and I turned to Catriona and pretended to be terrified, while she giggled in the back.

If I ever lose the feeling of wonder at an engine turning, barrelling along at a speed most people who've ever lived could only reach by jumping off a cliff, then I'll know I've lost something that can't be replaced. The road tossing pebbles against the underside of the car, the weary walkers who stop and watch and wish they could swap places, the scenes of fields racing past like a faulty projection, the vibration of the interiors, the movement in my body rounding a bend. It's hard not to imagine what it feels like, times a million, strapped inside a capsule, like a bullet shot at the sky. I put a flattened hand out the window and watched it, like a wing.

'Don't start about the rockets,' Siobhán said, accelerating on an open stretch, moving through the gears as if she was born to do it.

We pulled in outside Nuala's red-brick townhouse, not far from St Stephen's Green. Every time we visit, I see the big house and something gnaws at my gut, telling me that I sold Siobhán short. People look at Nuala and see a woman who used her beauty to marry as high as it took her. Only the eldest son gets the farm, and the rest of us were left with the tools we had. Cormac is a good man and, as far as I can tell, a good husband, though there have been moments through the years when I wondered if he's just a bit too settled in having the fine-looking wife and attentive mother to four children.

It's easy to imagine Siobhán coming out the front gate, dressed up and on her way to the city, meeting other women for tea at the Shelbourne. Heading up some committee created to rattle cages. Or a board member of some theatre. We went to the Wexford Opera Festival a couple of years back. That music touched parts of her heart and brain that I can't.

Nuala opened the door as if she was expecting us, in a navy dress and canvas shoes, her dark hair tied loosely, faint strands of grey threaded through it like a subtle decorative detail. My sister, getting older.

'Siobhán,' she said, leaning in for a hug, two from her flock roaring in the belly of the house. She kissed my cheek then crouched in front of Catriona, putting her hands under her arms as if to gauge any change in weight or size, then calling her all the things women call little children. 'Come in, come in,' she said, standing, warning us that the place was a mess. There were fresh flowers in a vase inside the door. I handed over a box of chocolates picked up on the way, probably half-melted. I gave her a card with some money for my goddaughter, Marie, who Nuala told me was at tennis.

'It's all change around here,' Siobhán said, looking back to the street.

'The families are moving out. In come the offices. Accountants, lawyers, and doctors,' Nuala said. 'We might look at someplace near the sea sometime. The boys get cooped up here. As you can hear.'

The two eldest boys stopped their shouting and came to investigate, both heads of hair styled in the same neat parting. Siobhán bailed me out of not being able to tell which was which. 'Fintan and Liam,' she said. 'Ye're after getting massive.' They stood taller as if to emphasise their growth spurts and led Siobhán to the living room, telling her about their rugby team. I tugged Nuala's elbow before she could follow. I made sure not to whisper, not wanting to raise suspicion. Not wanting Siobhán to realise the real reason for visiting. The last thing she needs to hear is me complaining about my aches and pains.

'Is the good doctor in?'

'He's in his study. Probably has his records on. Go on and bring him out.' She looked me up and down, appraising in the way that only a sister can, then went to the kitchen, keeping whatever she had deduced to herself. I watched her cross the chequered pattern like a Queen moving from one end of a board to another, her shoes gliding across the tile. She left me standing in the grandeur of their home, admiring all we didn't have, the crystal fingers of the chandelier above my head pointing at me, the eyes of the long-dead people in the portraits along the stairs looking at me as if I was the help. As Nuala and Siobhán's chatter dulled behind a closed door, I heard music. Opera.

I knocked once and turned the brass handle to the room to the left of the stairs. Cormac was sitting next to a wall of mahogany bookshelves, a glass of something amber in one hand, one foot up on the other knee. His ritual whenever he got in from the hospital and took an hour to himself. There was a steaming bowl on the table beside him. The smell of Vicks Vaporub singed my nostrils.

He looked up, expecting Nuala, then stood, smiling when he saw me.

'Jim, Jesus. I'm in my own world, I didn't hear you arrive at all. Nuala never told me you were coming.'

We shook hands, and I remembered his limp grip, like holding a damp cloth while looking for a place to drop it. He was a few years past his best, but ageing suited him, the greying sideburns giving an intellectual air, the furrow between his brown eyes bolstering the look of a man who spent a great deal of time pondering difficult questions.

'Ah, I hadn't told her, sorry to land in. It was a spur of the moment thing. Siobhán and Catriona are with me.'

'Well, ye're more than welcome. Let me get you a drink.' He turned on his heel and went to a cabinet at the far wall. 'I'm having a brandy myself,' he said, with his back to me, pulling the stopper from a glass decanter. 'How does that sound?'

'A small one sounds ideal.' He had it poured before I answered.

'Have a seat, Jim, we'll have this, then head out to the women.'

I sat in an armchair at the other end of the bookshelves, admiring his sanctuary and not able to stop myself comparing it to my simple workbench at home. The music and the brandy and Cormac in his tailored suit reminded me of important men in important rooms. I thought of a picture I'd seen of Kennedy and his brother Bobby – two dark silhouettes sitting close in a hotel room, deep in conversation. The books were mostly medical textbooks. If there was an order to them, I couldn't discern it. *Artistic Anatomy. Hypnosis in Modern Medicine. The Rheumatic Diseases. The Conquest of Plague.*

'You must think I'm very dull,' Cormac said, watching me scan the shelves. 'Coming home from the hospital to read about medicine. But it fascinates me. I wish I could have specialised in every discipline.'

'I can imagine. It must all be changing fast.'

He drank his brandy. 'Right you are. I was only reading about a case in Boston. A young boy tried to hop a freight train and had his arm ripped off, clean at the shoulder.' He made a slicing gesture with a flattened hand. 'They reattached it, every vessel and nerve, as if they were stitching a sleeve back on a jumper. A year on, and the boy can feel hot and cold. Pain.' He laughed. 'Given the gift of pain. He's even back playing baseball.' He waved a hand towards his desk and a bundle of pages and magazines, as if I might want to take the paper with me to read for myself.

'How's work?' I said, and took a sip. A mouthful of warm wood.

'Nothing as exciting as limb reattachment, but still, no two days the same.' He drank. 'My surgical colleagues have had a fair rise in patients after traffic accidents this summer. Are you finding that yourself?

'Drink, bad roads and bad light. We've pulled plenty from ditches. Everybody thinks they're great drivers as soon as they get the keys.'

We drank and when we swallowed, we'd forgotten whose turn it was to speak, so I got right to it.

'Cormac, I know you're off the clock, but might I run something by you?'

He sat forward, holding his glass between his knees which he'd set wide apart. He gave me a look of absolute concentration. If it was meant to encourage me to speak plainly, it had the opposite effect. Some fear of him thinking me a hypochondriac or a man not able to manage a headache. I found myself wandering into another deception.

'It might be nothing,' I said, dismissing any worry with a flick of one hand, holding the weighty glass on my thigh with the other. 'One of the guards at the station, a man around my own age. He's been having terrible headaches lately. The local doc gave him pain-killers. I asked him the other day if he was feeling alright and he said he's exhausted most of the time. That his joints are sore and his arms tingle as if he'd slept on them. I suppose we're working plenty these days. Would any of it concern you? For a man his age?'

Cormac was brushing the underside of his chin with the finger-nail of his index finger. 'Well, I'm a neurologist so you'll get a neurologist's answer. We always see what we're used to. So, from that point of view, something neurological could explain the tired arms and the sensation in them. But of course, headache and fatigue are some of the most common complaints doctors hear every day. Then he might just be getting a bruising on the football field or overdoing it at the pub.'

He laughed and I smiled, giving the lightness room to breathe, before probing again.

'Just some concern on my part. I'd like to steer him to the right help if he needs it. The local GP isn't up to much. You know I lost a twin years back, so I suppose something like meningitis is always in my head. That probably sounds silly.'

'Not at all. But it's difficult, Jim, the man could have a simple infection for all I know. Show a rheumatologist joint pain and fatigue and he might see rheumatism, show an endocrinologist fatigue and dizzy spells and he might see Addison's. You see my point.'

'What does a neurologist see?'

He drank. 'I suppose something like MS might make sense. Given the man's age and some of the symptoms.'

'MS?' I said, as if I'd never heard the letters.

'We know more every year, like everything. I won't bore you, but if you're that concerned you should get your man up to us. Or at the very least get him to a better doctor.'

'Will do.'

'They're lucky to have you as their sergeant,' he smiled. He emptied his glass put it on a side table then stood and took the needle from the record. 'Into the breach.'

I stood and left my glass next to his and looked at the title of the book nearest to where he'd been sitting. *Progress in Neurology and Psychiatry.*

'Tell me, Cormac.' He stopped, holding the handle. 'Is there any real progress being made in psychiatry? Or do we still just round them up like cattle and let them rot in asylums?'

He gave the question some thought. 'There are improvements, Jim, certainly. New medicines, greater focus on treatment. These places are far from perfect but also far from what they once were. A lot more dignity than there was even a decade ago.'

'Would you put a family member in one?'

He laughed. 'Maybe in another two decades.'

'Progress,' I said and followed him through to the kitchen, where Nuala and Siobhán were sitting behind cups of tea, discussing all the things Nuala had on her plate, with children swarming around like bees and the mysteries of neurology swarming around in my head.

# 18

Patrick stopped on the front step with a feeling that he was being followed. He'd loosened his tie and opened his shirt on the cycle, and had the dishevelled look of a man thrown from the pub at closing time. There was nobody at the gate and the yard was empty. The quiet of an ambush all around. The warm smell of newly cut hay coming from the west. He scanned the fields, imagining hidden eyes watching from trees and thickets. He went inside and locked the door.

In his bedroom, he shook off his jacket and trousers, then threw the shirt and tie on top of them. He pulled a canvas bag from beneath his bed and looked around the room, sparse as a prison cell, and decided that there was nothing of use, before dressing in his familiar clothes and packing a couple of shirts and trousers from his wardrobe. He left the room without looking at the painting.

He took some tools from the kitchen table – a chisel, a hammer, a screwdriver, a crowbar, a briar hook – things he likely wouldn't need but didn't want to return for if he did. His knives. Tins of beans and fruit in syrup. Oats. Newspaper-wrapped quarters of rabbit from the larder. Piled into the bag without order, testing its weight every time something was added. He packed needles and wool – green and red, then searched the brown suitcase, unsure of what he was looking for, and took some fine thread and paperclips, with no use in mind.

Standing in middle of the room, he imagined his father in his chair, hands joined loosely over his stomach, muttering prayers under his breath and circling his thumbs, while his mother carried dinner to the table. He saw himself, four years old, coming in the door, wearing shorts and muck on his knees, offering palms filled with dirt and worms to his parents. Being hoisted to the basin in the sink to scrub them. Colm somewhere unseen, working in the yard or shed maybe. His brother stared back from the picture on the wall. Where Patrick once saw a sort of contentment in Colm's eyes, he now saw contempt.

His mother's room was darkened by thick curtains. It was a long time since the window was opened and the air was thick and heavy. He stood perfectly still, with all the caution of a small boy afraid to be found somewhere he shouldn't be. He walked slowly, glancing at the bed, last made the day she died. He ran a finger along the small dresser, furrowing a path through the settled dust, then lifted a tin box, filled with creams and balms and ointments, and shook it, but nothing of interest loosened. He unscrewed the lid of a near empty tin of talcum powder and fingered the dusted rim. The smell brought no memory.

The top drawer of the nightstand held his mother's underwear. The second drawer held more secrets from a woman's world, Clairol hair dye and Lustre Net spray. A fur-lined hot water bottle like a hibernating animal. From the bottom drawer he lifted a bundle of papers. Empty envelopes and a couple of mass cards for his father. One from the Rossiters. One from Field, offering condolences and a few soft words about *Sean*. He leafed through the bundle and stopped on a page with his own name written on the top corner in his mother's neat handwriting. An application form for work with the ESB. In the same bundle, he found applications for Bord na Móna and an apprentice fitter post with CIÉ, companies she probably imagined were so big that they could surely find space for him. He thought of her, collecting the information in town, too proud to ask any local for advice out of fear they'd laugh and tell her that the ESB only hire the best and brightest and that her son hadn't a chance.

He moved to the middle of the bed, imagining himself between two ghosts as he held the papers against his chest and shut his eyes, thinking that even his mother, who wished him away almost every day, wouldn't consider sending him to Senan's for anything other than pushing a mop across the floor and collecting a bit of money for his efforts.

He lay in the dark room, taking some time to say goodbye to them both, his mind moving too fast to find a memory of good times. Running ahead to what he'd do next, running so fast it tired, and he fell asleep, the letters and application forms rising and falling with his chest.

He woke to a car door slamming. More than one. The pages fell to the floor when he turned from the bed and crouched his way across the room, even though the curtains were drawn. He knelt on one knee by the window and drew a curtain back an eye's width, slowing his breathing and watching, half-hoping to see Field come up the path, maybe Colm in tow, coaxed into negotiating some sort of agreement.

Flood and another guard came through the gate, trailed by Colm, Casey, and Doctor Murphy. He heard voices but not what they said. There was no sign of Field. Flood pounded on the front door while the others stood back. Murphy's sleeves were rolled and he wiped his forehead. Casey stood further back with his arms folded, overseeing things like a man who'd stumbled on the scene.

'Open up, Hatten,' shouted Flood, pounding. Colm stepped forward and Patrick heard him tell Flood that it was his house and that he could walk in if he wanted to.

'You don't know that mad bastard won't blow you right back through the door,' Flood said. 'Open this door now, Hatten!'

Patrick ran across the room and kept his head down through the kitchen, slowing to turn the handle on the back door and escaping to the rear of the house. It was late, but not yet dark. He scrambled around the back of the house, unsure if the banging he heard was on his front door or inside his chest. He hopped the wall and landed in Casey's field, then took cover behind the first tractor and watched to make sure that the men's eyes were fixed on his front door. He ran, cutting a diagonal track across the field, back bent and arms out and rigid, as if carrying invisible bags. He took the short side of the field at full pelt, and without breaking stride, he jumped at an oak, wrapping his arms and legs around the trunk and pulling himself up until he reached a thick lower limb, shaking birds loose from the tree like blown leaves.

From his outpost, he saw his front door through the treeline and saw that they had opened it. Casey and Murphy waited outside. The guards and Colm must have been inside, walking among his things, touching them, and he wondered if Colm remembered sitting at the table, or sleeping in the back room. If some memory might catch him off-guard and make him reconsider.

Murphy and Casey went to the door of the tool shed. The younger guard came outside and joined them. The trio hesitated as if scared of what might be inside. The guard put a hand on his baton. They deliberated for a while, making occasional gestures towards the door, until eventually, Casey slid it open and Patrick imagined the cat seeing Casey's huge shape fill the doorway. He closed one eye and wished he had his rifle, so he could see things more clearly through the scope. He imagined fixing the sight on Casey's back, so broad it was impossible to miss. Casey turned and said something, then turned in a half-circle, eyeing the landscape, and Patrick felt a murmur of satisfaction that out of all the men, Casey was the one who sensed him watching, the one who felt a shiver on the back of his neck. Murphy leaned against the wall of the bungalow, his interest in the venture lost.

The cat didn't appear. Flood came from the house carrying Patrick's rifle. A few seconds later, Colm followed and Patrick imagined that he'd stayed behind, taking one last look at the place. The men gathered in the doorway and talked for a minute until four of them left, leaving Flood behind. He heard the car doors shutting and an engine starting and he glanced to the grey fists of cloud, raised in a darkening sky, ready to release stores of rain. He watched Flood shuffle his feet on the front step and knew that when it came to waiting, he could beat Flood every day of the week.

Flood gave up his station not long after the rain came. For a few minutes, he leaned against the doorframe with his hands in his pockets. His cap and uniform gave shape to a silhouette that lapsed into restlessness, probably thinking of a warm bed. He pulled the door behind him and sank into the dark night before he reached the patrol car. Patrick saw the sweep of headlights while the car turned in the road, then hopped from the tree in time to watch the two bulbs of tail lights shrink away to nothing. He ran down the road and climbed his gate.

He stepped inside and wiped the rain from his face, then fingered the shelf inside the door in search of matches. He found the box and lit one, not risking the light, in case Flood had decided to keep watch from the comfort of his car, somewhere just off the road. He scanned the room and saw the bag, still near the stove like a sack of fuel. Anything else that might be of use was too big to carry. Something in the room was different. He lit another match, turning in a slow circle until he spotted the rectangle of space on the smoke-stained wall. He knew his brother had taken the picture and was glad that Colm had seen it as something worth holding on to, but knew it meant that Colm didn't ever plan on coming back.

He hoisted the bag over his shoulder, closing the door quietly. He went to the shed, where it was too dark to see if the cat had stayed or left.

'Goodbye, Cat,' he said to the blackness.

Avoiding the main road, he pushed his bicycle through fields and lifted it over wooden stiles. He left the bag in a watertight gap in a hedge, then joined the road at Corcoran's Cross, cycling without a light until he heard the Barrow whispering and saw long and short blades of moonlight on its surface. At its tightest bend, the river was so narrow he could piss into Kilkenny. Patrick stopped outside the high walls of Penrose's estate. He had his pocket-knife and a torch, and no plan other than getting inside and looking for what he needed, expecting that Penrose was tucked up in his bed with a full stomach and a head full of rich man's dreams.

The wall was an easy climb, with plenty of footholds between the old stone. He walked the drive, listening to secrets shared between the trees and the river. Sheets of rain passed over him, the drops against the leaves sounding like a gentle applause. He stopped at the smell of dogs and peered at a pen to the left of the house, likely to be full of jumpy bloodhounds. He veered right, stumbling on a low clipped hedge before rounding a conservatory and finding a side door. A gutter emptied a steady flow next to it.

He felt his way along a wide corridor, taking care not to trip on a long rug that softened his footsteps. There was a smell of some foreign herb or plant, and silver shields and masks on the walls took shape in dim light through a huge window above the stairs. Souvenirs from battles that no Penrose had ever fought in. Thick frames surrounded miserable oil portraits. The staircase was bolstered by a banister as thick as an electricity pole. A bulb burned in a room across from it. He looked in at couches and bookcases, then backed away, guided by nothing but instinct to go back the way he'd come, to the top of the concrete steps inside the side door.

The basement was colder than the rest of the house and he took his torch from his pocket. The light reflected against glass and temporarily blinded him. When he blinked back into focus, he smiled, and thought that after the day he'd had, he was due such luck. The glass was set in the doors of a cabinet that lined the entire wall, filled with shotguns and rifles, standing on their stocks like a troop of soldiers waiting to be called on. There were boots and wellingtons and baskets of clothes against the opposite wall, riding crops and saddles and helmets on shelves, falconer's gauntlets on a low table. The smell of oil. He went to the cabinet and pulled open the drawers, loaded with enough ammunition to defend against a brigade of IRA men who might want to come burn the place down.

He rested the torch on the cabinet and pocketed what he could, taking a mix of gauges. When his pockets were full, he tucked his shirt in tight and put more cartridges inside and the cylinders of the casings rolled against his damp skin. He opened the cabinet – unlocked, as Roche had promised it would be – and ran his hands up and down the long barrels and leaned to smell the polished stocks and the chemical solvent used to keep the barrels clean. Patrick reached for the gun that shone brighter than the others. Lighter than expected, the stock was polished to such a fine finish that he could just about make out the reflection of his eyes. It was fixed with a scope twice as big as the one on the rifle Flood had claimed. He turned it in his hands and read the Weatherby inscription, then ran a thumb over the white diamond-shaped inlay on the grip cap. It fit inside his shoulder as if it was tailored for him, and he turned in a half circle, the sloping cheek piece cool against his skin while he aimed it at the far wall, sure that it could blow a hole through the concrete. He felt a stirring of disloyalty and conceded that his old gun was best suited to small game and the hands of boys shooting their first rifle. The one in his hands was meant to cause altogether different damage.

# 19

We stayed too late at Nuala's. Catriona fell asleep in their bedroom after an evening playing with her cousins, all of them mad on Milky Mints and Bullseyes. They're good children, Nuala's. Energetic, kind, easily tired and selfish, like all the rest of them. I wonder is there an age that it sticks, all the shite and badness we put on them?

Seeing Nuala is a bit like stepping back in time. I'll always see my older sister and she'll always see the younger brother she knows better than. For myself and Siobhán, it's also like looking into a future we once imagined, with Catriona in a house full of children we'll never have. Siobhán loves visiting. The big house, kids running wild. I was wound tight as a drum until after dinner, stiff from the drive, thinking about illness and Patrick, convincing myself that I'd miss nothing. Nuala's mutton stew was divided into more portions than she'd planned. Apple tart, cold cream and warm custard followed. Then Cormac poured another brandy and I heard Siobhán's laugh and looked across the room and saw Nuala's youngest lad bouncing in her lap and that smile on Siobhán's face. I let myself enjoy it. Siobhán was like a wounded bird nursed back to health, set free to spread her wings. She talked and reasoned and argued with Cormac about everything from the death penalty, to McGahern, to the importance of technical colleges. She reminded me of her father, only even more spirited and better able to grasp the contrary opinion and smooth its sharp edges. Cormac raised his glass to concede more than once.

I shouldn't have been driving really, but it was late and the roads are quiet at that hour, even from Dublin. It was peaceful, Siobhán asleep next to me and Catriona dreaming in the back, wrapped in a blanket from the boot and a cardigan Nuala insisted her youngest girl had grown out of. Part of me wanted to drive as slow as I could, to make the journey last as long as possible, long enough for it to burn itself into my brain to draw on at some stage when I might need the memory.

I wondered would myself and my sister have to wave our own children off, the way our parents lost our brothers to seas and skies. Each of them gone long enough to become men that I only really knew when they were little more than boys. Off in Brooklyn, Maryland, San Diego. Laying concrete, hauling freight, guarding the peace like myself.

I read once that that nearly half of the people born here the same year that I was have left. What was here for Siobhán and myself that made us stay? Each other, I suppose, if you believe in love and fate and all those things people hope are true. Stuff that isn't easy to believe in until you find it, coming off an overtime shift on Christmas Eve in '49, keen to get back on the road after dropping my partner home, until his sister came into the room carrying a tray of tea and cake. From that second on, my heart was wherever she was.

Will we watch Catriona drift away from us or will we learn to take a stronger grip of them all? It's part of why the rockets fascinate me so much. It's why when we hit a long dark stretch, I looked through the windscreen, at Ursa Major and Ursa Minor and the huge coin of the moon as smooth and clear as a frozen lake, and the black sky spangled with dead stars, and imagined what else might be possible. As if I was the only fool to ever tilt his chin and look at the sky after a couple of drinks and believe that I could see the full width of heaven, as plainly as the road in front of us, only eternal and insurmountable.

I parked against the kerb, rain arriving a day early and pouring down since we got into Wexford, the wipers working like men scrambling to clear water from the deck of a sinking ship. I put my hand on Siobhán's face.

'We're home, love.'

She stirred and kissed me, her eyes still closed, the rain tapping on the windscreen like a thousand typists racing to meet a deadline. I told her go on ahead and put the keys in her palm and watched her go inside, leaving the front door open. I lifted Catriona from the back seat, still bundled up, and stood on the street, the engine catching its breath.

'Do you know what's up there?' I asked her, my eyes flicking between the sky and the side of her head. She managed to make a noise from her sleep. 'There's a woman up there now. She was sent up today. To float in space, all on her own.' I lowered my voice to a whisper. 'She's a Soviet.'

Her head turned and I saw her eyes open and scan the night. 'I can't see her,' she said, then closed her eyes again.

'Oh, she's up there, love. She's up there.'

My breath clouded around Catriona's head and I kissed her and held her to my shoulder, as if to tell her, even while she slept, that it was all out there for her to discover, just the same as her home would always be here for her when she came back.

# 20

Patrick reached Roche's in full darkness. Even with torchlight, he'd had to stop several times to get his bearings. He sheltered from the rain twice on his journey, then carried on when it didn't look like stopping. His clothes were heavy and wet and clung like a second skin. He wheeled his bike to the side wall, moving by memory through dense blackness. He considered sleeping in the shed and trying Joe in the morning, but remembered the pregnant cat and decided to leave her be, missing the cat he'd left behind. His bag gnawed at his shoulder, filled with salvage from home and the shotgun cartridges. The new gun stuck out of the bag and he wore a beltful of knives. He hoped the rabbit meat would be enough to soften the old man. He was hungry and tired and cold, and the chair in front of Roche's empty fireplace was more tempting than a night outside, even if it came with a scolding.

He banged on the door of the cottage, then looked through the window and saw his own eyes looking back. He called Roche's name and knocked again, then turned the handle. The smell that attacked his nose was so powerful that Patrick thought it might be all he ever smelled again. He imagined the raw and rotting stink knotting itself to every strand and filling every seam of his clothes, felt it curl under his fingernails and behind his ears, spreading like gas through his nostrils and into his throat and mouth, filling the pink flesh of his gums, seeping into his teeth and their roots. He gagged and covered his mouth and nose with a wet sleeve. He flicked on his torch and walked through the cottage like some cave explorer, about to find the body of a man who'd never found his way out.

Roche was where he'd last seen him, sitting upright on his chair, his pipe between his thighs and his face paled to an unearthly colour, made paler by the white light of the torch. The mouth was open, the single tooth like some fungus growing from the corpse. Patrick pressed one hand to Roche's chest and it felt like a skeleton wrapped in wool. He kept his hand there for twenty missing beats. The tiredness and darkness and smell seemed to have tripped his brain onto some dazed frequency and sitting with Roche felt like a macabre dream, his breath clouding the scene.

He went to the table and took his lamp from his bag and lit it. The boots were still waiting to be repaired and he set the lamp beside them.

'Now, Joe. I brought a rabbit like I said I would.'

On the far side of the room, he dropped the rabbit in a basin, then picked up the new gun.

'I took your advice.' He approached the old man from behind. Roche looked as if he was sleeping in front of a fire that had long burned out and Patrick put his hand on a bony shoulder then surprised himself by leaning to kiss the top of his head, like a son saying goodnight to a parent. 'You were dead right, Joe. Penrose's cabinet was wide open.'

He went to the bedroom at the back of the house, wiping his mouth and scraping his tongue against his top teeth as if to remove the taste of the dead man's scalp, the chaos of the day and night all seeming so unreal that he wasn't sure if it had happened. He was too tired to give it any more thought and lay back on the sour mattress.

He woke more than once in the night to what he thought was footsteps, wondering if he had it wrong and that Roche was on his way to find his bed occupied. Patrick went to the room twice, holding the new gun at hip-height, his bare feet made gritty by the dirt they lifted from the cold and uneven floor. Both times, he found the body unmoved and aimed the gun at the darkness around him, as if Roche's ghost might step out of it.

He woke to the sound of raindrops falling just outside the narrow window of Roche's bedroom. In his dream, the drops were the sound of a Garda's fist hitting his front door. The bed had a wooden frame and a mattress of meal sacks sewn together. He put a hand into a torn seam and felt a mix of feathers, straw, and bog cotton.

The window was divided into four dirty panes by a flaking wooden grille, and outside, the rain had stopped and the drops were jumping from the roof in ones and twos, landing on the lid of a barrel at window height. The ashes of something Roche had burned had turned to a grey paste in the dirt yard. The land behind the house was wild and rough, all weed and rock, wildflowers leaning in a breeze, giving way to the oaks rising on Carrickbyrne hill – dark and watchful, sheltered by heavy cloud.

He turned from the bed, pushing away a blanket as stiff as cardboard. Roche's room was probably no better than a cell in Portlaoise, but it beat a packed dorm in Senan's. A wardrobe stood against the far wall, slanting to one side. He opened it to a few old ties and a black suit, a couple of pairs of trousers bundled at the bottom. There was a washbasin in the corner, next to a wooden chair with a wicker seat mended with twine and folded up to reveal an ancient chamber pot. He crossed the room and found it mercifully empty, retired from its long career of receiving Roche's shite.

There was something wilder in the pitch of the bird calls outside, as if they weren't singing, but threatening. He thought of his house and garden and the jobs he'd planned to do today. The thought of his brother and Casey shaking hands stirred a violence that occupied every part of him, the same as when he pressed his finger to Colm's head in the Royal, or watched Casey from the branch the previous night, thinking how easy it would be to hit a target that size, to fell him with one pull of a trigger from distance, deciding when he took his last breath.

The top of Roche's head was visible over the chair, a pale and freckled turkey egg, his white hair thin and soft as down. The smell was less severe after spending a night in it. He watched the dead man and wondered if his passing would register any more than the loss of whatever creatures had lain down during the night and died in fields and forests all around.

'Now, Joe. What will we do with you?'

He rounded the chair and saw the hollow face, like something that had never lived at all. He moved the pipe and tobacco to the next chair, then straightened Roche's moth-eaten woollen jumper, with its unravelling strands hanging loose. He counted in a whisper – *one, two, three* – and lifted Roche from the side, one arm under thighs as thin as forearms, the old bones beneath the clothes rubbing against Patrick's own, and weighing no more than a bag of kindling. The fingers like long stalks, the nails the dirty yellow of honey fungus. The backs of Roche's hands, spotted and thinned by years of outdoor living. Patrick remembered the same hands, only a decade before, pinning a flailing, muscular pig that was fighting for its life, then slicing its throat. Time had shrivelled Roche like a rotten apple.

He set him down in the far corner of the empty byre and thought about saying a prayer, but instead folded Roche's hands over his stomach. Decomposed and blackened straw lay scattered around the body like a crude nest. He shut the door and faced the empty cottage, and the empty day, like all those days and weeks after his mother died when he had nothing but time to waste, and he remembered how it had nearly driven him mad.

He opened the cupboards and wasn't surprised to see that Roche had been surviving on so little that he wondered if he'd starved to death. Some porridge oats, eggs and a bag of flour alive with weevils. A loaf of bread that could sharpen a knife. The sink used an old-fashioned pump from a barrel, where flies floated on the surface of dregs of water. There were some cuts of wood on the ground next to the stove and Patrick suspected that Roche used them sparingly, their use not justified in warmer weather. Maybe he'd known he wouldn't make it to winter.

Outside, everything was painted grey. He rounded the cottage and looked to Carrickbyrne. Stories of the 1798 rebels were one of the few things that kept his attention at school and he thought of them camping out on the hill, springing attacks, the sound of gunfire across Wexford like Ireland's closest thing to cowboy films. He'd been up the hill a few times and on one clear day he saw as far as the Blackstairs. Kilkenny to the west, where he'd once cycled aimlessly, looking into fields on the off-chance he might spot Bullet, tied to a wall or fence, living out his days. Unseen and 30 miles east, the Irish Sea. He cycled there twice in the aimless weeks after his mother died, unable to sit still or focus on any task. The winter water was calm and grey and it unsettled him, having hoped to encounter a wild sea of waves, raging against the land in an eternal battle. He thought of his brother, somewhere across the still water, and wondered if he knew she'd died. He sat looking at the sea for a long time, until it turned to night and he cycled home in darkness, Christmas lights or candles in the odd home along the way, then spent days in bed shivering and recovering from a sickness that stole a few pounds of weight while Christmas and New Year passed.

He went to the shed. There was no sign of the piebald cat or any of her kittens, if she'd had them. He toed the axe and drank a mouthful of rainwater from the rusted trough.

On the far side of the shed, three ghostly chickens that a fox would turn its nose up at stood thin and still, their feathers tossed as if they'd just flown through a storm. Not even a hint of fresh droppings. He went to the back of the house and slid the wet lid off the barrel by the bedroom window and found a shallow pool of salted mackerel and his nose filled with ocean. At the far end of the house, a gutter was angled so rainwater poured into a second barrel.

He couldn't imagine Roche catching the mackerel in the frail state he'd last seen him alive, and though it had been a while since the fish in the barrel had seen moving water, they'd likely been caught in the last few weeks. The realisation that somebody else must call on the old man killed an idea that Patrick hadn't realised was growing. The possibility of staying and taking over Roche's place in the world, dead before it drew breath.

He turned in a slow circle, as if some necessary task would present itself, some purpose to pass the day. He looked at all the unworked acres, and remembered Roche helping his father with their few cattle, and for all their sweat and aches and pains, what had it earned them? He imagined the land years from now, the arms of heartless machines – with no need for blood, or muscle, or bone, or soul – moving and digging and tilling, doing the work of twenty men, piling crops onto scaffolds and tipping them into lorries, the work of the likes of Roche and his father seeming as primitive as drag stones.

He went back inside and took the new gun from the table, then propped open the window and let it frame his potential targets. He closed one eye and pressed his tongue into the gap in his teeth, then drew back and opened the bolt and chambered three cartridges. He remembered the first time he fired the Winchester. Not even ten, his mother raged for days at his father for not keeping it out of reach. He was in the shed with his father when a neighbour came for help with a calf, and Patrick sat with Bullet, waiting for him to come back. After an hour, he went to the gun, standing in the corner. He stepped outside and sighted a crow, crossing the grey in a steady line, and when he pulled the trigger the force of the gun jarred him and he lost sight of the shot but knew the crow hadn't even noticed it. He heard the chickens then, frenzied by the shot, and he went to their coop, watching the flock of easy targets pick their way across the ground. His finger curled around the trigger and just before he fired, he heard his father's voice behind him.

'Patrick,' he said, soft and calm, with a note of surprise, and Patrick lowered the gun and put it on the ground and went to his father and cried into his shoulder. It was the last time his father held him. Not long from being judged unfit for anywhere but Senan's, but still there to help his neighbour, and to comfort his son.

His breathing was deep and low and clouded the lower pane of glass. He scanned the middle ground and after passing over the crows on the roof of the shed, he saw the bottle green head of a pheasant moving in the dense cover of grass so dry it almost matched the feathers on the bird's side. He pushed the bolt forward. The bird's black eyes moved in the poppy-red face, and a blooddrop of wattle hung from its head. He fingered the trigger, then pulled it at the end of three long breaths. He drew back in time to see the crows scatter in fright. The sound of the shot caught him off guard, and the power of the gun left a dull feeling in his shoulder.

He went to examine the bird and saw little left for eating. He hadn't so much killed it as destroyed it completely. He crouched to examine the tangle of feathers and flesh, as if some apprentice had made a mess of butchering the thing. He stood with the gun in his hand and put its nose in the earth and a hand on its stock, leaning on it like a fencepost, shaking his head at its might, looking to the top of Carrickbyrne.

# 21

We walked around to mass, Catriona between us. Siobhán had some lemon cake from Nuala to give to Rita if we saw her. We took a hand each and lifted Catriona over the puddles. The usual line of bicycles against the wall, ponies and carts and the odd car along the road. Voices lowered to whispers within a few yards of the door. I had the feeling of eyes on me as I walked over the mosaic of Our Lady and found a pew with space for the three of us.

Father Crowley came out cloaked, flanked by a pair of altar boys. We all stood and the tiredness in my legs reminded me of the late night and long drive. Up and down we went, acknowledging our sins, listening to his Latin, celebrating sacred mysteries with amens and invocations, proclamations and responses. I took the bread and ate it, offered peace and lifted up my heart, then let my mind wander down the nave and out the double doors, back to the model V-2 and Sunday dinner. Before he let us go in peace, to love and serve the Lord, he asked us to join in prayer for the soul of Donncha Reilly, a retired schoolmaster, who last I saw walking at Arthurstown with his hands behind his back and a whistle on his lips.

Outside the church, there was whispered talk about Donncha Reilly's teaching days and how he had lost weight the last time he was seen and how much he'd love to have seen Kennedy. Men huddled together, gathered around some invisible truth that they all leaned an ear towards.

Siobhán spotted Rita Kirwan, making a slow and lonely exit through the side gate. She told me she'd meet me at home and led Catriona by the hand, weaving through the bodies to tap Rita on the shoulder. I saw Rita's smile spread while she crouched to examine Catriona and the small parcel of cake.

On my way through the gate, I met Flood in his Sunday clothes and Colfer in his uniform, and knew they were waiting for me. They glanced at each other and then at me, then at their feet, like a pair of schoolboys caught with a packet of Player's.

'Why do I get the feeling I'm about to be kept from my roast?'

Flood glared at Colfer, who cleared his throat. 'We were out at Patrick Hatten's last night, Sergeant.'

'What brought you out there?' I looked around at the thinning crowd, as if I might see Patrick there to explain his side of the story.

'Peter Casey. Himself and Colm Hatten. But Patrick wasn't there.'

'He'd made a threat,' Flood said, his gaze fixed on Colfer who he judged to have left out the most important detail. 'In the middle of the Royal Hotel, Jim. Told his brother he'd shoot him in the head. He'd pointed the rifle at Eamon and pulled a knife in Gallagher's too. It was time to act.'

'Good Jesus,' I said and took off my hat. 'Not here.' They kept a half-step behind as I walked to the station, through the sound of hooves and goodbyes and the chat of the women queuing at Gleeson's and Riley's for the Sunday shop.

'Do I have this right,' I said, as soon as I sat at my desk, Colfer and Flood opposite, with Colfer holding a couple of pages. The station was cold and quiet. 'Ye were part of a troop out at Hatten's last night? With the intention of what, throwing a net over him like some animal and carting him off to the zoo?'

'Under the Mental Treatment Act, Jim. We had a written application from a family member and a certificate from the medical officer.' Flood looked pleased with himself and I saw Colfer turn his head away a fraction, as if to distance himself from the words.

'You don't need to explain the law to me, Flood. Tell me, when did the medical officer examine him? Since you know the Act so well, you'll know that any medical certificate is to be issued up to seven days before the family application is made. Christ knows what Murphy was doing there. Appointing himself medical officer, I suppose.' Flood stirred in his seat, a petulant schoolboy on a final warning, trying to decide if giving some cheek back would be worth it. 'Do you know what this is? This is Peter Casey and Colm Hatten, ticking boxes any old way, the law be damned. How well they knew to chance it while I was away. Because you can both be damn sure I'd have reminded ye of what the job is and isn't.'

Colfer looked at Flood, who was staring at my desk.

'He made the threat in the Royal, Sergeant. Against his brother,' Colfer explained.

'Ye said that already.' I pointed a finger at him. 'Did you do any thinking for yourself? Or did you just do what Peter Casey told you to do?'

'I went to your house after Colm Hatten came in with the application. There was no answer.'

'And who reported this supposed threat?'

'Colm Hatten was with a waiter, Gerard Breen.' He slid two typed and signed statements across the desk.

'Why do I feel like a school principal instead of a sergeant?' I rubbed my temples and took one of Murphy's tablets from my top drawer and threw it back without water, feeling it in my throat after I swallowed. 'How many brothers do you have, Colfer?'

'Three, Sergeant.'

'What about you, Flood?'

'The same as Colfer. Three.'

'Have any of them ever said they'd kill you?'

They said nothing. I put my elbows on the table. 'They came in looking for me, but found you, and reported that Patrick Hatten had threatened to shoot his brother. You took their statements,' I said, holding up the pages, both signed by Colfer. 'And then what?'

'Hatten and Breen left. That was in the afternoon. When myself and Flood were finishing up around six, Casey was leaning against his car outside, with Dr Murphy in the passenger seat and Colm

Hatten in the back.' Colfer looked me in the eye as he explained it. Flood looked at Colfer.

'What had Peter Casey to do with anything?'

Colfer held eye contact. Flood didn't.

'There was no trace of Patrick in the house?'

Flood shook his head. 'The place was empty, but in a right state. I stayed for hours, in that rain you know, but he never came back.'

'Anything else?'

Colfer shook his head.

I let a long breath escape my nostrils. 'Go on. Get out. Ye're to come to me if Hatten pops up or if Casey has any more bright ideas. If either of you do something like this again, I promise I'll have ye pedaling around the Aran islands for the next decade.'

Colour rose on Flood's cheeks. They stood together, Colfer leading them out. Flood turned in the doorway.

'Jim,' he said, his voice low, like a man confessing some private shame. 'He came here looking for you.'

'Who did?'

'Patrick Hatten. A couple of hours before his brother came in. He didn't say what it was about, only that he wanted to talk to you.'

I thought of him. Cornered and with nobody to turn to, then settling on me. I remembered telling him he knew where to find me if he needed me, and forgot Flood was in the room. They could have had him in Senan's by this morning.

'Jim?' he said, stirring me from my thoughts. 'Can I put those hours at Hatten's down as overtime?'

The look I gave him was enough for him to bow his head and shut the door after him.

I stood and pulled my coat on, the joints of my shoulders, elbows and wrists hurting as I shuffled into it. My day of rest. I was passing through the station, showing the lads a cold shoulder, when I saw Trevor Penrose at the front desk, the trousers of his fine suit tucked into wellingtons, saying something about a stolen Weatherby Mark V.

Colfer took the report and I sent Penrose on his way with a reminder that if he's going to hoard enough guns to arm every guard in the district, then he should have the good sense to lock them up. If it's been stolen, smart money would say it's somebody that knows his gun room well – a cleaner or some fella who joined him on a Sunday trek once, blowing animals to pieces before tea in the conservatory. Patrick was there in my thoughts too, gone missing at the same time as the rifle.

Turning between the huge wrought-iron gates, their gateposts crowned by the golden shapes of horses' heads, I realised that it was my first time at Casey's stud. A flat slab of granite stood on a plinth to the left of the gates, the name of the stud not yet carved. The driveway was smooth and tarred, with empty paddocks on both sides, fenced in and lined with young birch trees.

Rounding the last bend, a farmhouse came into view, modernised and painted, windows decorated with flowerboxes like something from a postcard. A glossy black door with a golden handle in the shape of a horseshoe, to match the gates. I parked in front of it, next to Casey's Jaguar. A couple of Land Rovers with tow bars were parked further along, before a row of horseboxes that had been recently washed and stood in drying pools of water.

I stood out and breathed sawdust and varnish, the warm smell of horses and straw. Across the way, Casey emerged from the stables, in a flat cap and waistcoat, shirtsleeves rolled up, trousers tucked into wellingtons. Rose sloped a couple of paces behind like an old dog following its master's scent. Casey spotted me and said something over his shoulder to Rose, who went and sat next to the feeding station, beside a round yard of smooth sand. Beyond it, a small man-made lake mirrored the sky and in the far distance where the land dipped, I could just about make out the row of trees that shielded Casey's eyes from the sight of the Hatten house.

'So, this is it,' I said as Casey neared.

He smiled, and say what you want about the man, it was a smile like a child's and the closest thing I've ever seen to sincerity in his face. He had the same energy as Siobhán at the Opera House.

'Come on,' he said, patting my shoulder as if we were old friends. 'I'll give you a tour before we get down to why you're here. Unless you're here to invest, that is.' He laughed at the notion.

He told me that the main building would house offices and a bar. He looked over the fields and talked about soil pH levels and grass and straw in scientific terms that suggested feeding this variety to his thoroughbreds would lead to offspring that would be closer to unicorn than horse. He cast a hand towards the paddocks, six in total, with field shelters at the southern end of each. He talked about expansion plans and didn't bother explaining what direction it would be taking, since we both knew. He might as well have owned the sky above us.

'When will you be finished?'

'We'll never be finished. This place will be breeding winners long after I'm gone. But the first chapter will close once we've bred a Grade One Champion.' He pointed behind me, in the direction of the car park. 'There'll be a big bronze statue of our prized possession there eventually, to remind everybody in future decades about the standards we set from the beginning. That's how sure I am that he's going to sire some of the best racehorses in the world.'

Rose wandered over, looking from me to her father.

'Hello, Rose,' I said, and of course, she said nothing.

'Say hello to Sergeant Field, Rose,' Casey said and some sort of noise came from her. 'She has her exams next year. Isn't that right, Rose?' I felt him tighten at her silence, as if he wanted to take out the riding crop and lash her into life. I thought of Catriona floating above me like a weightless astronaut, laughing down while I move her back and forth. I wondered how Casey could feel such contempt for his daughter.

'Well, you'll need brains and hard work, Rose,' I said. 'I was never one for exams.'

'Ah, you can buy brains,' Casey said and put a hand on my back, steering me away from her and towards the stables.

'On that we disagree, Peter.'

He laughed, a short boom he likely used regularly, for guests to the stud, or salesmen who'd just named their opening price. 'Add it to our list of disagreements, Jim. We're working hard to refine her a bit. I have a bright young woman that comes to her three times a week. Rose loves the horses too. She gets that from me. When you know there's something they want, you can get them to work for it. So, when Rose does well, she earns more time around here. That business with Hatten woke me up to how bad things could get if I didn't take a tighter hold of the reins. She's coming along well, thank God.'

The stables were cool and cavernous, an arc of light at the other end where the doors were open. It was like an enormous, hand-carved warehouse, with stalls either side of a wide aisle and an indoor wash stall at the far end, woodwork tried and tested for centuries holding Casey's vision together – mortise and tenon, dovetail, and birdsmouth joints made by a master. I had the feeling of stepping into a grand hotel or home of old money, or even sitting in Cormac's study, allowing myself to believe that it was my life, just for a second. I'd never as much as been to the races, and there I was, picturing myself in a three-piece and pocket square, clutching a race card trackside, watching my own horse bound for the finish line.

'How many stallions?'

'I'll have twelve when the place is ready for them. Just the one now and we'll do well to ever have one as good.'

Everybody in New Ross knew about Casey's prized horse. I'd heard it spoken about in whispered voices, as if something sacred was being discussed. We stopped walking and he turned to it, a black horse looking out from its stall, the skin tight around muscles and visible veins that curled through its neck and legs. Near 17 hands high and about 80 stone of muscle and bone that it had the strength and heart to vault over ditches, racing around tracks at near the same rate as my Zephyr, all while carrying a man on its back. I was moved to silence, as if I'd travelled back in time to see something from folklore, something mythical creature that people doubt ever existed. And there it was, under Casey's total command.

'Altair,' he said, reading the name engraved on the gate.

'The brightest star in the Aquila constellation.'

He smiled. 'Very good, Sergeant. I'm reminded that you have your passions too.' He turned back to Altair. 'An incredible horse.'

'I've seen horses nearly every day of my life, Peter. Pulling carts, or tethered to fences and staring into empty fields. I'm not sure that's what this is.' I resisted the urge to reach out and touch it, preferring to keep the part of me that wanted to believe it wasn't even real. I saw my shape in its large eye and couldn't help but feel that it was a wise and quiet animal, making sense of me that I couldn't make of myself.

Casey spoke as if we were standing in front of an altar. 'His sire won the King George. Grandsire won the Gold Cup. This,' he said, reaching out a hand and patting the horse, 'is as fine an animal as you'll find anywhere in the world. This is how big Ireland needs to think, Jim. Kennedy needs to represent the beginning of something more. He has to. We've to seize this moment.' He looked at the horse with all the pride he hadn't extended to Rose and his eyes burned brightly with the certain success of its future, whereas Rose's exams would likely end with him even more unsure of what to do with her, bought brains or not. I wondered if he'd ever ridden a racehorse, or if his size had made it nothing more than a dream. He lifted a stray horseshoe from the top of the fence and held it up.

'I've a farrier who makes these, in demand from here to America. This place locks up tighter than the cells in your station, and I've a Roscommon man who knows his way around a shotgun coming on as full-time security. He'll live up there.'

I followed his finger to the ceiling, then spotted the wooden stairs to the living quarter.

'Is he up there now?'

'I'm here now. There's no man stupid enough to try. Here,' he said, handing me the horseshoe, heavier than I expected. 'Give this to your little girl.'

Walking out from the stables was like the slow resurfacing from a dream. A breeze passed and we looked out at a sloping field, littered with daisies. He turned to me and raised his eyebrows to alert me to the end of the tour.

'You were busy while I wasn't around last night, Peter. What was the plan? Kidnapping?' I pocketed the horseshoe.

The laugh again. 'Colm Hatten was concerned for his safety. You heard about the threat, I'm sure. He was terribly shaken by it. I had a meeting with him yesterday and it's all he could talk about. He wanted to act as soon as possible. You no more need a doctor to tell you that his brother isn't wired right than I need a vet to tell me that my horse has what it takes hanging between its legs.'

'A doctor and two guards with you. What did you think would happen?'

He shrugged. 'He could have opened the door with a shotgun for all I know.'

I shook my head. 'Didn't I tell you he'd be better kept where he's not causing any harm?'

He tossed a hand. 'If I never see that lad again, it will be too soon.'

'You might not ever see him again. But that doesn't mean he won't see you.' He studied my face, a confused half-smile on his own, unsure if he'd just been threatened or warned. He swallowed and raised his chin in defiance.

'Tell me, Peter. How do you know for sure that he can't see the pair of us right now? Do you feel safe now you don't have a clue where he is?'

He scanned the horizon and the boundaries of his little kingdom, rocking on his heels with his hands hidden in his pockets. The thin mask of confidence couldn't hide his doubt.

'Imagine somebody came and took all this away from you.' I eyed the land and he stiffened, indignant at the notion even being put to words. 'That's what you did to him. You might not think his home is fit to house your dogs, but to him, it's worth more than what you've built here. You didn't even need it, Peter. That's where our disagreement really is. An old house, somewhere beyond those trees, well out of sight. Why bother with it?' I took my keys from my pocket. 'Come to me if you get even a smell of him. Lock your doors at night or you might wake with him looking down at you. Don't let that idea keep you from your sleep, and don't ever pull a stunt like that again. Thanks for the horseshoe.'

I left him to think about it and he called after me.

'Chief Superintendent Broderick was telling me how important the next couple of weeks are for the guards in this county.' Of course, Casey knows my chief more than I do. 'The eyes of the world on you all, or at least on the man ye'll be looking after. I know Broderick is feeling the pressure something awful. You know he's a big horseman? Oh yes, he was out here only recently, in fact. He told me a man's career could be made or broken by how he handles himself while Kennedy is here. An uncovered sneeze could see him stuck on his rung of the ladder at best, or pushed off the ladder at worst.'

He bit his lip as if to trap any more words inside, and it was his turn to leave me to think about something, while he returned to scanning where his land met the sky. On the way out, I slowed to let a van come through the gates, with three workmen behind the windscreen. Two of them I recognised – Matty Whelan and Eamon Doran, who Patrick had supposedly aimed a gun at. The skinny one behind the wheel, I didn't.

# 22

The setting sun through the window made it seem as if the cottage was being lowered underground. It was his first evening in Roche's and he held his mother's knitting needles in his right hand, rolling them together. He used to visit on his way to town in the morning, and before that, his father was always well warned to be home before dark – one of his mother's conditions in allowing them to visit Roche at all, who she regarded as a man hardly worth her disgust. She'd concede a thin smile on the occasions he helped to kill the pig, then trot him to the door and send him away as quickly as possible, with the ears and snout for his efforts.

He sat and remembered her as he saw her most clearly. In her cardigan and blue dress, knitting or lacemaking, her hair short and mannish. He remembered the lengths she went to before heading to town, wearing clothes she bought with money from selling the land, head-scarfed and perfumed, her face powdered and blushed. How she wore it all uncertainly under his gaze, as if she knew that he understood her efforts were for people who wanted nothing to do with her. The well-off and respectable. How he wanted to tell her she looked well, even if he didn't really know if she did or not, but knew it wasn't the sort of thing boys tell their mothers. In life and in death she remained a mystery and seemed to carry the weight of some secret whose telling would be her undoing and whose keeping undid her just the same. He remembered coming up behind her once, while she was hanging clothes on the line and didn't hear him approach and for the first and only time, he heard her sing, some upbeat song he couldn't remember the words to. He watched her tapping her foot on the grass, her head moving side to side and backed away, not wanting to break the scene. She may as well have been a stranger, an apparition in spring sunshine.

Outside, he lifted his face to the sky, with the new rifle across his shoulders and a hand curled around each end. A fine mist of midges hung in the air by the shed. The pregnant cat had abandoned the place, probably scared off by his coming and going, missing the peace and quiet Roche had given her. He drank a couple of handfuls of water from the trough and wet his chest and back. The sky would soon run out of daylight, which meant he could move unseen as he neared his home, over land that was less sparsely populated than Roche's outpost. Land where people might lie in wait.

He left his bike, not wanting to carry it over stiles and walls and hedges, and turned to look back at Roche's as he found his footing in the first rocky field. In the half-light, the place looked like the land itself, dark and ravaged by time and weather, the thatch like a forgotten bale, sagging at its centre.

He crossed some of Wexford's least fertile fields, the rifle in his left hand. The ground softened after a couple of miles and he was watched by the gloomy faces of unsheared sheep. Their dark droppings littered his path. If they recognised a rifle, they pretended not to. He climbed between fields of crops and cattle, the cool air soothing his skin through the open buttons on his shirt. He crouched by a spring so still and so clear he was only sure it was water when his hand broke the surface. He rinsed his hands and wiped them across his face and hair, the edges still stubbled by Gerry Foley's razor. On the near side of a small wood, he took a knee next to the remnants of a fire left by some other wanderer. The ash was still warm to touch.

The sky lowered like the lid of a coffin, darkening the county. He passed the unvisited graves of men, women and children – held captive then set alight by rebels and deserters at a barn in Scullabogue nearly two centuries back. He imagined those fleeing the blazing barn like screaming stars, the four points of their legs and arms burning like sticks of firewood. Their skin melting to bone until they were shot by muskets or skewered by pikes and the flesh-fuelled flames were stamped out by vengeful boots. He wondered if there was a field in the country that hadn't seen a life extinguished by violence or hunger, or seen a man reduced to his knees by the blighted crop it offered.

The road to his house was familiar and foreign, and returning was enough to distract from the empty stomach that slowed him for the last mile. He felt like an unwelcome guest as the charcoal roof came into view. In Casey's field, the Masseys had retreated from the wall and were taking their rest. A pale moon shone on the damage done by their day of work. The trees that lined the east of his home as far back as his father's birth were felled and stacked like firewood that could sustain a never-ending blaze. He looked at the space for a long time, as if he might make them grow again. A gap in the limestone wall beyond. A mound of earth and rubble piled next to it. A wall that had been built by Hatten hands over a hundred years ago, knocked in an afternoon's effort. Patrick imagined its builder, sitting on it when he was finished, sore, proud and exhausted, believing it might stand forever.

A breeze carried the smell of sawdust and wood oil from Casey's stables. A van idled in his yard, back doors open and the engine running. He heard voices through the open front door of the house. He crouched behind the bucket of a tractor and watched as three men went in and out, laughing and carrying things from inside, recognising two of them as the men who drove the tractors to his wall. They loaded the van with whatever they could pass off as presents for wives or mothers, or sell for the price of a drink. He imagined his father's slippers, askew on a folding table at some country market, next to his mother's perfume, being pawed and smelled and inspected and bartered for.

He thought about going to them and telling them to unload the van before he went to Sergeant Field, but decided against it, reasoning that three against one were odds that meant he'd either be caught, or forced to use the gun. He couldn't even be sure that Field didn't know what they were up to, that Field wasn't part of the whole thing.

The tall man had hands big enough to carry all his mother's old pots and pans. The smaller one came out with a milk crate cupped in his arms, clinking like a broken music box, and Patrick knew it was stacked with her cutlery and cups and saucers. The third man emerged, and the others laughed and bent and slapped their knees as he walked straight-backed to the van, wearing his mother's good hat, a berry-coloured thing that she only wore to mass. She'd have worn it to see Kennedy if she was still around. The man's arms were full of her clothes and an old greatcoat of his father's fell from his left shoulder. Rage filled Patrick as if he was drawing it from the ground, so that it filled every limb and extremity. He clenched his teeth so tight he thought they might crack. The men's laughter sounded like wild animals.

He rested the barrel of the rifle on the bucket of the Massey, feeling its power extend to his index finger, then chambered a round. He thought that the bullets he fired from the top of Carrickbyrne in the morning might still be travelling, overtaking ships in the Atlantic by now.

The man tossed the clothes in the back of the van and then bent to pick up the coat, holding it in front of him like a magician's cloak. He folded it to reveal himself again, and Patrick pulled the trigger before deciding that he would. The power of the shot trembled through the bucket and the bullet cut through air and blew the man's left knee apart. Patrick felt the recoil in his shoulder like a balled fist and the sound rang in every direction, as clear as the bell on St Michael's. He looked at the gun as if he was surprised to find it in his hand then looked through the scope again. The thief writhed on the ground, pleading like a broken-legged horse that had clattered over a hurdle, his pained cries like something from some backstreet operating table. His partners looked at each other then dragged him to his feet, ducking their heads while they loaded him into the back of the van to bleed over everything they'd stolen.

The van pulled out of the yard with its lights off, hitting the gate on its way, the engine roared through the gears and as the sound faded, Patrick saw the lights switch on and the van sway as if it might topple, racing to whatever doctor they could find.

Patrick walked through the gap in the wall and stood in the electric light, so much brighter than the lamps at Roche's. His hands were shaking and he realised after a few seconds what he had done. He'd turned himself from an outcast to a fugitive. Near the doorstep, he saw some wet blood and imagined the man's knee, blown into as many pieces as the pheasant. He bent and picked up his father's coat and pulled it on.

He righted a chair that was knocked on its side and sat at the corner of the table facing the ransacked room, with the rifle on its end between his thighs. The whole place felt lighter, after Casey's men decided that scavenging the place was a perk of their job. He held his hands out and watched as their tremble slowed to stillness, coming to terms with having shot a man for the first time.

It hadn't felt different to shooting anything else. There was no change in the mechanics of the task, no extra resolve needed to steady the weapon and take aim. No hidden strength needed to pull the trigger. Once that was done, the bullet did the rest, hurtling off on a journey that only ended with its target. The target this time a tall and skinny thief, who bled just the same as all the winged and four-legged creatures.

He was back in Roche's, the paraffin oil burning and a plateful of beans and potatoes in his stomach. He'd taken anything he didn't want ending up in the hands of Casey's men. They'd almost stripped the place. He salvaged a couple of his mother's brooches and his father's flat cap. Her knitting book and some of his poor attempts. He tied the laces of the old boots he'd planned on giving to Roche together, and hung them around his neck for the journey back. Leaving things behind had been one thing, leaving them behind for thieves was another. He laid them on Roche's table like a sorry altar shrine, a miscellany of near-worthless and sentimental items like things reclaimed from a battlefield's dead.

He wondered who the men thought was shooting at them, or if they believed it to be one of the Hatten ghosts, stirred from the grave to put a stop to their desecration. When their fear had passed and the light of day helped them to see sense, they'd come to the conclusion that there was only one likely shooter. Whether or not they'd tell the law how it came to happen was a coin toss. The more he thought about it, the more he realised that it didn't matter. He was a man who was already found guilty without judge or jury. Casey had fixed it so he couldn't resurface and Field's men were part of it. Even if Field hadn't been part of his eviction, he'd have no choice but to involve himself now, after a man's leg was shot to pieces.

The thought stayed with him while he lay in Roche's bed, a fox barking somewhere near the hills. He scratched his torso and legs, tossing and turning. They couldn't punish him any worse than what was already planned. It was as if a peculiar freedom had been granted. He was a man who'd been given his sentence, then told to pick his crime – would he like to be hung for a sheep or a lamb?

He turned from bed and lit a lamp, keeping the flame low so he could only see inches beyond where he held it. He closed his eyes and relived the moment of firing. Of standing unseen in the darkness, the fate of those men in his hands. How the two he left standing had turned and looked into the wall of night and couldn't see him, though he stood with the gun still aimed, looking directly at them. The burning smell from the barrel, the stock set against his shoulder. How in an instant, he could have picked either one of them to blow apart as easily as blowing out a candle.

He went to the fireplace and scooped out a handful of dry ash then took it back to the bedroom. He opened the wardrobe door and put the lamp on a shelf inside and looked at his face in the scarred mirror. He rubbed his hands together then daubed his face, like a man washing in reverse, so that when he looked at himself again, he resembled a miner just returned to the surface. He kept his mouth shut and used his fingertips to spread the charcoal ash into the folds around his nose and back to his ears, then he stepped back a couple of feet, so that all he could see in the mirror and lamp light was the whites of his eyes.

# 23

Donncha's funeral was like practice for the Kennedy crowds. The latest estimate is that we'll have thirty thousand here, but I still think it'll be more. People coming from far and wide, half of them with no place to stay the night and no plan on how to get home until the following morning, two or three to a bike, whole families to a truck bed.

There weren't thirty thousand out for Donncha Reilly, but it was as big a funeral as I can remember. The man taught someone from every family within twenty miles at one stage or another, and was remembered more fondly than plenty of schoolmasters might be. Myself and Siobhán joined the slow march of mourners following the hearse to the graveyard, along streets where businesses were shut and curtains were drawn. Catriona walked part of the journey and I carried her the rest of it.

Peter Casey positioned himself right behind the Reilly family, his hat pressed to his chest. There were tears, and grandchildren, and spits of rain. Father Crowley stayed true to form in making the rite of committal as miserable as possible. For a faith that believes in life after death, it hardly seems less likely when watching a box lowered into the earth. The hollow sound of dirt tossed on the coffin coming from the grave like coughs, while a priest reminds us of our sins before men come with shovels to bury the departed in soundless sleep.

After the plywood was slid over the grave, I let Siobhán and Catriona fall in step with the rest of the crowd, telling Siobhán there was someone I needed a word with. I hung back and watched them leave through the gates, carried away with the sound of whispered grief from the crowd so I was left listening to the breeze and jackdaws in the yews. I walked through the maze of graves and stopped in front of the simplest stone in a row near the west wall. *Sean Hatten 1900–1956. His wife, Maura Hatten 1910–1962.* I don't know what I was hoping to find.

Maura wasn't buried long enough for her grave to be in ruins. How long since I visited Declan's? At least a year, when I went with my mother and she tried to cry but didn't manage it – tears dried up by time. The Hatten plot was ragged all the same, streaks of bird shit down the headstone, and the stalks of rotten flowers wrapped by a thin red-ribbon knot. A dozen or so tiny, damp patches of wool, poorly knitted and frayed at the edges, scattered on the grave like petals lost to the wind. I bent and picked one up and the stitching near came apart between my fingers. I dropped it back where I found it, not sure if it was just wind-tossed debris or some sort of tribute to Maura. I put my hand on the headstone, Sean's handkerchief soft between my fingers, and said sorry – knowing there was nobody there to hear me. Sorry for what I did to him and sorry for not doing a better job of looking out for his son. There was rubbish burning somewhere nearby and the smell of smoking rubber ghosted between the gravestones.

All six feet six inches of Nollaig Quinn were beyond the gate, the bulk of a man who'd played hurling at county level, bent by time, and bruised by the shoulders and elbows and hurleys of every opposing midfielder in Leinster. I suspected he was waiting for me and wondered if he had watched me go to the Hatten grave. A sergeant, three months past retirement, coaxed into staying on to help the newly built station in Glynn find its feet. He was uniformed, with grey hair parted to the left, and a neat and thick black moustache. A constellation of freckles dotted his forehead and he had a sickle-shaped bald spot in the stubble of his jaw – the result of a cigarette end pressed to his face during an arrest.

'That's a man who'll be missed. I saw you at the church, Jim. How's the family?'

'They're grand, Nollaig, thanks. What about your own?'

He tossed his chin. 'My lot are halfway to talking with American accents. Both lads are in Boston since last year. Anne-Marie has been there three years with no sign of coming back. They all tell themselves they'll be back. Something to keep them warm on the crossing.'

We shared a silence to acknowledge his loss and he watched memories of his children disappear down the road.

'How are you getting on with everything?' he said. 'Not long now until the famous son returns.' He tapped a cigarette from its box and pulled it out with his teeth, then cupped his hand to light it. 'Have the Yanks been in to check and triple check? I'm surprised they haven't asked to strip search everybody on the day. Or better yet have us all show up bollock naked.'

'I think we're being sold short with the number of guards. I'd say we'll be policing fifty thousand in town.'

'You might be right. Drinking, celebrating and fighting.'

'You'll be drafted across yourself, I'm sure?'

He exhaled his smoke. 'We both have that to look forward to. People vomiting and pissing up against walls, singing the Star-Spangled Banner. So Kennedy can come and tell us how lucky he is that his family fecked off out of the place.'

I saw no point in trying to convince Nollaig of the significance of the visit. Of the difference between a congregation that looks to Kennedy, and one that looks to Father Crowley.

'How's the new station?'

'Years in the making, the ribbon's been cut, and the place still isn't finished. One flushing jacks, still no telephone.'

'Anything lively?'

He smiled. 'Quiet as always, thank God.' He released another cloud of smoke. 'One bit of noise though. Do you know Matty Whelan and Eamon Doran?'

'They do odd jobs for Peter Casey? I only saw them yesterday evening, over at the stud.'

'The very men. They were off hunting with some wild fella from up the country last night. Must be after they'd finished with Casey. Susan had them land into the hospital at all hours with this lanky character – Drummond is his name – strapped around the thigh and below the knee, some botched effort at mending him. Howling the place down he was.'

'What happened?'

'Well, it looks like one of the brainboxes shot him by accident. Susan said the fella's knee is shot to more parts than a jigsaw. And that it's missing too many pieces to be put back together.'

'Which of them got him?'

Nollaig laughed. 'Hopalong says it was his own gun that went off. He won't give a name. Those three want the Guards involved about as much as a man wants Kennedy involved with his wife, so it's all written up as an accident. Suits me fine.'

'Maybe it was?'

He looked doubtful and scratched the corner of his moustache. 'Maybe. But Susan says the stories were too similar, as if they'd practised how they'd tell it. They said they were after rabbits, looking at each other while they gave the doc their spiel. I've never seen a man shoot his own kneecap off with a hunting rifle.'

'Whelan and Doran, though. They've never given trouble. If it wasn't an accident, they'd have no reason not to come out and say so.'

'Unless they were up to something they shouldn't have been. But what can I do? Drummond is bandaged up and won't be walking in a straight line any time soon. I thought I'd say it to you, on the off chance they were up to something around here.'

'Thanks, Nollaig. I'll keep an eye out.' He flicked his cigarette to the ground and twisted a shoe on it. 'How well do you know Casey?'

He folded his arms. 'Ah, not well. You know he made it to the All-Ireland handball finals as a young man? Beat me in an early round. Of course, he had youth on his side and I was carrying more injuries than a war veteran – a left knee made of glass, the right stiff as concrete. By God, Jim, it was like sharing an alley with a fucking bear. A big, sweaty, mean bear who thought every single inch of the court was his – even the bit you were standing on.'

'I don't doubt that for a second. Say hello to Susan from myself and Siobhán.'

He called after me on my way to the car. 'Jim. Donncha looked better in that box than you do today. Take care of yourself,' he said, pulling his keys from his pocket and walking away with the sound of them jangling, a thin ribbon of smoke dancing from between his lips.

Siobhán hadn't turned a page in her book for ten minutes. I'd taken *The Exploration of Space* from my bottom drawer and was struggling to re-read essays I'd read years ago. It made little sense then and made less now. The science of it is beyond my comprehension, but I reassure myself that my lack of understanding only heightens my sense of wonder. Maybe if I understood it all, down to the composition of dust on the moon, it would cheapen it somehow, and remove the mystery. I read the same line over and over and it wouldn't straighten itself out. I put the book on the floor.

'That was a long day,' I said and she kept a thumb in the book and closed it. 'What has you stuck in the book?'

She looked at the cover as if she'd forgotten what she was reading, then shook her head. 'Ah, nothing. I'm distracted is all.' She put the book on her nightstand and turned off the lamp. It took a few seconds to adjust to the darkness.

'What is it?' I reached over and ran my hand through her hair, my fingers apart so the soft strands felt like water flowing over them. She hesitated. 'What is it, love?'

'I want to take Catriona to Mammy and Daddy's tomorrow. I know you can't go.' She said nothing more, just let her words take flight to see how they landed in the dark. I stopped rubbing her head and sat straighter, knowing that there was something wrong.

'We're not long back from visiting. It's a rotten journey without a car. Is everything okay back home?' I thought of the empty envelope and wondered if the letter had been a summons of some sort.

She turned to her back. 'Everything's fine. I don't know, I'm not saying it's because of it, but today was Catriona's first funeral. I wonder how many more times she'll see them.'

'Christ, love, they're only in their fifties.'

'I know,' she said, sitting up. 'But time goes so quickly. Do you remember Daddy holding her for the first time? Terrified, he was. Like she was made of paper. Now she's losing baby teeth. It won't be long and she'll be going off to university – at least she will if I have anything to do with it.'

'You'll worry these years away. She'll be with us a long time. Twelve years until university.' I took her hand. 'Think of it this way. It's not even twelve years since you broke the heart of a young policeman. Look at us now and all that's happened. A lifetime's worth.'

She sighed and took her hand away. 'I stole those years from us.'

'Rubbish,' I said, face to face in the dark. 'If you had never left you might be here with me now, wondering how things would have worked out if you did. Or maybe you wouldn't be here at all.'

'Do you not have any regrets?'

I swallowed and was glad that the darkness hid my hypocrisy. Preaching about making peace with the past, when I carry it with me every day.

'One or two.'

We lay in the quiet. A floorboard sighed and pipes tutted.

'What do you think, pet? For a few days while she's still off school. You're busy anyway. You might be glad to have us out of your way.'

'Come on, love, you know that's not true.'

'Isn't it?'

'How do you mean?' She said nothing, only sighed. I rolled to my back and found the light switch. 'Where's this coming from?'

'Well, you were out most of the day on Sunday when you were supposed to be off. Your head was someplace else at the funeral. It's Peter Casey, or it's Patrick Hatten, or it's JFK, but it's rarely us. Jesus, pet, when was the last time you took her for a spin, just the two of ye? You know she loves it.'

I said nothing and she rubbed her forehead, seeming to have overestimated her energy for the argument. She pushed back the blanket and turned from bed. I looked at the shape of her back, cloaked in a white nightdress, her sunburn fading.

'What's going on, love? You haven't been yourself since Cork.'

'I am myself, Jim. This is me and this is the life I have, and I love Catriona and I love you. But you're too busy running around over Patrick Hatten to see that most of my life happens under this roof.'

'Love, I've been telling you to go back to work. I think it's the right thing to do. If there's something I can do to change things, tell me.'

She stood and took her dressing gown from the back of the chair and put it on.

'Siobhán, it's not as if I've been away fishing or drinking down in Ryan's. I've been working.'

'I know your work very well and I know what the limits of it are. You act like some sort of missionary for that boy.'

'Because nobody else will help him! What about you? You say you want to help women like Rita, but how many times did you go out to Maura Hatten? Wasn't she a woman left on her own?'

She raised a finger. 'Maura Hatten wouldn't let help near her doorstep, as you know well. You can tell me all you want that it's your job, but tell me this – why aren't you doing the same for every other misfortunate creature like him? Do you pay them their dole when they forget to collect it too?'

I looked at her and before any words could form, she went on.

'Oh yes, Jim, I know what's missing and when it's missing. Every time you tell me he's forgotten his dole I notice that we're down money ourselves. How easy it is for you to lie to me. Do you think I can do the shopping and keep the house running without knowing how to balance the bloody books? How much money in total? How much that could have been set aside for Catriona? Or for us.'

Her voice trailed off at the last and I knew she was right. That I was a great man for making plans and not sticking to them, promising to head someplace nice and how I could go on making promises until we run out of road – the future always one step ahead of us while I fill it with more and more promises.

She had her head down like a woman without the fight for any more words. 'You're right, love. I'm sorry.'

I put my arms around her and felt her tears on my shoulder and knew she was crying as much for all the promises the world had broken as for the ones I had. I held her tight and kissed the top of her head and felt as helpless as a man can.

'I'll drive you to the station in the morning, love. Take Catriona away for a few days and relax and let Con and Margaret help. When all of this is over, I'll make sure we get back on track.'

She looked as if there was something else she wanted to tell me, but stopped herself.

I lay awake for a long time, listening to her sleep. Imagining heading away with them for a week off west. Eating Margaret's porridge thickened with honey, reading the papers after Con is finished with them, then talking out the state of the country, two men analysing what they read. Long walks through the countryside and along the towpath. I thought about it, could taste it and smell it, but the image was blurred by the feeling that there was some reason she needed to go without me. I turned to her back and put my hand on her sleeping shoulder and thought about what it was she didn't want to tell me and eventually I fell asleep, none the wiser.

# 24

Patrick had another restless night. The sound of footsteps every time he woke, stopping as soon as he sat up. The feeling that there was something else in the house, learning to live with his occupancy, moving in the rooms he wasn't in. He left the bedroom more than once, but never went into the byre, just tugged on the door handle to confirm it was well shut then went back to bed, the rifle along his body while he drifted in and out of sleep, tortured by the thought of Colm remembering old Roche and saying something to Flood or Casey. Imagining them laying siege to the cottage like something from a western, and how he'd go out firing if they did.

He left the house at first light, hoping that the rising sun and fresh air would clear his head of fear, and spare him a morning in the house, talking to himself and wondering if Roche's ghost was listening. He narrated every action as soon as he left his bed, then began forming random shapes and sounds that sounded like words, listening for how they echoed in the cottage. *Aaaaooiii. Oooooii-iuuunn.* He thought about burying the old man but decided that it wasn't his right.

He crossed the land behind Roche's then went on through a small gathering of trees and stepped from their shade to the bone-coloured light of morning, like some wild and hungry thing escaping the woodland, his face a mask of dark ash etched with unknowable signs and symbols from where he'd been scratching between bouts of sleep.

It drizzled between fields and he remembered the ash on his face when the rain diluted it and he tasted it on his lips. He stood and showered his skin in the rain, wiping the run-off away like a flood of dark tears, taking his shirt sleeves to his face to dry them.

He walked south-east. He suspected that most people were at mass. A person could get away with missing the odd sermon back in town, but deeper into the county, nobody missed a moment of worship. He passed a couple of stone cottages, replicas of one another. Corrugated roofs and whitewashed walls. Spiked armies of wheat stood tall in fields. Orderly green heads of beet looked healthier than last summer, when the mangold flies came in their millions and blistered the leaves, wiping out the crop while farmers stood in doorways in town shaking their heads and cursing the plague. He'd harvested a few of the insects, transparent and headless, and kept them in a jar in the shed, only to forget about them after his mother died. When he eventually remembered the jar, he went to examine it, and the flies had turned into air.

'Into air,' he said, detouring from the road, happy to let his gut guide him. He tried to invent a reason to wander, to escape another day staring at the world from Roche's door and avoiding the byre. At the end of a muddy trail, he came to a rusted gate. Beyond it was a farmhouse, not much different to the one he'd been chased from. He stood at the gate for a couple of minutes, watching the windows and doors, no sign of life beyond the trio of crows on the chimney top. Midges came to inspect his ears. He hopped the fence and walked the dirt path to the front door.

'Good morning to all inside,' he shouted after knocking. Nobody answered.

He turned the handle and stepped into a hallway with walls yellowed like the pages of an old book and loose skirting boards and worn rugs on the flagstone floor. A bucket to the left caught a drip from the ceiling. A man's coat hung from a hook on the wall and a pair of paint-splattered boots stood under it. Christ, as always, staring from the wall and lit by a dull red glow. The floor was sticky and made a sucking sound as he crossed it. He stood in the doorway to the kitchen. A two-day-old newspaper was open on the table, a fly tiptoeing across a block of butter, no trace left by legs as fine as silk. There were breadcrusts on a plate, shaped by the mouth that had bitten at them. Patrick touched the cup next to the newspaper. It was cold, a mouthful of tea at the bottom with some crumbs floating in it. He sat at the table and ate the crusts and swallowed them with the remnant of tea. He flicked through the paper. Ads for cars and touring holidays. Showtimes for films. Some politician in Dublin shifting blame for a collapsed building that had buried two young girls. A black and white photo of a priest standing in the rubble, giving the last rites to some poor child, breathing her last dusty breaths beneath the ruins. Kennedy, Kennedy, Kennedy.

He opened cupboards and drawers, sliding a steel knife-sharpener into his belt. He wondered how many people in the country looked at the ads in the paper for cars and holidays and homes off west for escapes in fine weather. Why was it that Peter Casey could spend more on a horse than everything inside this house was worth? And if the horse broke a leg, he could put a bullet put in it and still end up with money in his pocket from selling the carcass. The likes of Casey can lose and still win. Men who could do with a lesson about what loss really means.

He took the stairs slowly, every step groaning. An empty bedroom to the right, the covers unmade, a pair of trousers on the floor. A basin and shaving mirror. A fist-sized hole in a floorboard.

The curtains in the middle room were open and he stepped into the light and stopped at the sight of a white-haired woman, lying half-upright and staring at him.

'How are you, missus?' he said and went to the window, which looked over the trail he'd come by and the damp fields around it. The room smelled of her waste and he spotted the chamber pot on the far side of the bed. 'That needs to be emptied.'

'Who are you?' the woman asked, her mouth so dry her tongue was sticking to the top of it. She had no teeth.

'Ah, sure it makes no difference who I am.' He sat at the end of the bed and looked at her. Her hair was so thin she looked almost bald, a scab of red at each corner of pale pink lips. 'I'd say you must be near a hundred?'

She looked out the window, fixing her eyes on something miles away.

'Have there been any guards calling to your door?' She said nothing and he watched until she shook her head, a movement so slight it could have been missed.

'Where's your husband?'

'Heaven.'

'Who's the man who doesn't eat his crusts then?'

'My brother.'

'Is he good to you?'

'What do you want, boy?'

He ran his hand over a lace blanket by her feet. He recognised the intricate pattern of flowers and leaves and admired the eyelets and fringe and imagined the care and patience needed to make it. All the skill he didn't possess and never would no matter how long he spent at it.

'Did you make this?'

'That's Mount Carmel lace. From New Ross.'

'My mother used to make New Ross lace. She spent hours at it, copying patterns and starting over if she made a mistake. She used get awful worked up. I'd look at the scraps then and could never spot the mistake that annoyed her so much.'

'The nuns taught me. That lace was once wanted all over the world.'

He went on, as if he hadn't heard her. 'She made a handkerchief once for my father. I remember him wiping his head with it one day in town when I was small. He looked a right gentleman. This light little thing with the same pattern as that blanket. I asked him where he got it and he was awful proud – telling me that my mother had made it for him. For their thirteenth wedding anniversary.'

He swallowed and smiled then ran his hand across the blanket, stained yellow by life and time. He left a faint charcoal smear. He stood and went to the wardrobe, opening it and fingering through coats and dresses the woman hadn't worn for years. She'd probably wear the black one to her grave. He closed the wardrobe and turned to her.

'There's no money here,' she said.

'Money's no use to me these days.'

'Your face is sinful filthy, boy.' She shook her head and looked around the room as if searching for something he could clean himself with.

He smiled. 'I was practising. A disguise.' He pawed his face and leaned against the wardrobe and she looked at him, as if she was deciding how to answer, then deciding not to.

'You believe in heaven, you said. Your husband is up there waiting, is he?'

She blessed herself and whispered some holy affirmation.

'And my father? And mother? They're up there too do you think? Herself letting him have it still?'

'I don't have any answers. If your parents were good, holy people then they'll be at peace.'

'Do you think you go to heaven if you kill a man?' She met his eye again.

'I don't know,' she said. He saw her struggle with the dryness of her mouth. 'There's no man worth killing to find out.'

He chewed his lip and considered her words, then went downstairs and took the kettle that was hanging over a dying flame and poured a cup of water. He added some sticks to the fire to spare the brother the effort of restarting it. He brought the water upstairs and left it by the bed, where the woman was asleep, her chin down and her yellow skin sagging like melting candlewax.

He took the belt from the trousers on the man's bedroom floor then went outside and stood in the breeze, thinking of his mother making that perfect patch of lace for his father, something bringing on a bout of softness and kindness towards him and he supposed that it must have been something like love or affection and all the things the likes of Colm preferred to pretend had never existed between them.

From the trail, he looked back at the house. The woman's window reflected spools of grey cloud and the crows had flown from the chimney.

# 25

I woke to Siobhán singing to Catriona in the bathroom, 'Siúil a Rún', above the sound of water splashing and Catriona laughing. I went downstairs and boiled eggs and cut soldiers of toast and they joined me, packed and ready, as I was putting breakfast on the table, the pain in my head nearly knocking me off balance when I turned to them. I helped Catriona take the top off her egg and dipped the toast with her, stealing a few bites while she laughed and protested.

'Why aren't you coming, Daddy?'

'Your daddy is too busy,' Siobhán said. 'Making sure everything is right for President Kennedy. Are you feeling okay?' She put her hand on my arm and I told her I was fine.

'Kennedy,' Catriona said, raising her arms, a yellow trail of egg dribbling down her chin. 'Kennedy, Kennedy.'

I wasn't the only one suffering on the way to Waterford North. I had to pull in to let Catriona get some fresh air while I worried about missing the train. She sat in Siobhán's lap for the last few miles and the silence was full of our voices arguing last night. I reached across and put my hand on her thigh and wasn't sure she noticed.

A young woman gave me their tickets and my change and told me the platform number, and I carried Catriona through the hall and outside, where other passengers admired her and got a smile in return. Men in suits, men in construction gear with sandwiches wrapped in wax paper, the odd American – about to learn that the smallest of islands can make the longest of journeys. I lowered Catriona and kissed her head, then lifted their case on board. It was Catriona's first time on a train, something we hadn't thought of until we saw her face shift from excitement to terror and back again as they climbed aboard the coughing, dark green carriage, the smell of fuel thick on the platform.

'Now,' I said, taking the change from my pocket and reaching to where she stood inside the door. 'You can get yourself something nice in Cork, if you're good for your mammy on the train.' She took the change in her small hand and made a fist so tight it looked like it might never open. Siobhán took her other hand and told me from the door that they'd only be away two or three days and I said goodbye, then watched through the dirty windows as she led them along the carriage to their seats. She took Catriona in her lap and they waved together. She gestured for me to head away, but I stood there like a lovesick schoolboy, my hands in my pockets, watching people board and listening to CIÉ men calling out instructions while the train growled like an empty stomach, ready to eat up the miles of track to Cork.

The long blow of the whistle cut through it all and I looked at them again, their faces close to the glass. I watched the train roll along the platform until the two smiles were carried out of sight and off west.

There's been enough said about love by men smarter than myself. I've nothing that'll improve the world's grasp of the subject. If I hadn't taken up Michael on his offer to stop in for tea that Christmas Eve, I'd likely never have met Siobhán and I'm sure I'd have managed just fine. I might have had a grand life of steady bachelor loneliness, or I might have met some woman here in New Ross or Enniscorthy. We might have had a family and a life most men would be happy to look back on. But I can say with close to certainty that there's not another woman in the world who could leave me standing on a platform, altogether aimless in her absence, with trains headed north, east and west. A grown man, wishing I'd taken more chances to tell her that I love her, regretting every argument and every moment that I was short, or cold, or distracted. Wondering what secrets she was taking away with her and wishing that no secrets existed between us. The heart really has no shame.

Sitting on a bench in the shade, the station quietened around me. I closed my eyes and let myself miss my two girls fully, as if doing so would hurry the feeling through my system. I thought I could sit and wait there until they came back. But I knew that being a man who waits like a lonely dog was not one of the reasons Siobhán had given me through the years for why she loved me. I stood and put on my cap, with plenty to do while they were gone.

Casey's men had made a start on the place. I knew before I turned off my engine that Patrick was gone, and wondered how I had missed all that anger building in him. A family lost, a job lost, a home lost – and there I was, a fool, thinking a soft word would be enough to see him right. The east wall was knocked through, some trees felled to allow a clear path from Patrick's doorstep all the way to Casey's stables. The house looked different for being opened to the world, light falling on the end of that had been shaded by trees for years. There were tyre tracks in the gravel and a dent in the gate.

It was near stripped inside. The old gun was gone from the corner of the kitchen, the tools were gone from the table, and the family picture was gone from the wall. I went to the doorstep and stood, saying a silent prayer that he'd head off up the country, and find some work at a hiring fair, making some use of his shooting and whatever skill on the land he'd inherited from Sean.

I paced the front of the house, to a shed at the far end. A rusted door was open and inside smelled of cat piss and fish. A saucer against the wall was stained with milk, and a small, half-starved orange cat stared up at me as if it expected somebody else. It didn't follow me out.

On my way back to the car I stopped and knelt to inspect a brown stain in the loose stones. Even after a mix of drizzle and sunshine to dilute then dry it, I've seen enough blood to know a recent spill. A darkness passed over me and I wondered just how far Casey, or his men, would go. If there'd been a struggle, or a refusal on Patrick's part – if he'd stood in his doorway like some outlaw making a last stand – Casey's men might justify anything to themselves.

When I stood, my knees burned and the pain moved me to sit against a windowsill. The shirt I'd hung over the front fence was still there. I leaned forward and wrapped my hands around my knee as if I might squeeze the pain out, then remembered the man Nollaig had told me about and knew that the blood in the gravel belonged to Larry Drummond. The man I saw driving into Casey's, now lying in the General, his knee all but lost to a bullet.

On my way back the road, I was almost run into a ditch by a Land Rover that nearly toppled as it rounded the bend. I skidded to the side of the road and held my hand against the horn, almost certain it was Flood behind the wheel.

Drummond was whiter than the bedsheets he was lying under. A wounded leg sticking out, bandaged at the knee to twice its thickness. I spotted him as soon as I walked in, stiff and slow, my back rebelling against all the driving. He was the only man in the ward with a leg bound and elevated. I made eye contact with a couple of the others. A fat man with glasses too small for his face, whose injury was buried somewhere under his bedding. An old farmer whose wellies were ready and willing at the side of his bed, as if he couldn't leave his fields much longer, arm in a cast or not. The side of his face was purpled, a lake of bruise pouring from his eye and I wondered what accident he'd had – trampled by his cattle, trapped by some machine, or penned behind a fence. A couple of semi-conscious others, probably recovering from crashing their cars into trees or ditches. It seems a week can't pass now without hearing about a life lost to the road.

'Larry,' I said, standing at the side of his bed. There was no sign of anything left by any other visitor, no holy water or newspaper by his bed.

He opened his eyes and turned his head stiffly then stopped, as if even a quarter-inch more would be too much to bear.

'I already talked to ye,' he said, his accent from the west.

'How's the leg?' I said, looking at the bony thigh and shin, either side of a thick dressing that was iodine-yellowed at the edges.

He shook his head and his eyes were wet.

'I'm Jim Field, Larry. Sergeant over in New Ross.'

His chin pointed at me like an accusing finger. 'I told you–' He cleared his throat then swallowed with his grey eyes closed as if the pain from his knee had climbed up to rest in them.

'I told you, I already talked to Quinn. Can you see my leg? Can ya? I'll not walk right again. I'll not get a job again on account of being crippled. Can a man not even suffer in peace?'

He managed to fit 700 years' worth of Irish suffering and hardship into his voice.

I pulled across a chair and sat. 'I had a chat with the nurse on the way in. She says you have half a chance of getting out of things alright. That you might be able to keep working. Though there's hardly enough work for men these days, hurt or not.'

'Says yourself with your grand job and pension.'

'You don't like guards, Larry. Can we just take that as understood? Tell me, what part of the world are you from?'

'You wouldn't know it.'

'Ah now, don't be selling your home short.'

'Crossan,' he croaked.

'You're right. I don't know it.'

'Roscommon,' he said, and the word seemed to comfort him, as if it brought to mind some able-bodied memory where he'd love the chance to start again.

'I used work with a man who went up to the Roscommon races every year. He said that no race is ever certain until the winning post in Roscommon, on account of that incline.'

He ignored my attempts to soften him.

'What was it that brought you here, Larry? Work or a woman?'

'Women,' he tutted, and swatted away the notion.

'A job, so. I know you're doing a bit of work for Peter Casey.'

He fixed his eyes on the ceiling and said nothing. The bit of colour that returned to his face gave him away.

'Is that what you were up to when you were shot?'

'I shot myself. Did you not hear that part, from Quinn or the nurse or whoever you've been talking to? How is it a pair of ears that size hasn't heard that?'

'You were doing a job out on the stud, with Matty and Eamon. You don't remember that it was myself who slowed to let you drive in the gates a couple of evenings back. It's good manners to salute another driver. Around here it is anyway.'

'What of it? We did an honest day's work and then went shooting.'

'I see ye cleared that treeline and knocked the wall to Hatten's.'

'Never heard of any Hatten. I didn't ask whose wall it was.'

'Getting the place ready for Casey to level, I suppose. And you're the same Roscommon man he pays to watch that stallion? It must be like looking after Kennedy.'

He scratched the end of his nose and I sat forward.

'Do you know what I think, Larry?'

'You're going to tell me anyway.'

'I think ye did yere day's work and thought ye'd have a look inside the house. And ye thought that if it's being knocked anyway, then what harm is it taking what's inside. Who'd give a shite?'

The ceiling became even more interesting to him.

'And I think ye were spotted by probably the only lad who really does give a shite. And that a bullet came out of the night and took your knee away with it as fast as it came. And you know that if Casey finds out you were out thieving on his watch, while you were supposed to be back protecting that horse of his, then you'll not only be down a knee, but the nice pay and shelter he gives you to do it. Does that sound about right?' I stood, not needing him to say it out loud. His face gave him away. 'What happened to Hatten?'

He looked at me. 'You've too little work to do is what I think.'

'This is the only chance I'll give you to tell me what happened to him. If I find out ye did anything to him after I walk out that door, you'll regret not taking it.'

'I don't even know who you're talking about. For fuck's sake would you ever just leave me alone.'

'Alright, Larry. I hope you heal up.'

I left him to the ceiling and met Susan Quinn in the corridor. She looked at me as she would a patient arriving down in the emergency room.

'Jim. How are you keeping?'

'Grand, Susan. I was in having a word with your patient.'

She looked over my shoulder and through the door then rolled her eyes. 'That man,' she murmured. 'I shouldn't say a thing, Jim.' She held up her hands and exhaled and forced a smile. 'There are patients who test your patience.'

'I don't doubt it.'

'Nollaig said he met you at the funeral. I couldn't get off work. He told me you were looking run-down.' She looked at me the way she might assess her patients. 'He was being too kind.' She pressed a cold hand against my cheek, then my head. 'You've a temperature. Do you know what you're going to do for me?' she said, looking up and down the corridor, in that way women have, as if they're keeping an eye on all the moving parts. 'You're going to go down and have a seat in the last room on the left, and I'll send someone to have a look at you.' She objected to my protest before I'd put it to words. 'I won't hear no from you. Go on now, off you get.' She lowered her voice. 'It's Dr Mullins on today. He'll have to do.'

I walked the corridor like a schoolboy sent to the principal's office. The room was small, with a pale overhead light, and shelves filled with clean bedsheets and bedpans. A smell of disinfectant so strong it was as if the entire hospital was kept clean by the fumes seeping under the door. I sat and waited for Mullins, my eyelids gaining weight every time I rested them. I nodded off while thinking of

Patrick Hatten, hoping that he was alright, and that if he was, hoping that he'd come to terms with shooting a man without developing a taste for it.

I was woken by the smell of fresh laundry. A young doctor stood over me, his shirt and coat sparkling white. He made it clear with every sigh and avoidance of eye contact that he was far too busy to be seeing walk-ins on the say-so of some nurse without a medical degree. He questioned me the way I've questioned prisoners, the small storage cupboard like a holding cell, a place to confess my symptoms and await his judgement. I felt like the biggest inconvenience of his week and sat testing the weak grip of my hands on my thighs, chastened, until I woke fully from my nap and stood a good three inches taller, with the uniform and hat giving me another imagined few inches and he softened and let the whole unpleasant back and forth of questioning me end with a scrawl on a prescription pad.

In the corridor, I called after him. 'Doctor,' I said, and he turned, back on sure footing out of the small space. 'Do you know anything about MS?' The look I got in response was as if I'd asked him if he knew where the kidneys are.

'What about it?' He put his hands in his trouser pockets in a way that flared the white coat outwards behind him, backlit in the corridor like some angel I should be bending the knee to.

'Do you think I might have it?'

'No more than you might have any number of other things.' He turned, carrying with him this unquantifiable range of fates, as if he knew which one was ahead of me and that I wasn't going to learn on his watch. I watched him vanish down the corridor and knew he had the same challenges as the rest of us. The more we know, the less we know. The more we find out, the more questions we have to ask and answer. He was taking a punt on a heavy dose of antibiotics, and it seemed as good an answer as any.

*

Pheilim Riley was all chat for the couple of women in front of me. Whistling away and offering cooking instructions for the chops and sides of bacon he tossed on the scales then wrapped up in butcher's paper. He caught my eye mid-flow, then settled up with the women, who had armies of sons and daughters to be fed.

'Sergeant,' said Pauline O'Keefe as she passed.

'Sergeant,' echoed Aine Grealish.

'As good as it is to see you, I'm sorry it isn't your lovely wife in to me,' Pheilim said, leaning forward on his countertop, a rumpled white hat askew on his head of grey hair. 'It brightens my day when she walks in that door. What'll it be this evening?' He clapped his hands and rubbed them, eyeing his offerings as if deciding what I'd eat for my dinner.

'I'm after a bit of liver, Pheilim. Just for myself.'

'Oh? A bachelor's dinner, is it?'

'Siobhán's off at her parents.'

'Righto. Half pound do you?' he said, leaning in with a stainless-steel scoop.

'That sounds right.'

'Let's call it three-quarters for our sergeant, it'll keep until tomorrow.'

'Good man, Pheilim.'

I paid him and asked if he was near closing time. He doubted there'd be anybody in after me. I turned from the counter with the little parcel of liver cold in my hand, like a pathologist taking it off for examination. Empty hooks hung in the window, where there were sometimes a couple of rabbits or joints of other animals – pink and sinewed, purple streaks of veins and arteries beneath flesh like old parchment, strung up as if designed to spoil your appetite.

'Have you seen Patrick Hatten lately?'

Pheilim had taken his white cap off and had a mop in his hand. He looked old. I wondered would another butcher take over, or would it all end up coming from the British supermarkets Maurice Gleeson fears so much. 'Not for a couple of weeks. Saying that, he's never been a customer, just a supplier. That lad could trap his dinner with a carboard box and shoestring.'

'Did he ever ask about work in here? He might have been well suited?'

'He did. I didn't have the work for him. Even if I did, Jim, I can't say he'd have been popular at the counter. He's a frightful looking thing altogether, God love him. But I promised to take a couple more rabbits off him every month and to pay him a bit more for them. I haven't seen him since. I hardly need them, but there's no harm in helping the poor creature.'

I was glad to hear of somebody else trying to do right by Patrick, reminding me of the goodness that exists all over this town. This job can make you see badness in people who might be guilty of nothing but the business of their own day to day, their time and attention too taken up by their own troubles and triumphs to take the likes of Patrick's on board. People who deserve better than a broad brush. I headed for the door. Pheilim called after me.

'You said he *might* have been suited, Jim?'

I turned.

'And you asked if I'd seen him. Is he missing, or are you looking for him for something in particular?'

'Have a good evening, Pheilim,' I said, while he chewed his lip and leaned on his mop, his eyes puzzled by mysteries of his own making.

I fried some onions in butter and threw the liver in on top. A tin of peas on the side. The liver is a treat while Siobhán is away. It's one thing she won't eat. I never had the heart to tell her, but her mistake is overcooking it, blasting it on the pan as if trying to scorch away the taste. A little pink in the middle is best.

I sat at the table, the cat looking up at me while I washed my dinner back with milk. The sound of the water rinsing my single plate and knife and fork filling the house as if the place was mocking my loneliness. Tiredness on me like a heavy jacket.

I went to my workbench and sat behind the rocket, with the final few parts lined up and ready to assemble. I put on the little magnifying lens Siobhán got for me. It's meant for jewellers, but she said as soon as she saw it, she thought of me – squinting while I decorate the pieces like a man staring into the sun. I tried to put my distraction down to the empty house, to overdoing it with the extra quarter-pound of liver, to the long day of driving – but I couldn't concentrate, the parts of the rocket wouldn't come into focus and a pain came down from the top of my head and settled behind my eyes. I stood quickly, as if I could outpace the ache, but still there it was, gnawing away and warning that there's something wrong with me. I swore and cursed like some drunk or madman raging at his empty house, slamming my fist against the bench as if I might be able to batter the pain and tiredness out of me, until my hand was sore and red and I stood back, with the V-2's suction line and turbo pump broken into pieces.

There was nothing for it but an early bed, long distance runners ready to race around my head for the night. Thoughts of Siobhán away at home, back in the room where she was once a young girl dreaming of more than we have. I thought of Peter Casey, chatting with Superintendent Kerins and Chief Broderick, my chances of making Inspector in his hands. I thought about Larry Drummond and imagined him waking from dreams where he was walking in an unbroken stride, only to find it was the pain from his knee that woke him. I thought of Declan of course, as I always do when I'm left with too much time for thinking. And then a son who never fully comes into focus – a boy I'd take driving tomorrow with Siobhán away, or who I'd bring for a tour of the station, locking him in cells and showing him old badges and batons and the things boys love so much. Sean Hatten came to shame me for a spell. And there, keeping pace with the rest, was Patrick, hurt, dead, or stalking the countryside – sleeping in some shed or other kind of shelter, burning to make his brother and Casey regret their plans.

# 26

Patrick jumped up and down, his bare feet clapping against the dirt. Birds were busy in the hedges and a sparrowhawk sped up and down along a row of bushes, turning sharply and looking to claim a victim, before giving up and moving on. He'd seen one at its most vicious years ago, picking a magpie slowly to death, while the poor bird squawked and pleaded like a thief caught in the act by an angry mob. He went to the rainwater barrel at the end of the cottage and hoisted himself up and swung one leg over. He held his breath and lowered himself into the barrel of cold water, moving his legs as much as the tight space would allow, and his breath staggered out in bursts of instantly vanishing clouds.

He ran his palms all over his body, then worked balled fists into his armpits with solid turns. The water darkened around him as the dirt melted away. When he was used to the temperature, he let his head sink under, and held his breath, eyes shut while the sound of water closed around him. He stood in splashes, gasping when he could hold his breath no longer, then went under again.

He dried himself on the back step, using a crusty towel from Roche's wardrobe, then changed into his familiar trousers, shirt and boots. He went to the mirror and tried to fix his hair but it had set in a shock of curls, the parting Foley had made for him barely visible. When he pressed a stray clump down, it slowly returned to the way it had been, like a squeezed sponge.

He rolled up his shirtsleeves and did up the buttons, leaving the top two open. He pocketed his best attempt at a knitted rose, a small stem of green wool and a red crown that looked like something had trampled on it. It was the best he could do and he hoped that by keeping it small, he'd made it harder to spot any mistakes. He left his guns and knives on the table and shut the door. It had no lock. They'd met on days like this before, dry and sunny, or idle midweeks when Rose was supposed to be at school. There'd been no planning, just some instinct that led them to be by their tree at the same time. The instinct had failed him so many times in the last two months that he no longer trusted it, but he longed to see her again, before whatever came next.

He took the long way, keeping to the grass-lined centre of shaded roads and cutting through fields of beet and pasture, coming at Corcoran's Cross from the north-east. The soles of his feet were hard and hurting, as if he'd worn them through to the bone, and he cycled as much of the way as he could. He waved from a distance to a couple of old men or shawled women walking the road. His skin behaved itself, the cold bath and the breeze keeping the itch at bay.

His heart worked harder when he saw the crown of their ash. He came to the wall and looked around and of course she wasn't there. He leaned his bike against the wall, then sat with his back to the tree and closed his eyes, taking some rest, remembering a couple of traps that he could check for rabbits while back in familiar surrounds. He had a snare and pit trap within a mile, though any catch had likely been there long enough for some other animal to rip it to pieces.

When he opened his eyes he wasn't sure how long they'd been shut or if he'd been asleep. She was about fifty yards away, walking through the field of rapeseed, her hands in front of her, turning something in her fingers.

He closed his eyes and when he opened them again, she was still there, a grey cardigan over a navy dress. He stood. She turned as if she sensed him, moved slowly, parting the rapeseed, holding a strand of bitter vetch in her hand, its purple petals torn as if nibbled by insects.

'Rose,' he said and she stopped in front of him, close enough for him to see the new band of freckles across her face. She looked older. Her hair was straight and combed and held back with a neat hairband.

'Pleased to see you,' she said and he pulled his head back as if to dodge the formality of her words. 'You got very skinny.'

He looked down at his chest. 'Did you get your pincushion?' She shook her head and he swallowed, wondering who stole it. 'I left it here for you. Somebody else got it.'

'Well, thank you for thinking of me,' she said. 'I've come here a few times.'

'So have I. Hoping to see you.' She reddened. 'Will we sit a while?' He went back to the tree and sat as he'd been and she sat in front of him, fixing her dress as she curled her legs under her. 'Imagine the chances of us meeting again. Just like that.' He clicked his fingers and she looked over her shoulder as if it might have alerted something in the field to their presence.

'Did you hear I've been put out of my home?'

Rose looked at the vetch.

'By your father, no less.'

The rapeseed swayed and they watched until it stilled. A faint sweetness came and went.

'I'm being sent away,' she said.

'What do you mean? Where are you being sent?'

'To a girls' school. Up the country. He's had a woman in helping me get ready. Miss Hendrick.'

'Help you with what?'

'Lessons. El . . . elocution,' she said, sounding it out.

Patrick shook his head and looked across the field. His stomach threatened to send his breakfast back up. He breathed slowly and let the feeling pass. 'He does anything he wants. Did you get any say in it? I bet you didn't. Who's this Hendrick to tell you how to walk and talk?'

She sprinkled the shreds of the petals and watched them lie in the dirt. 'She says I'm doing well.'

'We could run away.' He said it before he'd thought it through. Once the words were out the air tightened around them.

Rose kept her eyes on the ground and said nothing.

'We could be gone a hundred miles in any direction before he even noticed.' Patrick raced to keep up with the idea. He saw them by the sea or on horseback on some field out west. He saw a small cottage fixed up and a fire that he'd never let die.

'Daddy's going to meet Kennedy,' Rose said, changing the subject and watching her finger scrape a circle in the dirt.

Patrick leaned forward. 'He what? Why would he be meeting Kennedy? Why? What would Kennedy want with him?'

'There's people invited to meet him. Daddy says he's going to Dunganstown and will get to shake his hand. He's getting a special licence.'

'A special licence for what?'

'To be on the road next Thursday. All the roads are closed unless you have the licence.'

Patrick clicked his tongue. 'You sound impressed.' It was the most they'd talked without long silences and it had only led to a distance between them.

Her finger burrowed a deeper groove in the dirt. 'People have come over from England to see Altair. Daddy lets me see him when Miss Hendrick gives me a good report. I brush him and feed him.'

Patrick's eyes were fixed on the end of the world. He hardly heard her.

'I stole a key to the stables. I could show him to you. Remember you told me about your horse? What was his name?'

Patrick felt her gaze but didn't return it, hurt that she couldn't remember. 'Bullet.' He remembered seeing Casey's horse once, being led across a field by some stable boy. Like something from another world, the huge black head and silhouette set against the sky. He cleared his throat and thought of all the long nights he'd imagined this moment, talking with Rose, and here he was, with Peter Casey's shadow standing between them, spreading its arms.

He took the knitted rose from his pocket and held it out to her. 'I made this for you. Bought green and red wool special.'

She took it and looked at him. 'Thank you, Patrick,' she said and he'd never known what his name sounded like until she said it.

'It's a rose.'

She laughed. 'I know.' She took a small round purse from her cardigan pocket and unzipped it, then folded the rose and put it inside, to live in darkness.

'We might never see each other if you go away to school.'

She looked at him and shook her head, her lips a tight seam.

'You know if your father was dead, I'd still have my house and you wouldn't have to go anywhere.'

She straightened and furrowed her eyebrows, then brought her knees to her chest. 'You shouldn't say things like that. One of his men was shot. The man might lose his leg.'

Patrick smiled and when Rose looked to him, he laughed.

She frowned. 'It's not funny.'

'It was when it happened,' he said, and cocked an invisible rifle. 'Bang. Down he went.'

Rose edged back, shaking her head, like the near-mute girl he'd known before her lessons and her progress and Miss Hendrick.

'If I shot him for taking my mother's things, then imagine what I'll do to the man that tries to take my home.'

She stood and he rose with her.

'Stop it,' she said. 'Stop saying these things, Patrick.'

Patrick pushed his tongue firmly into his canine space and the muscles of his jaws pulsed like a pair of small hearts under the skin. He moved nearer. 'That man has taken everything my family had. And here you are, defending him. Proud of him and his horse and men over from England and his licence to meet Kennedy.'

'He's my father,' she said, leaning away from Patrick's pointed finger.

'He has it all, doesn't he? And still he had to come and take from me.' His voice travelled across the empty field.

'You're being unfair, Patrick,' she said.

'You're just the same as the rest of them.' He leaned towards her, then stepped away. 'The very same. You can tell him that he'll wish he never got his special licence. Tell him that from me, will you? Get Hendrick to tell you how to say it nice and clearly so he understands.'

She was running then, looking over her shoulder once and carving a new path through the field. 'He'll wish he was never there,' he shouted.

When she was gone, he went to his haunches and scratched his back. He lifted her coin purse from the ground and pulled out the rose and threw it to the field. Inside, there was a couple of coins, a folded note, and a single shining key. He pocketed it and wiped his forehead and spat and cursed.

He took the short way out of the field and pushed away on his bicycle. After fifty yards his skin was on fire, sweating and itching while he ripped the buttons on his shirt and scratched with one hand until he'd left a maze of red marks across his chest. Somewhere near Raheen, he climbed off his bike and bent in the road, his breakfast pouring out like floodwater, dark and thick, the retching like a punch in the gut, the sound from his throat like guttural calls of feeding ravens. He walked to a shallow stream and knelt in it, washing his face and neck with the cold water.

He near knocked Roche's door off its rusty hinges, racing to the back room to pull the chamber pot out of retirement, then spent the late afternoon vomiting and pouring everything he had out of himself in streams of waste that he tipped out the window, just in time to refill the pot all over again. The memory of mouthfuls of water swallowed while washing in the barrel was enough to make his body bend in confirmation that it had been his mistake.

When he was sure that nothing more could be purged, he lay at the foot of Roche's bed like some dehydrated and near-dead salmon who'd misjudged its leap and landed on a bed of dry rock just above the water level.

He left the room on his hands and knees, like something crawling from a cave. The filth of the floors was made plain up close, leaving his hands blackened and his prints left in thick dirt and dust.

Something sharp caught his palm, and he looked down at the yellow dagger of one of Roche's teeth. From his lower level he searched for some cure he might have not spotted earlier. He'd had a sickness like this as a boy and could remember the feeling of shame at the smell while his father came in and out of his room, putting a wet towel on his head and pouring something unknown and foul into his mouth with a spoon.

He saw a small drawer on the underside of the table in Roche's kitchen and was on his feet, bent at the waist as he went to it. He slid it open and found a mix of rubbish – nails, screws, a handful of buttons of different colours and sizes, and a red diary from 1961 with a pencil coming from the pages like an antenna, the nib worn blunt, the end dented by marks left in the days when Roche still had teeth fit for chewing.

The diary had served in '61, and was reused in '62 and '63. Days with entries were amended to confirm what day it was each year. He flicked through it, scanning unconnected weights and numbers written on faded pages. There was no documenting of Roche's thoughts, just a scatter of numbers, an occasional name with some cryptic clue next to it, as well as lists of things that were needed. He saw the name Hatten written every few weeks with a question mark next to it, old Roche trying to identify some pattern to his visits.

He turned the pages to June where the most recent entries were written in a more vivid shade of slate. There was an entry in barely legible hand, crossed out then re-written on the following date. Everything on the page for 27th June had a line through it. The page for the 28th read '*26th or 28th Mackerel/Trout. 1 s owed. 1/4 lb this time.*' He leafed backwards through the notebook and found similar entries and saw the pattern. Fish delivered on the last Thursday of almost every month.

Patrick closed the diary. It might as well have been an eviction notice. Whoever was bringing fish to Roche was due back on the 26th or the 28th. When Roche wasn't there to take them, it wouldn't be long before the fisherman came inside or returned with somebody else. Patrick wondered why the date had been changed – then the 27th registered in his sick body as the date repeated so often in recent weeks. Kennedy's visit. Even this fisherman was delaying his deliveries to be part of the crowd lining the streets and filling the quay. Everyone from doctor to debt collector, from labourer to lawman, putting their lives on hold for a glimpse of this man – Kennedy, whose great-grandfather had climbed onto a ship a hundred years before, desperate to leave the sorry, starving island behind him.

He was moved to the byre by his own smell, the bitter stench of sickness filling the cottage so that somehow even Roche's corpse was less troubling once covered with a bedsheet. The body was purple and black and green, the skin slipping back the head and the shape of the skull undisguised. Patrick tucked the sheet tight around it and had no energy to clean the floor before crawling to the opposite corner, looking at Roche's covered body like a family member keeping vigil by a hospital bed. If he stared long enough his eyes tricked him into believing that he'd seen a fraction of movement around the chest or a foot shifting. He was stirred from his thoughts by the pain in his body reminding him that Roche was dead, his intestines feeling like a length of knotted rope being pulled even tighter.

He went outside and cut fistfuls of heather then left some smouldering in each room, including the byre, where he lay down and watched the sweet and woody smoke curl around the room. His throat was sore from the retching and his mouth stored a sourness he wasn't brave enough to wash away, still fearful of water. When his energy returned, he'd go to the spring. He felt like something shrivelled and in need of rain and imagined falling into the cold water. The cramps in his stomach eased but still stirred every now and then, like something turning in its sleep.

The only light came through a gap between the ceiling and the wall and he watched it darken slowly, hoping that recovery would find him in the night. He pulled the blanket around him.

'You're better off gone, Joe,' he said to the darkness. 'There's no place for men like us anymore. Isn't that just it,' he said, imagining

Roche shaking his head at the changing times and the unfairness of a rising tide, lifting all boats apart from those grounded or anchored by things beyond their control. 'Isn't that just it?' He closed his eyes and turned to the wall, his back to Roche.

'I'm going to kill Casey, Joe,' he said, his eyes shut tight – as if he could pass the thought off as being said in a dream. He opened them. 'I'm going to kill him.'

Somewhere outside a long-eared owl chick screeched like the gate back home and he thought of those great hunting birds, so well camouflaged by their feathers that it seemed as if the trees themselves were doing the screeching.

His stomach settled enough by mid-morning for a breakfast of boiled water and a firm heel of bread which partly restored him. He brought an armload of items to the table and set them down, then sat and began by cutting the inner lining from his father's long coat and sewing it to the hem, adding length, so that when he put the jacket on it fell just above his ankles. He tightened it at his waist with the belt from the stranger's bedroom, and at the chest, thighs, and calves with the rope he'd used to fasten the stag's head to his bike. He stood in the small yard behind Roche's, lunging and turning and crouching, attempting a weak trot. He loosened the knots at the thighs and felt an improved freedom.

He took off the belt and ropes, then took the coat to the trough of water which he'd half-filled with shovelfuls of dirt. He dipped a hand in then pulled it out, brown filth the consistency of cream sliding from his palm. He pushed the coat into it and stirred it with the wooden handle of a rake, like some laundry worker of old, working clothes in a tub with a plunger, only the coat would come out dirtier than it had ever been on his father's back. He left it to stew.

From among the items from home, he found a knitted balaclava that would fit him better if he had a second head. He fed a length of fishing line between the stitches of dark wool, traversing the forehead and jaw like nerves or veins, until the entire thing was crossed by transparent line. He picked the best from a bundle of foraged leaves – sycamore, beech, oak – and packed them under the line.

When the front and sides were decorated like a summer wreath, he pulled it over his head and went to the mirror in the bedroom. He twisted and teased parts that looked unnatural or squashed, shifted leaves to cover any black wool, then admired his head in the mirror, the warmth of his trapped breath moistening his face. He was as thin as a branch, his bout of sickness leaving little between skin and skeleton, and Rose's comment returned to mock him. Satisfied with his green crown, he went outside to work on the suit.

He took his father's coat from the water and squeezed it gently – a stream of filth spilling between his feet – then draped the coat over a clothesline of rope to dry in the sun, washed pale and floating on the far side of Carrickbyrne as if overcoming its own sickness.

# 27

I felt like a man who'd drunk too much the night before, nursing a hangover of worries and memories, examining if the broken pieces of the V-2 could be patched up with some glue and creativity, or need to be remade when I had the time and inclination. Maybe it was all a waste of time. I stood in the doorway of Catriona's room, tempted by the towel-covered bundle in the corner, but resisted the urge to check under it. I wondered if whatever they'd been working on would be finished for Thursday, or if the plan had been abandoned in Siobhán's need to get away.

It was a mild morning, a whiteout of cloud and sunlight, and I knocked on Mrs Rattigan's door to check if she needed anything. I knocked again but got no answer, then, blinking in the sun, made my way downhill and through town. The wooden podium on the quay was finished and a few men stood around it, as if deciding who should stand on it first. There were workmen running wires, painting and varnishing. Metal barriers were dragged across the ground, screeching like circular saws. A banner hung from the third-floor windows of the Co-op – *Welcome Home Mr President.* A tricolour stirred on the roof.

The lobby of the Royal was warm and the receptionist eyed me with the same alarm the uniform usually sets off in hotels or restaurants, or any place the proprietor doesn't want a guard seen hanging around for too long.

'Morning,' I said, reaching her counter.

'Good morning, Guard. How can I help?' She blushed as if she had committed some infringement of her own.

'I'm here to see Colm Hatten.'

She smiled, almost like relief, and looked down at a ledger, then turned a couple of pages and ran her finger down a list.

'Just in time. Mr Hatten is leaving us today.'

'Have you seen him this morning?'

'I haven't, but we can call to his room if you'd like?'

'If you wouldn't mind.'

I turned my back to the counter and scanned the lobby, while she clicked across the tile to a young lad in a waistcoat and bow-tie. Just as the youngster was swallowed by a pair of wooden doors, Colm Hatten came from the dining room, suited and fed, one hand in his pocket and *The Irish Independent* rolled under his arm. I saw the resemblance to Patrick, but the difference that leaving had made was clear. In his posture and his tidy haircut and healthy face. In his watch, strapped below a white cuff and in the twinkle on the toes of leather shoes. He slowed his step when he saw me but kept walking, sure-but-not-sure that I was there for him.

'Colm. A quick word if you don't mind.'

He stopped and sighed at the inconvenience.

'All sorted,' I called across the lobby and the receptionist waved a hand of acknowledgement.

'Do you remember me at all?'

'I do, Sergeant Field. Of course. You were Garda Field when I left.'

I smiled. 'And you were a boy when you left. I'll walk out with you.'

'I don't have long, I'm afraid. Long day ahead.'

'That suits me fine.'

He stalled on the footpath as if he didn't want me to see what way he was headed. Two American men came out behind us, talking about the weather, their accents making me wonder if my brothers had picked it up.

'Plenty of Americans inside these days I suppose?'

'They're good for a round at least. Happy to put a drink on the expense accounts.'

'There'll be plenty more on the way. Kennedy doesn't have a shave without them writing about it. It won't be enough to tempt you into staying a bit longer?'

He looked me in the eye for the first time. 'An Irishman in London can't afford to stand still.'

'You've done well for yourself, Colm. Fair play. You know I didn't recognise you when I saw you first – you're a far cry from the skinny youngfella I remember.'

'You haven't changed much,' he said and I felt it a polite way of saying anybody would be able to recognise these ears no matter how many years had passed.

'Any family?'

He smiled. 'A boy and a girl. And a wife from Laois. Yourself?'

'One girl. And a wife from Cork.'

'That's right. Somebody told me you were married to the best-looking woman in town.'

'I don't blame you for selling up, Colm. No more than any man could blame you for leaving when you did.'

'What's this about, Sergeant?'

'Patrick should have been looked after. He has nobody else – no wife from Laois or Cork.'

He lifted the end of his tie with an index finger and examined it, then patted it back into place. 'You know, I couldn't believe the cut of him when I saw him. If I didn't need the money, I'd have left him to stay there.' He sighed. 'Listen, I'm only trying to do what's best.'

'Having him sent to Senan's? That's what's best?' I shook my head. 'I hope you never have to set foot in one of those places. Christ, we'll look back in shame. We hear about how badly some Irish are treated over in America or England, but is it any wonder when we treat each other like that?'

'I didn't believe it would come to that. History repeating. I thought he'd heed the warning and take what was offered. You know I was there when they made the same plans for my father?'

'When who made plans for him?'

'My mother for a start. Your old sergeant – Kilcummins. Casey too, of course. She told me to wait outside the station, not realising the window in the office was open and that I could lean against the wall and listen in. She was always so keen to be in Casey's good graces, to get invited up to the house for one of his parties. Christ, it used drive me mad that she couldn't see where she wasn't wanted.'

'What has that to do with Sean?'

'She wanted rid of him as soon as he showed signs of failing. She wore that wedding ring the way Christ carried the cross. I'll never understand why she married him, other than not wanting to end up a woman on her own. We know what Casey wanted of course. Daddy was a quiet man, but if his mind was right, he'd never have let the last of his land go. He was so proud of the place. But once his mind was gone.' He clicked his fingers. 'There are men who do whatever Casey wants.'

'That there are.' I thought of Flood.

'Not you though.' He looked at me.

'Not intentionally anyway.' I always knew that I was a pawn in Peter Casey's game. Did exactly what he'd set me up to do and swept Sean from the board. 'The same old greed a decade on,' I said, to myself as much as to Colm. 'When does a man have enough?'

He gave the question thought, as if we might arrive at an answer to explain this great flaw of men. 'I left Wexford when I was nothing more than a boy. I neither knew nor cared that she'd left that house to me until one of Casey's men walked into my office a few weeks back and handed me a solicitor's letter. London – it's full of men who think a dirty young Paddy or Mick shouldn't even be in their country, let alone have the gall to go toe-to-toe with them.' He hardly stopped for breath and he tapped his chest as if in time to a racing heart. 'There are nights I can't sleep, worrying how I'll keep a roof above my children's heads. Then I get this gift from the grave – land and a house that I can sell. Think of your own daughter, Sergeant, and tell me you wouldn't do the same. I thought Patrick would take his share and that would be the end of it. I didn't know he was so far gone. When he told me that he'd put a bullet in me, I didn't doubt him for one second.'

'Do you've any idea where he might be?'

He exhaled long and slow through his nose and shook his head, then opened his mouth as if an idea had come to him. He paused. 'I'll probably never see him again. I hope he finds some peace. I don't think I'll ever see you again either, Sergeant Field. Give this to him if you see him, would you?' He took an envelope from beneath the newspaper and handed it to me. I could see him battling the tears. 'Good luck.'

He slapped the rolled-up paper against my arm and was crossing the road before I could say anything else, headed towards the river. I opened the envelope and counted through a thick bundle of notes. Eight hundred pounds. The price he got for the land and house, split right down the middle.

# 28

He stood in front of the mirror wearing the balaclava of leaves, ash darkening the skin around his eyes. He wore his father's still-damp coat, soiled brown and tightened with belts and rope and shrouded in greenery. He spent most of the day sewing leaves to it with green wool. He smiled, wishing he could see himself with his eyes closed – no whites to give him away – a human-shaped shrub, a man turned into nature.

He travelled south towards Newbawn, swapping between fields and roads, looking for a place to test his disguise. He carried his gun, garlanded with greenery of its own and twice he crouched into the thick hedgerow. First for a car that continued its journey without slowing, an expensive-looking rig of the sort Casey might own. The second time was for a man on a cart behind an ancient old workhorse. The man and the animal came so close he could smell them and he heard the man singing to himself *as Gaeilge*. If they saw him, on his haunches by the road, they gave no clue.

He walked on until he heard the calls of men and the rattling engine of a TE20. He knelt and looked through the hedgerow to a field where around a dozen men were at work. Some moved in a line behind the tractor, tying sheaves. A bent old man worked alone, swinging his scythe with the rhythm of a clock, as if he was racing the machine to prove a point, slicing the grass while a young boy held the pole. They were too far away to hear what they were saying, but in the drone of voices he could make out the comradeship of shared labour, like those who went to war, or battled sporting opponents together. An unwritten and unspoken contract between men – all that needed to be said was said in the act of helping and protecting one another, and he longed to be among it.

Looking over his shoulder to make sure nobody was following, he stopped at an enormous oak in a distant corner of the field. He watched the men and thought that in their toil they looked the picture of peace. They'd finish stiff and blistered and hungry and feel all the better for it. He remembered once being part of a team like that – his father shaking him awake before first light, too small to be of much value but doing as he was told by men with red and wrinkled faces and smiles and jokes for one another. The flies and the dusty smell of the field, the weak tea at break time, his father giving him two sandwiches and eating nothing himself, despite cutting more than every other man.

He grabbed a low branch and secured a footing against the trunk, then hoisted himself up. He was far enough away to doubt that they'd spot him even without a disguise. The heart of the tree swallowed him, made him part of it. He steadied himself, then stretched across the thickest branch and pulled himself along it, the gun slung over his back, and a scattering of leaves came away from his suit and fell to the ground, the dry smell of bark in his nose.

'Take it easy, Patrick,' he whispered, staying still for a couple of minutes, slowing his breath, as if to allow the tree to get used to his weight and presence. He wrapped his legs tightly around the branch and moved his right arm slowly to draw the gun to his side, then raised his head and chest and positioned the decorated weapon under his shoulder so it extended from him like a smaller branch. The movement caused another shower of leaves from his suit and he knew it needed alterations.

The men worked on, as they would until the sun was squeezed close to the land, drained of every drop of light. He took aim at the sky and even though it was an unmissable target, an endless span of pink and orange and white, he followed his usual routine of counting three slow breaths and pulling the trigger just after the final exhalation.

The shot sent birds flying from every tree and the men straightened, looking to one another then in every direction. Only the old man and boy kept working, sensing a chance to make up some ground. After a pause they carried on, the sound of a gun nothing new. He fired again, and again they stopped working, this time turning in more deliberate circles like men who might be under attack and still no look lingered in his direction. They returned to work and Patrick moved the gun to his back and lay in the tree and watched them until they left through the corner gate in near darkness, clapping backs and shaking hands, bundles of fresh cutting lining the field in rows like flowers left on unmarked graves.

# 29

I was the only person in the station, other than Frank Sheflin, who was asleep in the corner of a cell, dirty brown saliva dripping from his mouth to make a damp boutonnière on his lapel, like a rotten flower. In another life he might be wearing a red rose to a daughter's wedding. Flood had hauled him in before five, a few hours earlier than Frank's usual. He'd found him at the side of Ryan's, where Frank had gone to piss against the wall, then fallen asleep in his own puddle, the last of his decency sagging out of his open fly.

Flood had denied ever having driven a Land Rover and seemed to enjoy that I knew he was lying, pulling his shoulders back as if he was daring me to resort to beating it out of him. One quick way to get rid of me.

I went to the phone on the top floor and I could see the sunset, strung like copper-wire between a gap in the buildings across the way.

I sat on the desk and heard the call connect.

'Hello,' she said, her voice familiar and distant. I imagined her, standing in the back room of the pub. What Con once called his office – now a sort of second storage room, with kegs and lost hats and scarves and coats, old election posters rolled up and scattered around the big desk with the phone, that plenty of locals still came to use.

'Hello, love. How are ye getting on?'

She laughed. 'Daddy had Catriona in behind the bar today, standing on a stool and taking orders then calling them out to him. She was playing to the crowd by the end.'

I smiled and sensed she could hear it. 'Just like her mother. How's Margaret?'

'Still wrapped in her apron. Still doesn't know how to stand still. Up and down to the well every day.'

'Going strong, so.'

'Oh, she's definitely strong. You know, I was counting it up.' I heard her sit and take a breath, closed my eyes and saw the glow of light in her eyes while she came to her point. 'Two five-gallon buckets. More on washing days, less the odd time. Near enough every day for 35 years married. That puts her up at about one hundred and thirty thousand gallons carried.'

'I wouldn't bet against her doubling it.'

'Nor me. I haven't had to carry any for years. Maybe that's how we should measure improvements? Tomorrow I'll calculate how many pounds of turf Daddy has cut from the bog.'

'They grew up tough, there's no doubt about that.'

'You know Daddy's only a decade older than Kennedy? You wouldn't think it. They haven't been out of Cork since they came to see our house. Once in a decade. Once in a lifetime as far as I know.'

'That's Cork people for you. Have you decided on a train back? I could come and collect ye?'

I heard her hold the phone away and tell somebody she wouldn't be much longer. 'I was thinking of staying for a week. Mammy and Daddy are going to go see Kennedy in Cork and I thought myself and Catriona could go with them. There's a convoy going from around here, lifts being arranged and seats being claimed as if they were the last lifeboats.'

'Come back and see him here. I thought it would be something special for her in time, seeing Kennedy in her hometown. With her mother. She'd likely never forget it.'

'We might as well be in Cork. And you'll be working anyway. It'll probably be Christmas before we're back here and Catriona loves it around the farm.'

'Well, think about it. Ye're badly missed – I've only Frank Sheflin here for company. Mrs Rattigan didn't even answer the door to me this morning.'

'She does her devotions in the morning. How's that headache?'

'On and off. I'm on an antibiotic since you left.'

'You went to a doctor?'

'Not exactly. A doctor came to me. In a storage room. I was over at the general to talk to somebody and Susan Quinn spotted me. The quickest way out was to do as she said.'

'Did he say what's wrong with you?'

'He was the sort of doctor who was certain what it was, but decided it was best kept secret. Something invisible anyway.'

'But was he worried?'

'He was worried about how quickly he could be rid of me. It's nothing, love. I'm sure the tablets will clear it up. Between what Murphy gave me and what this man gave me, they'll do something.'

'There's something else troubling you.'

'You mean apart from being on my lonesome? Without my girls.'

'What is it?'

'Ah. You're sick of it.'

'Hatten again?'

'He hasn't been round for a couple of days at least. The house has been sold, and Casey's work has started. There's a man in the hospital missing a kneecap that I know has something to do with it all. I'm worried that either something has happened to him, or while everybody in this town is looking one way, Patrick Hatten is going unwatched. And that he'll soon have their attention. If there's any trouble on the 27th we might as well plan on retiring here.'

There was a quiet on the line. A horn droned down at the dock. Downstairs, Frank Sheflin banged on the door of his cell.

'Maybe he's just left, Jim. What other choice had he?'

'No. He wouldn't.'

'Jim, pet, there's a woman here wanting to use the phone. I better go.'

'Yeah. Tell my little girl I said hello, will you?'

'I will of course. Bye, love.'

'Siobhán?'

'Yeah?'

'Before you go, let me ask you a question.'

'Go on.'

'Who's more handsome, myself or Kennedy?'

She laughed and then groaned. 'Let's see. The one who looks so good in a suit, with a fine head of hair, a great smile, and a little girl that he loves.'

'And a beautiful wife?'

'Yes, that too.'

'So, which of us is it?'

Another laugh. 'Bye, love.'

'Bye.'

I took Murphy's medicine from my pocket and swallowed a day's worth dry, then went downstairs and took what was left of my liver and onion sandwich from my desk and a bottle of Powers from a cabinet in the staff room – left over from some Christmas party or retirement-do, or a long, slow nightshift when the lads broke the rules. I poured a drop into a cup then locked it away again.

Frank was sitting on the narrow bed when I opened the hatch.

'I've been banging on that door. How is it ya didn't hear me?' He staggered across the cell as if he could smell the drink. I could only see his big belly and his stained shirt, buttoned up wrong. I passed the cup and sandwich in.

He let out a slow laugh that sounded like a death rattle.

'You're a good man, Jim Field.' He swallowed the whiskey and the cup appeared in the hatch. 'Very good, sir,' he said, in his best British accent. 'Bring the bottle.'

'Sleep tight, Frank.'

There was music coming from Ryan's and evening birds circled the town in time. The sun glowed along the horizon beyond the river, like a lit fuse, burning its way around New Ross.

Colfer's love interest, Claire O'Gorman, walked along South Street, arm in arm with Ronan Casey. Poor old Colfer hardly stands a chance. Though I suppose the same was said about me.

The incline of Craywell Road tested me and I stopped once, to watch the brown slurry of the Barrow flow in the opposite direction. I turned to face the town and tried to imagine what Kennedy might think – a summer breeze on his face, CBS boys chasing his car in their white shirts and trousers, the patchwork of Wexford fields on the far side of the river. Turning onto John Street, pulsing with tricolours, stars, stripes and thousands of cheering and smiling faces, greeting him like a long-lost son or brother. There are still people who'll tell you it will mean all but nothing to him. But standing there in the near-dark, with midges shimmering all around me, after months of talk and planning and scrubbing and painting and cleaning, it was as if the whole town was sparkling with a one-time-only sort of magic.

I wanted nothing more than for Siobhán and Catriona to be part of it.

# 30

Patrick cleared Roche's table – putting the unrepaired shoes neatly against the wall as if their owner might come to collect them, then moving a scattering of rubber bands, the rusted head of a claw hammer, a bladeless Stanley knife, two sticks of chalk and a nail clipper to the chair at the end of the table. He held Rose's purse tight, with its couple of coins and single key, and left it safely in Roche's bedroom.

The tabletop was an uneven and pockmarked sheet of plywood and Patrick remembered the painter's board as he took the darkest pencil he could find from the drawer under the table and drew the Barrow on the western end, weaving the pencil through a blanket of dust, the river's outline like a vine from top to bottom. He marked O'Kennedy Park with a crude star, then the Kennedy home in Dunganstown with another, recalling the men in the barbershop amazed that Kennedy would stand in that yard and sit in that old house sipping from cups of tea. South of the football field he marked the quay, then drew a second, thinner vine of road connecting the three spots. He moved east across the table and marked Carrickbyrne and Roche's as accurately as he could estimate, then drew the tracks, trails, waterways, and roads that connected each location. Places mapped and unmapped, known only to him. Circles marked Casey's home and stables and the house he'd lost.

He tucked the pencil behind his ear and climbed onto the chair, his head almost touching the low ceiling, looking down at the map which marked the limits of the world he'd known his whole life, stretching from one end of the table to the other, nothing around it only an uncertain fall. The little place he'd drawn, a small town that seemed so big when he was a boy, would soon be known all over the world, but not for the reason its people wanted. In England and America, in France and Germany, they'd write about the man shot in front of Kennedy's motorcade. Children and grandchildren of New Ross would never hear about the famous afternoon without the Hatten and Kennedy names forever joined by a bullet.

'What do you think, Joe?' he shouted in the direction of the byre.

He ruled out going near town, knowing it would be swarming with locals and uniformed and plainclothes guards and visitors from every corner of several counties, journeying from damp peninsulas and blanket bogs, down from hills and up from valleys to see the entire world in the shape of one man. A crowd would be easy to get lost in, but hard to get out of. The roads would be closed and only the most direct route between town and Dunganstown would stay open. If Peter Casey was going to Dunganstown, Patrick would wait all day and through the night before to make sure he didn't miss him.

He could picture it clearly. When he saw Casey, sitting in a passenger seat with his window down to make sure all those people lining the roads saw him, he'd fire from whatever perch he chose and people would hear the sound and wouldn't be sure of what it was until Casey's driver floored it and somebody screamed at the sight of a bloodied passenger. The crowd would scatter and run and by the time anybody was sure what had happened, nobody would be able to say *where* it had happened, and he'd have long shed his suit and run away from the scene with the rest of them.

He stepped onto the table, then walked his map slowly, thinking, thinking, thinking, then he stepped over his version of the Barrow and jumped to the floor as if he was jumping into the cool, rushing river.

His coat was draped over a chair and had lost most of its foliage during its trial run. It looked like some ragged and diseased tree, shedding leaves like an autumn oak. He knelt and inspected it. Some leaves were sewn too close to their edges and others would be torn away while climbing or rubbing against the ground while hiding. He knew what was needed to improve it, and knew where he could get it, and get it tonight. His calves and back ached. Days of walking and cycling. Of hunger.

'We're not finished yet, Joe. Not by a long chalk.'

# 31

I wasn't ready for sitting in an empty house worrying over Patrick. There's something about a Friday evening that demands company. I headed in to Ryan's with a stomach full of liver, after leaving some leftovers in the cat's bowl and rehearsing what I'd say to Casey if I saw him. How to ask him straight out if he knew where Patrick was and if he didn't, warn him again that it's in his best interest to keep his eyes wide open.

A few heads clocked me before the door of the pub had even closed – out of uniform, arriving on my own for a drink. I raised a finger to John Ryan who was mid-pour. A drone of talk and laughter and glasses touching played out of time to the music coming from three men in the corner – an accordion and fiddle playing fast, fingertips falling like raindrops on the holes of a tin whistle. Feet tapped on the floorboards and there was a pair of young couples in a snug, pints and gins on the table. There were more women in the bar than I'd ever seen, and the chorus of British and American accents explained it. Women who didn't know or care about the judgement they'd be subject to for being in the pub. Their presence added a charge to the place that I'd never known. Men stood shyly in groups of two or three hoping a dignified distance might attract the women's eyes, while others were like excited puppies, eyes shifting from woman to woman as if it was the last night on earth. Scanning the crowd, I saw Patrick's face between bodies and behind shoulders, and every time I looked back, it wasn't him.

Local women dared to join, emboldened by their foreign peers, and they shared looks and nods and smiles as if they were all complicit in some organised rebellion. John Ryan's had an international air and he'd drafted in his two unworldly sons to help behind the bar, while Tracey Gaughan was pouring a trayful of whiskeys and ignoring the advances of two smartly suited Brits, who wouldn't have been long backing off if they knew how brutally Tracey's grandfather had fought their countrymen a few short decades ago. Who'd have thought it back then, that English and Irish would be drinking together, breathing the perfumed and Brylcreemed air of Ryan's while waiting for the American President?

I found a stool at the far end of the bar and John put a Guinness in front of me and told me the first pint of the weekend was on him. I sat and made a silent promise to take Siobhán out some night she was back. Not just out, but away, to Dublin or even London. On the boat, or if I make Inspector, a plane – where we could join hands as the wheels came up. A group of men at the table behind me toasted Donncha Reilly and I raised my glass.

Three American women leaned against the countertop at the middle of the bar, sipping some concoction that John Ryan had likely never made before. I imagined their lives back in New York or Boston or wherever they'd come from, and imagined Siobhán in their company, in some city of millions, wearing the same sort of dress, tight at the waist and flaring to just above their knees, or even daring the slim trousers that one of the women wore, mystifying a few old boys at a nearby table.

I was well into my second stout when the musicians were silenced by a man standing on the lower rungs of his barstool, tapping two glasses together. The man had deep black hair swept back, with a single length of grey down the middle, and raised his arms with a showman's posture. John slung a tea towel over his shoulder and folded his arms, gauging how long he'd allow the floor to the man, who wiped his mouth with the back of his right hand then picked up a glass and held the amber liquid to the dim ceiling light and projected his voice like a tenor.

*'Now all you Irish people, just listen to this rhyme*

*With paper and with radio, we've kept touch all the time,*
*The Irish nation celebrated the historical event*
*When Senator Kennedy was elected President*
*All of us know the crises grow*
*We hope heaven this man has sent*
*So here's to the great O'Kennedy, the US President!'*

He raised his glass towards a cobwebbed corner of the ceiling and everybody cheered the same as they would for a winning point in Wexford Park. I drained my pint and when I set my glass down, Colfer was squeezing onto the empty stool next to me, aftershave as potent as an oil spill.

'Colfer. Good timing as always.' I pointed at my empty glass.

'Same again?' he said, trying to meet one of the eight eyes behind the bar.

'Same again.'

The youngest Ryan boy put two pints in front of us, with more head than a seasoned barman would have been happy with, and I swatted Colfer's hand away. 'The first one of the weekend is on me. Rules of the house.'

He lifted his glass. 'It's not the first. But thanks. Sláinte.'

'Sláinte.' I wiped the foam from my top lip after a long swallow, and remembered Claire O'Gorman walking with Ronan Casey. 'No love in the air tonight?'

He turned and put both elbows on the bar. 'I'm sure there is somewhere.'

I drank again. The music slowed and it darkened outside, and the smiles and faces were half-lit and full of mystery and promise and I wondered if Colfer knew that sitting with a broken heart on a Friday evening, in the midst of all that summer longing, was as sure a sign of life as there can be.

'How do you see it going?' he said, when his eye drifted back from one of the American women.

'We'll be okay.' I leaned towards him to be heard above the noise and took another lungful of aftershave. 'We better be.'

He looked around the pub, at the bodies squeezed together, a mix of dancing and pushing through and heads tossed back in laughter knocking into heads bent to listen more closely. 'It will be like this, times fifty thousand.'

'Like emptying Semple Stadium onto our streets for the night.'

'You'll be in Dunganstown. Right up next to him.' He turned on his stool, with the excitement of a boy talking to a man about to be strapped into a shuttle and launched at the moon.

'I will.'

'Will you say anything to him?'

I drank to disguise my embarrassment, as if Colfer might read my mind and the list of questions I've imagined asking Kennedy about the space programme while I shook his hand. In reality, I'll be a background figure, watching on while Mary Ryan butters scones and tells Kennedy about his ancestors. 'Not a word.'

'I still can't get my head around him coming here. Can you imagine something going wrong? His car getting potholed.' He laughed. 'Secret Service lads getting out for the spare. Or the platform falling through mid-speech? Or some fool of a protestor making a show of us. We'd never live it down.'

I called for two Jamesons.

'To nothing going wrong,' I said when we touched glasses. We knocked them back and he turned as if to confess some secret and I saw the glaze of drink over his eyes.

'Jim, can I ask you something? It's a bit embarrassing.'

'It sounds like we'll need two more.' The Ryan boy was already coming with the bottle, having watched us make the others disappear. He poured and I paid.

'How do you show a woman that you're good enough, if everybody thinks you're not?'

'Is there any particular reason you're coming to me for this advice?'

He reddened. 'No, Jesus, no. It's just I thought since you're a guard too and you're married and all. And since your wife is such a – well, such a fine woman.'

'I know why you're asking me, Colfer.' I thought about what to tell him. Felt him looking at me like I had the keys to everything in my pocket. I thought of telling him that even if you get her, there's no guarantee you'll keep her. That I don't know why a woman loves, and that all he can do is want her for the right reason. If it's because she looks a certain way or comes from a certain family, it's a waste of time. If the reason is right – that he loves her – then he has to love her so much that he doesn't need to say the words for her to know, but says them anyway. He has to be sure enough that there's a reason she feels the same, and when he finds himself second guessing it, he has to do it privately, in some quiet corner of his mind. He has to understand that years move on, and while loss and challenge changes them both he has to keep falling in love with every new version of her that comes along.

'It's one of life's great mysteries, Colfer.' He said nothing and drank his Jameson. 'Christ, let's get out of here before somebody hears us.'

The cold hit me like stepping out on the deck of a ship at sea. Standing upright after a few pints gave me the feeling that the town was passing over waves. The singing and music and revelry were dulled and I walked away from the door. Colfer came out after me, his hands in his pockets, looking up and down the road. There were young lads down at the river, unseen, their drunken choir reaching us.

'I'm not going in after any of them,' Colfer said, nodding towards the water.

'I'm worried about this week.' I looked back to the door of the pub where an auld fella was leaning against the wall, his chin to his chest.

'Something in particular?'

'Patrick Hatten.' I turned to Colfer and his face was serious enough to not make me feel a fool. 'There's a gun missing from Penrose's that could take a plane from the sky, and a man in hospital with a gunshot wound that I'm near certain he got on Hatten's doorstep. Patrick can move around the countryside like air. He's as comfortable in it as you and I are in our beds.'

'So, what are you thinking? That Patrick Hatten is going to have a pop at Kennedy?' He laughed, but only for a second.

I looked at him and realised that I hadn't allowed the thought to cross my mind until I heard it out loud. 'It's Peter Casey I'm worried about. Assuming Peter Casey doesn't get to Hatten first.'

'I get the feeling that Flood has been out doing some searching for Casey.'

'You and me both.'

'What can we do only let Casey know? And let Kennedy's people know – that's the protocol.'

I shook my head. 'You know there's been three threats made against Kennedy? Keep that to yourself. Remember, he's visiting Dublin, Cork, Limerick and Galway too. What'll I report? That some youngfella is roaming the countryside with a gun? And that this same youngfella has never uttered a threat? They'd do nothing different. Every second fucker in America owns a gun.'

'There's no harm in trying to find him.'

'Good man, Colfer. Ask around without stirring people up. Find out if there's anybody he could be with. I spoke to his brother, who left us today. Family is a dead-end so don't waste time looking for aunts and uncles. They never wanted anything to do with him. Think local. There's only so much time we can spend on him this week though, so don't take your eye off the ball. And remember, if you do find him, he hasn't done anything that we know of yet. There'll be no carting him off to Enniscorthy without us having a good long talk with him. What time are you in tomorrow?'

'I've to be in for ten.'

I patted his shoulder. 'Colfer, you should go back inside and see if any of our guests want the company of a young Irish guard. You might never see a night like that in Ryan's again.'

He smiled and I headed for home.

'Sergeant,' he called after me. I turned to him. 'I should never have gone out to Hatten's without checking with you first. I'm sorry.'

I turned and left him to it. To the perfume and aftershave and cigarette smoke, to the sweat of men straight in from their fields, their unwashed hands and toothy grins, in the same space as made-up women with accents and confidence and all the boldness our own are raised to hide.

The cat followed me upstairs and I kicked off my boots and lay under the covers on Siobhán's side of the bed, looking at the black ceiling until the drink started to make it turn and I felt weightless and alone, as if I was floating through space.

# 32

The cycle took less than an hour. The blur of street lights looked like stars hanging close to the sprawl of town as he freewheeled down Wexford Street. There was a man struggling with his key in the door of a terraced house. He shouted something at the upstairs window and banged on the door. Patrick veered his bike to the opposite side of the road and when the man turned and looked at him, he let his bike wobble and warbled a jumble of words of some invented song as if he was just another drunk making his way home. The blade of the church steeple glinted as he rolled into the heart of town and slowed to an easy pedal.

There were more people on the streets than he had expected. A handful of drunk men refusing to accept that there was no more drink to be found. The occasional couple looking for a quiet doorway or laneway. Patrick pulled his cap down and pedalled on, then turned onto the unlit lane behind the tackle shop. He stood his bike against the wall beneath a long, high rectangle of window. There was nobody on the street, or watching from the windows of Nolan's drapery.

He stood on the crossbar, reaching up his left hand to steady himself against the window ledge, and slid a crowbar from inside his trousers with his right hand. The claw end of the crowbar shattered the window in a single swing. He climbed down and returned to the side wall, then to the front. A man was walking in the opposite direction, past the platform that had been built by the river. Patrick waited until the man was swallowed by darkness and listened to the quiet.

He ran the crowbar around the window frame and shards of glass fell into the shop and others fell outwards like blades of rain and he shielded his head with his left arm then reached down and hooked the crowbar over the handles.

He pulled himself up, his fingers grabbing the windowsill, his worn boots struggling to grip the wall. He swung a leg up then hauled himself to the window so he lay across the sill, looking into the back room of the tackle shop.

The small bulb of flame from a match lit the space. Against the far wall there was a desk with stacks of books under it. There were unopened boxes and rods and a shelf lined with folders and note-books. He climbed down and lit another match and crossed the room to where some landing nets were bunched in a corner, standing on their wooden handles. Next to them was a spool of cotton net that McCrann would have a hard time selling. Stuff of the past. Patrick pulled at the loose end of a roll of nylon net, then used his pocket-knife to cut away about two yards' worth and stuffed it up his jumper.

He turned the handle of the door to the front of the shop, surprised to find it unlocked. He stepped inside and found himself behind the counter, and put his palms on the wooden surface and closed his eyes, imagining the ringing of the bell and the sound of coins being dropped into the till.

'Can I help you, sir?' he called out to the shop, rehearsing as he had when the job was promised. He rounded the counter and almost stumbled over Moll's empty bed. 'Oh, it's the very finest. That line is like a magnet. You'll catch more than you know what to do with.' The simple dream of work felt like a lifetime ago.

In the back room, he took a chair to the window and put his head out. The lane was empty. He looked out at the grey buildings and could almost hear people snoring, and babies crying, and brothers and sisters sharing beds in tiny rooms, and he saw the town itself as evidence of its inhabitants' stupidity. Given the choice of how to live and what did they do? Build great big ugly towns and cities and pack people into them to live and breathe and get sick and die on top of each other. Hundreds of thousands of acres of countryside that a man could live happily on and they act as if it isn't there. His bike was untouched below the window. He let himself hang then dropped to the footpath. He tucked the crowbar back into his trousers and felt its cool length against his thigh as he made his lamplit journey back to Roche's without stopping or looking back. He fell asleep as soon as he lay on the bed, the bundle of net still inside his jumper.

# 33

Nollaig Quinn was at the side of his home, slamming a sliotar against the shed wall and catching it on the rebound. He wore a white vest over trousers, and stopped and turned at the sound of my engine, his silhouette backlit. It was easy to imagine him, just for a second, in his prime, lining out for the county team.

'You never lost it,' I said, coming up his driveway.

'Jim, I lost it decades ago.' He massaged a freckled and bulky shoulder, hinting at some injury from his playing days.

The bungalow had been painted yellow since I'd seen it last. The neat garden of a couple preparing for retirement. A bench to the left of the front door, where they'd sit and look across the part of the world they'd claimed as their own.

'I'm not so sure. It looks like you might put a hole in that wall if you keep at it.'

He turned and looked at the side wall of the shed, then smiled. 'Susan wanted to cover it with ivy. I told her it would cause havoc for the slates. Sometimes all you need is a ball and a wall to hop it off. Do we ever lose the love of the things we loved as boys, or do we just forget about them?'

I thought about the sketches of rockets and missiles and the string of planets in my school copy books. 'I'd say some people have no choice but to forget them.'

'True enough.' He looked beyond my shoulder, no doubt recalling the sorrier cases he'd seen in his career. Poor souls whose childhood loves were buried like culled cattle. 'Jim, you were either hard at the drink last night, or something was hard at you.'

'A bit of both.' I'd seen myself in the mirror after waking, some watered-down version, my ears looking even bigger against a drawn face, with no appetite for breakfast and every joint feeling as if the bones were grating together. 'I talked with Larry Drummond.'

Nollaig eyed the sliotar, then pucked it over his shoulder. 'I know you did, Jim. Susan told me. I hope you're not stirring up trouble.'

'I should have run it by you. I had a feeling I knew who shot him and wanted to confirm it, that was all.'

'And?' He collected the sliotar.

'I'd say I'm right. Not that Larry will ever change his story. Where did Casey drag him in from?'

'The wild west. What brings you out to me, Jim, other than to tell me you were talking with a man whose case I shut?'

'Did you ever come across the Hattens, out my way?' He shook his head. 'I haven't had sight or sound of the young lad since he lost his land and house to Peter Casey. Have you had anything strange out here? Sheds or outbuildings broken into? Any food or guns stolen? Anything at all out of the ordinary.'

Nollaig shook his head again. 'One of the quietest stations in Ireland. We had a dog attack a couple of nights ago, though, you might have heard. Nothing quiet about it. A massacre. Seventy sheep dead when we got there, ripped apart. The poor farmer's livelihood gone.'

'Christ.'

'You know the worst of it wasn't the dead ones. There were live ones, standing there with their faces peeling off, as if they were waiting for us to help them. They were in shock I suppose. I had to walk around with poor aul Lorcan, putting bullets in his animals.'

'Any sign of the dogs that did it?'

He spat and gripped his hurl so tight his knuckles whitened. 'This wasn't wild animals. It was pure sport. Those dogs are somewhere now, muzzled and in the back of a van, and won't be heard of again until some other poor fucker's flock is hunted. You can only hope the bloody dogs turn on whatever bastards are keeping them.

I wouldn't mind being called out to find the owners with their stomachs eaten out of them.'

'Jesus, Nollaig. Don't be going soft on me near retirement.'

'Other than that, divil a bit. This Hatten lad? You think he shot Drummond?'

'I do. And I'm worried about him, or what he might do next.'

'If he shows up or if I get as much as a smell of him, you'll be the first man I call. You have my word on that.'

'Thanks, Nollaig.'

I turned to go and he scooped up the sliotar and hopped it on his hurl a few times, then swung and connected with the sound of a gunshot. We watched as it travelled over my head, this little airborne globe of cork and leather, spinning through the blue sky and over the road beyond the gate, crash landing someplace in the opposite field. I turned back to Nollaig, who'd raised the hurl above his head by way of goodbye.

Colfer was at the hatch when I got to the station. The full cup of coffee next to him was unlikely his first of the day, though the percolator was rarely used, with coffee a distant second to tea. Colfer looked like he'd had a late one.

'Sergeant.'

'There's lipstick all over your collar, Colfer,' I said from the doorway and he blushed and pulled at his ever-immaculate shirt. 'I'm joking, Colfer. You weren't wearing your uniform last night, remember?' I went to the counter and looked over my shoulder at the empty public office, feeling a wave of weakness roll over me. 'Quiet morning?'

'Yes and no. Yes, because only a couple of heads have been in. No, because both made some noise you might be interested in.'

I reached over the counter and took his coffee. 'Make yourself a fresh one.' I drank a couple of gritty mouthfuls and wished I hadn't. 'Lord, that's foul. Who's been in?'

'Ann Nolan came to report a window broken at the back of Tom McCrann's. I know you had work lined up there for Hatten, so thought there might be something to it. Sullivan went around for a look, but McCrann said nothing was taken and seemed bothered that any report had been made at all.'

I smiled. 'Why do you think Tom McCrann didn't come in to report it himself?'

He waited for me to answer my own question.

'Any rumours you've heard about McCrann's reading material are true. In case you're in the market.'

'Sergeant?'

'He didn't want to come in to report a bunch of missing dirty books.'

Colfer turned a page in his notebook, taking a couple of seconds to gather himself. 'I had a farmer in then. Jimmy Burke.'

'Last time Jimmy was here he was in a cell. What was wrong with him?'

'He says there's people poaching on his land. Said that yesterday evening he watched a man crossing his field, head to toe in leaves, even his face covered.'

'A ghillie suit.'

'A what?'

'Camouflage. A suit of leaves – hunters use them. Were any of Burke's animals shot?' I was thinking of what Nollaig told me, sympathetic to a farmer's struggle to keep animals alive long enough to kill them with plenty of meat on their bones.

'This is the interesting bit. Burke says nothing was shot on his land, only that he saw this man cross it. He admits his eyes aren't what they were, but says that the gun that leaf-man was carrying was bigger than a shotgun, with a barrel longer than any he'd seen before. He guessed a hunting rifle.'

Saying it out loud seemed to confirm to Colfer that whoever Burke spotted might be carrying Penrose's Weatherby, blending into Wexford by wearing the county's flora. I knew it was Patrick. Colfer straightened, ready for instructions.

I asked him for a road map and tore out the relevant rectangle of Ireland. I marked Burke's land and wrote the names of every farmer and landowner I knew down that way, then drew a border to mark about two hours' worth of walking from Burke's in every direction, taking in Corcoran's Cross, Campile and Carrickbyrne.

'Who else is on today?'

'Sullivan and Hanley. Flood is in later.'

'Get one of them on the hatch.' I double-tapped the map. 'Talk to these men. Ask them if they've seen anything like Burke has. And keep your eyes open while you're going door-to-door. Stick your nose into any shed, shack or ruin that looks even close to habitable. If you see any smoke – in woods, fields, bogland – I want you to tell me if there's a fire under it.'

'You think it's Hatten?'

'I think it's worth finding out.'

I went to my office and sat, not sure what part of myself to reach for first. Hot pain filled my shoulders and elbows. My muscles felt like they'd taken a beating for fifteen rounds and the headache fought on so strongly that I forgot what it was like to not have it. I took a couple of antibiotics from my pocket and some Murphy tablets from my top drawer and swallowed them with the coffee, then told myself to get out and share the workload with Colfer, but my body said no and kept me waiting for the pain to ease. Kennedy's words blurred slightly on the wall and I mouthed them to myself as best as I could remember.

The phone rang as soon as I stood.

'Jim Field,' I said, standing straight, testing my body.

'Jim, Billy Kerins here.'

'Superintendent. How's things?'

'Ah, up the walls, you know yourself. I need a good dose of winter, not this weather that can't decide. Anyway, Jim, I won't keep you. I've promotion exam results here, they'll be coming in the post anyway but thought you'd be interested.'

'Of course,' I said, standing and thinking of Siobhán and what news I'd be greeting her with. A step closer to Dublin, or clinging on to the sergeant's rung, staying close to Patrick's world.

'Flood's after passing the sergeant's exam with flying colours. Somebody high up must like him, so you can congratulate him and tell him he'll have his stripes soon.'

'Oh, great stuff, I'll tell him as soon as he's in.' I waited for him to get to my results.

'You don't seem made up for him?' Kerins said. 'When I was sergeant, I took all the credit for any of my men doing well.'

'I am of course, fair play to him. I thought you were about to tell me the Inspector results.'

I heard him move the phone away and the rustling of paper and some dull chatter over the line. Then he came back. 'Sorry, Jim, no. I've nothing in front of me yet.'

'Right. Would you expect them soon?'

'Jesus, I wouldn't say so at this rate. I can't see another piece of paper without the name Kennedy on it even being looked at until he's gone. Keep the head down and make sure it all goes well.'

'Will do, Billy.'

'Good man. Talk soon.'

'Bye.'

He hung up and left me with his hint. Make sure the visit goes well. I sat on my desk and imagined Flood making the office his own if it didn't. Taking Kennedy's words from the wall and replacing them with a shrine to Peter Casey, while I learned about policing sheep farmers up in Donegal, Siobhán and Catriona captives of the Atlantic rain.

# 34

He woke late and ate more than he had in weeks. Beans, porridge and two hind legs of rabbit cooked over the fire. He cooked the shoulder, saddle, loin, ribs and two other legs to eat later, not wanting to have smoke rising for longer than needed, then quenched the fire as soon as he was finished. He drank pints of water carried from the spring and felt strong and rested.

He lay his suit across the boards, stretched out like a body at a wake, the leaves removed and stacked roughly by order of colour. He cut a length of fishing net and wrapped it around the suit until it was almost fully covered, then sewed the loose ends of net inside the coat and trousers and around the cuffs and collar, humming as he worked, like some master dressmaker at ease with his cloth. He stitched thin strips of sackcloth to the suit and used his knife to make three slits in each sycamore leaf then looped the green wool through the slits and tied them to the net, some inside and some outside, working slowly and patiently through hundreds of leaves with the care and focus of his mother with her lace. He packed more leaves and twigs tightly between the net and the clothes, occasionally lifting the coat and shaking it, satisfying himself when no leaves were shed. When he ran out of leaves, his fingertips hurt and almost all the suit was covered, like a rustling green pelt.

He planned to pick more leaves over the next couple of days to add some depth of colour. He'd chosen sycamore because of their June thickness and heavy lower branches, and because of the enormous sycamore near Dunganstown, where cars slowed for a bend within easy range.

On the doorstep, he shut his eyes and sounds grew sharper. Birds and breeze, burnt wood cooling in the stove. He imagined Casey, slumping in the car, a flower of red blood appearing on his chest then spreading outwards while his heart let out its final few beats. The newsmen following. The chaos. The road closing and Kennedy rerouted, helicoptered away and never to return, the whole visit clouded by death, New Ross shamed in front of the world. In London and Washington, and Berlin and Tokyo, they'd report on the President's near miss and the little town in the south-east of Ireland, where wildness reigned and all the locals' high opinions of themselves came crashing to earth.

He let thoughts of being caught, or being spotted and having his head blown off, pass without entertaining them. He imagined that for decades to come, people would talk about the visit and the wealthy man who died. Around fireplaces, and in kitchens, and at bar counters, in huddles in snugs and schoolyards, people would share theories and the conversation would never pass without somebody mentioning the name of Patrick Hatten. The boy cast out by the town, who had the best shot of any local who ever owned a gun, who left a bloodstain on New Ross that could never be scrubbed clean. He imagined that some old head would always toss a hand and dismiss the notion, arguing that Patrick Hatten could never have done it and been smart enough to get away, but every now and then, those same men would find themselves alone in their fields or walking home from the pub on a dark night and stop, just for a second, at the thought that a pair of eyes was watching.

# 35

I skipped mass on Sunday morning and went for a drive, wishing Siobhán was with me, with Catriona in the back, promised ice-cream and asking us about all the things she was seeing for the first time. None of the farmers had anything to tell Colfer and I saw little point in dragging him in on a Sunday to follow up on my gut feeling. He wondered if it had been some tourist with all the gear but no sense of direction, after taking a wrong turn. I'd spent some of the night driving roads and byroads out by Byrne's and Rossiter's, looking for a face or flame in the dark, finding nothing but boulders of hayricks in the fields.

I drove north of town while mass was on, to O'Kennedy Park, where it will all kick off when the helicopters land on Thursday. Where some CBS boys will sing for the President, while their classmates lie in the damp grass, spelling out the word *Fáilte*. Kennedy will smile for a troop of newspaper men, among a political crowd there to greet him – ambassadors and minsters and councillors all looking to shake his hand in case any of that magic is contagious. And of course, the Secret Service men will be easy to spot, scowling and cloaked in black trench coats and polished shoes, the inner circle in this great mission to protect him.

I stayed in the car but rolled my window down to let the breeze in. Behind the goalposts at the far end of the pitch, tall spruce and pine lined up like opposing teams and I imagined Patrick camouflaged in the branches.

I turned the car and drove the route the motorcade will take. Down to the waterfront, past the barred windows above JV Kelly's, the raised platforms for cameramen and the céilí band. South and out of town, beyond the sharpest bend in the Barrow, the roads swept clean, even the trees glistening as if committees and volunteer groups had undertaken the job of going out to polish every leaf. The road narrowing in bends so tight people will be trying to reach into the car, while Kennedy blinks against the daylight flickering through tall flanks of trees. The electricity poles and their black string perches with crows standing sentry, the bales in fields like barricades. The gates that will serve as seats and stands, the slope of fields to the right, falling into the disappearing and reappearing Barrow – never out of sight for long. The endless foxholes, bunkers and ditches. The rise and fall of the land, the unblocked expanse of flatness after rounding the second last turn before Mary Ryan's, just sky and cloud so close you could touch it. The road there little more than a track, then the entrance to a farmhouse as humble as any in the country. Nothing different or special about it other than the result of one man's departure just over a century ago, when he walked out that gate for a final time, leaving his footprints in a dirty trail – the first steps on a journey to a different land where he had a son, who had a son, who had a son, who became the President of that new world.

I kept the engine running, and in the quiet, I imagined the ghost of that man rounding my bonnet, and wondered what he'd think of it all. Would he recognise the road, where footprints and hoofprints gave way to the wheels of carts and tractors, then cars like my own, and God only knows what next.

When I got home, there was a young girl standing outside our door and I wondered if it was some child whose mother or father was in trouble, sent for help. It took a few seconds to recognise Catriona. My Catriona. I stood from the car and in the moment it took for her to turn and smile and run to me, every ache and pain was gone. I lifted her and spun her and felt her soft hair on my face and her laughter in my ear and I felt like a sort of fairy tale witch, drawing life from the young.

'My little girl, you've grown,' I said, lowering her and crouching to meet her eye. 'You've grown at least three feet and put on at least three stone. How long have you been gone? Three years, was it?' She laughed and corrected me. 'Where's your Mammy?' I said and before she could answer, I saw Con and Margaret coming up the hill, suitcases in hand.

I forgot to say hello, only looked beyond them, waiting for Siobhán to appear.

'Granny and Grandad are here,' Catriona said.

Con smiled. 'Well, aren't you going to let us in?'

'Of course.' I unlocked the door and shook his hand and hugged Margaret, then let them pass. They put their suitcases by the stairs and stood looking around the hall as if there was plenty to see, while I looked back at the empty footpath.

Catriona led Margaret around the house, showing off her bedroom and her few dolls, a new one under her arm, while I followed them.

'Let's put Rose to bed, Granny.' She set the new doll among the old ones, muttering something to them, before warning Margaret not to lift the towel in the corner, then came downstairs and stopped at the threshold of my workshop. 'You're not allowed in here. This is where Daddy builds his spaceships.'

I sat at the end of the table with a view to the hall, while Con made a pot of tea. He insisted on having a full pot on the table before telling me where Siobhán was.

'Now,' he said, sitting at last. 'I'll tell you one thing for nothing, if they don't improve the rail and roads, there might as well be an ocean between the east and west of this country. Just coming from our place to here would add years to you.' He poured three cups. Heaped sugar into his own to remind me of Siobhán.

'Con, come on now. You have me worried. Has something happened?'

He shook his head. 'Nothing has happened, Jim. Before you start arguing with me, let me tell you that we asked her not to go. When that didn't work, we asked her over and over to at least talk to you about it, but she said you'd only worry.'

'Worry about what? Where is she gone?'

'She's away up North.'

'Up North?' I searched my memory, through flashes of conversations, trying to remember anything she'd ever said about a friend or relative up there, but nothing came other than the empty envelope.

'To Tyrone, Jim.' He showed his palms as if begging me not to ask him to make sense of it. 'She's gone with a few other women, up to some protest about housing. There's poor women there living in squalor, most of them young mothers. Siobhán says she's part of a group going there to help them protest. It sounds to me as if those Tyrone women need no help at all. They're making a hell of a fight of it. Do you remember the pram parade a few months back? These women, pushing their prams to council meetings, squatting in empty homes?' He drank his tea as if it were a toast to their fortitude.

'Did she say when she'd be back?'

'She didn't, just that she would be. There's no way she'll miss Kennedy though. She wants to be there with Catriona.'

I sat with all he'd said, a mix of relief and worry and admiration, and could do nothing only trust that Siobhán would come home safe and lick my wounds over her not telling me.

'She gets it from you, you know? All that fire.'

He smiled. Proud of it. 'I know well. Jesus, seeing her so worked up about it breathed some life into me. I might leave the side-line yet.'

Catriona and Margaret came in, the tour completed. Margaret sat across from me and Catriona climbed into my lap.

'The place is looking well, Jim. What about yourself? Siobhán said you were under the weather.'

'What she's saying is you're gone awful shook-looking since ye were down to us. What's going on with you at all?' Con pushed a cup of tea towards his wife.

I reached around Catriona for my cup and drank, uneasy with their eyes on me. 'Ah, some sort of bug. The doctor gave me something for it. I'll take a break after Thursday.'

Margaret looked unconvinced.

'Come on,' Con said. 'I saw a television in there. We'll go and see if my daughter has made the news.'

Chairs scraped and Catriona went to her grandfather to show him how the television works. Margaret eyed me while my body unbent and pain moved down my legs like liquid, pooling in my ankles. I followed them into the room like a man walking in shackles.

Catriona sat on my knee while we watched the news. The television was a fine way to waste money, sitting on its stand in front of the couch where Siobhán reads or where we sit together and listen to the radio when Catriona is in bed. There wasn't a word about the protests up North. Con sat on the edge of his seat, scanning the screen as if Siobhán might appear, looking over at Margaret now and then to confirm that she was as impressed by the technology as he was.

Then Kennedy appeared, touching down in Germany, striding across some airport runway, handsome and confident and smiling broadly, and there was a charge in the room as if we'd all just seen somebody we know. A brother, or son. Even Catriona recognised him.

'Well by God,' Con said. 'He's getting closer.' He settled into his seat and I knew he wouldn't move until the screen went blank.

When the news finished, we chatted for a while about the bar, and the farm, and the woman we were all missing. I told them I'd head for an early bed and Margaret thought it was a good idea, once I'd explained away that I'd eaten earlier. I told Catriona it was past her bedtime and she looked at Margaret, who said she'd bring her up.

I was sitting on the edge of the bed, shoes off, when Margaret knocked and let herself in. She had something tucked under her elbow and had a glass in her other hand, steam curling from it and something green floating in grey water, as if she'd just dipped the glass in a stream to see what it would collect. She put it on Siobhán's nightstand.

'Drink that, will you. It will help.'

'Margaret, it looks like there's tadpoles in there.' I lifted the glass and examined it.

She handed me something, wrapped in brown paper. 'Siobhán asked me to give you this. Lord knows what it is, but she had us traipsing all over Cork the other day, looking for it.'

I put it on my thigh and thanked her.

'Get some rest, Jim. She'll be back.'

She shut the door after her and I pushed myself up the bed, to Siobhán's side. I unwrapped the paper and when I saw what she'd sent to me, however she'd found it, I missed her as much as those early days of love from a distance. A green cloth hardcover, its spine chipped and worn, its pages yellowed. *The System of the Stars*, by Agnes Mary Clerke. Inside the cover, a little slip of paper. '*With all my love, Siobhán.*'

I put my head back on her pillow, then took the concoction and held my nose and drank it all down, like a meadow in a glass, muck and all.

I woke in sheets as wet as if they'd just been washed and didn't know what time it was. My stomach ached along one side and an earthy smell came from the empty glass beside the bed. I closed my eyes and when I opened them again, I wasn't sure if I was awake or asleep.

I'd been dreaming, fevered dreams of lions tearing sheep apart and Sean Hatten standing bruised in the middle of a queue of old farmers in identical coats and wellies, lined up at my desk begging me to help them with some unnamed problem that had driven them all to the edge of madness. When I tried to stand I couldn't and the farmers took turns trying to lift me from my seat and I could still feel their coarse and calloused hands even after I woke. In one dream, Patrick Hatten stood over where I lay in brown grass. He was wreathed head to toe in leaves and he extended his hand and lifted me the way the other men couldn't, then turned into Colfer as soon as I stood, and Colfer was crying in the dream, saying he didn't know what to do and we were side by side looking out at a graveyard, where Nollaig Quinn was hammering his hurl against a coffin as if he was trying to crack it open.

I turned from bed and the soles of my feet burned as soon as they touched the floor and my back groaned when I bent to pick up the book. I went to the window and put my head into the cold night. The town was silent and so dark I could have been looking out to sea.

Across the hall, Catriona was bundled up and sleeping. Con was snoring in the other room. I felt as if I'd fall asleep standing up if I closed my eyes and went back to bed and while the rest of the town slept, I said a prayer with the guilt of a man who'd skipped morning mass and only prayed when he needed something. I asked whoever might be listening to keep Siobhán safe, and asked for whatever was swimming around in my blood to drown, and leave me in some state to see Kennedy.

# 36

Patrick believed that night came up from the ground the same as it fell from the sky. That it seeped through the earth, appearing first as shadowy pools around the grass and flowers and shrubs. Standing at the back of Roche's he looked across the land and watched the patches of shadow and light do battle until the balance shifted and the light lost its strength and gave up. The trees and wildflowers drew up night like water, in darkening stems and trunks, closing their petals and quietening their branches where birds hid in sleep.

He looked at Carrickbyrne and thought that it might be the last time he ever saw it like this, at the end of a hot day, rounded in a clear and darkening sky, far enough away that the last circling birds looked like flies buzzing around a resting head. He walked the yard and considered that he might be the last person to ever live in the place Roche had called home. He imagined it years from now, in ruin or rubble.

The front wall of the house was still warm from the day's sun. Patrick wondered if the place had ever housed a woman or child or if the yard and sheds and fields had ever known lightness and then he remembered himself as a boy, playing lonely games while his father and Roche played cards and he wondered if that boy could ever have imagined this night, with Roche's body inside, rotting like fallen fruit.

In the shed, he sat on the axing stump. He wished he smoked, and conjured the comfort that lighting a cigarette in that moment would bring, inhaling its warmth and watching the smoke blend with the sky, becoming it. He stood and made a neat bundle of the irregular pieces of chopped wood for no reason. He went to the far end and tilted the trough and watched the brown tide of water pour out and splash against the ground then race away, its whispers filling the shed.

Inside, he took a cloth and wiped the tabletop, erasing his map. He rearranged Roche's clutter on the table and pushed in the chairs. The rifle stood by the door, the polished and expensive weapon as out of place as a diamond ring. Next to it, he'd left a small cloth sack, with a change of clothes, his army knife, Rose's purse, some tinned fruit and a couple of apples and pears he'd foraged on a walk that morning. Parts of a rabbit he'd wrapped in paper were already starting to turn.

He looked around the room then turned down the lamp and went to the bedroom. He lay on the bed and closed his eyes and listened to insect wings against the window and when he tried to remember his father's face, he couldn't. Whatever came to him was some interpretation, changed year on year and coloured in by mistakes and flaws of memory. He turned to the wall and never felt more alone.

# 37

When I walked into the kitchen in my uniform, Margaret turned and looked as if Christ was appearing to her.

'Jim,' she whispered. 'Don't tell me you're going to work? You should be up in your bed. I looked in on you earlier and thought you might be dead.'

'I was up in my bed all night, Margaret. Whatever you gave me seems to have done the trick.'

She was right to look unconvinced. I felt like I was wading through sand, every joint too tight, as if the long bones leading into my knees and elbows might be crushed.

I poured a cup of tea and leaned against the countertop to drink it, knowing that sitting would give away the extent of my stiffness. There were two small plates on the table, crumbed and streaked with egg yolk.

'Where are Con and Catriona?'

'Oh, up and out. There's no stopping her. Gone for a walk to the river. Con will get the paper, I'm sure. There was talk of going for tea.'

'Sorry I missed them. Did ye get on okay last night? I'd have had a bit of food in if I'd known ye were coming.'

She started to clear the table. 'Con went around and got us fish and chips. It was a treat. Though you should have food in whether people are coming or not, Jim. You've to eat properly and look after yourself.'

'You got me at a busy time, that's all.'

'Well, I can see there's no point trying to stop you, no more than trying to stop your wife. Ye're just the same. I'll only ask that you take it easy. Come home at lunch and we'll feed you properly.'

I finished my tea and put my cup in the sink while Margaret took a damp cloth to the countertop. 'What will you do for the day?'

She stopped wiping and put a hand on her hip and gave the question a long thought. 'I honestly don't know. Back on the farm you have your routine. There's always something to be done. I could go mad with idleness in a house like this. Looking out the window at people on their way to work.'

I thought about Siobhán's days. 'I think it's me that should be telling you to take it easy, Margaret. Call it a holiday.'

She started wiping again, in defiance of the idea. 'A holiday? Did you ever hear the likes of it. Go on away, get out of my sight.'

Colfer crossed the day room, wringing his hands. 'Sergeant,' he said in a loud whisper. 'He just pushed his way in and sat in your office.'

'Who did?' I said, and for a moment as short as a blink, I thought he meant Patrick.

'Peter Casey. And he's more of a bollocks than usual.'

I went through to my office and Flood was sitting on the edge of my desk, arms folded and still grinning at the news of his promotion. When he saw me, he stood and adopted his professional face, looking at me as he went by as if I was a classmate he'd just told a tale on.

'I'll see you again, Peter,' he said and myself and Casey watched him leave.

'Sergeant,' Casey said, looking at me then the empty doorway. 'Though that could mean either one of you soon.' He wore his coat and hat, and didn't stand.

'Peter,' I said and sat, my legs thanking me. 'What can I do for you?'

'Didn't I bloody tell you?' he said, sneering, making no effort at civility. 'You had to try do things your way, with your soft gloves.'

'I need you to start making sense, Peter.'

He leaned forward and pressed an index finger on my desk. The tip of the finger bent and whitened. 'That fucker. That little fucker was at my daughter again. And do you know what he told her? He told her that he's going to shoot me. The lunatic that your heart won't stop bleeding for.'

'Slow down, Peter. When was this? Where?'

He leaned back. 'Thursday. I was away in England until last night and only got it out of her then.'

'And what did she tell you? Was he at your house?'

'Nobody saw him if he was. And if any of me or my boys do see him, he'll be sorry he let us. You know you're to blame for this?'

'What else did he tell her? What did they talk about?'

'Oh, they were all talk. She can't open her mouth from one end of the week to the other, but managed to tell this mad bastard that I'll be going to Dunganstown on Thursday. I came to you when all their talk started. And I told you he was a danger. You could have acted, but you just wouldn't, would you? And when I tried to do something, you wanted to stop that too.' He stood and I didn't rise with him. 'It's time you get in line with what's happening here. That boy will end up dead or in Senan's. I don't care which.'

He turned, and I called after him, knowing the anger I was about to provoke, doubting I had the energy to deal with it.

'You won't be going to Dunganstown, Peter.'

He turned back. 'The days of you telling me what I can and can't do are gone, Jim. I hope you like being a sergeant, because it's all you'll ever be.'

'Peter, you won't be going. This isn't personal.' He took a step closer, looking at me like somebody he recognised but couldn't quite place. 'You're after coming in and telling me that somebody has made a threat against your life. If you think you're going to be within shouting distance of Kennedy while wearing a bullseye on your suit, you're sorely mistaken.' It took all my will to not wince as I stood and a spear of pain plunged into my lower back. 'I'm saying that to you as a sergeant, something I do indeed like being. But it won't just be me you hear it from.'

He weighed his words. 'Better men have regretted the day they crossed me. Regretted it powerfully.'

# 38

He thought about leaving without saying goodbye, until the idea of Roche turning to bone stirred a loneliness he'd never known, and he decided that the man deserved a word.

There was a foul smell of waste and rot in the byre. When he pulled back the sheet Roche's head was barely recognisable as a human thing and Patrick wondered if six feet was deep enough for a grave. Life twitched under the skin and insects played out battles on Roche's corpse, the maggots moving in rippling waves and feeding on flesh, attacked by flies and beetles. Patrick covered his mouth and nose and his eyes watered and he knew it was a sight never supposed to be seen. He pulled the sheet back over Roche and knew he would never remember the man he'd known in any other way.

'I hope you're not still here to see yourself, Joe,' he said. 'You didn't know many people, but you knew my father. You knew me. And I knew you. You were a good man.'

He shut the door after him.

In the main room, he pulled on the lower half of his camouflage and folded the jacket and head covering into the cloth sack with the balaclava and a bundle of fresh leaves that he'd wet in the barrel.

He took the bicycle north, knowing it would be its final journey. He saw very few people and the ones he did see were busy and distant.

On the road towards Lacken Fairy Woods, he passed dense treeline and imagined his old home behind it, untouched with no more work carried out since he'd seen it last. He'd lost his memory of his father and Roche at their best, and he didn't want to risk his memory of the house. It would stay with him as he'd known it that morning in the sunshine, when he was on his way to talk to McCrann.

An old man he didn't recognise was fixing a lock on a gate and eyed him and his trousers of greenery and didn't say anything until Patrick said hello and he said it back.

He pushed his bike through the woods. The place was in full summer, berries and mushrooms and wildflowers, the thick canopy offering shade and silence and Patrick carried his bike over lower branches, through green light, winding his way to the centre and a spot so deep it felt as if he'd slipped through a tear in the world and into another. When the bike was too awkward to carry further, he sat against a tree and took his army knife from the cloth sack. He took the wheels off and then took apart the seat and lay the parts on top of the frame and covered it with leaves.

Small shards of sky dangled over him. He put on the jacket and balaclava, then put his head against the tree and waited. He closed his eyes and thought of all the times he'd been in this wood. Of how he knew the land for miles around as well as he knew the lines and ridges on his own hands. The product of wandering since he could wander, first with his father, then to escape the house after his father was gone. Then to survive – hunting and fishing and washing. And now to hide. He wondered how long it would take to get to know some other place so well, if such a thing was even possible.

# 39

The two wiry inches of grey eyebrows rose into John Ryan's wrinkled forehead when he saw me near the counter, with Con at my shoulder.

'You're becoming a regular.'

'This is my father-in-law, John. Con Sheehan.'

The men shook hands over the dark wood bar. Con complimented the place and introduced himself as a fellow publican, then called two pints. He spotted a snug and went for it as if he might be beaten to it even though the place was near empty. A few after-work drinkers at the far end, no band, no music, and it seemed a different pub to Friday night.

I followed Con over and he took off his jacket and folded it, then rolled his shirtsleeves and clasped his hands on the table. I felt like a constituent, meeting my local politician about some problem to do with land, or right of way, or a poisoned well, or potholed road. Con seemed to be rehearsing for a return to the world of politics, energised by his daughter and Kennedy.

A pint was his suggestion. I'd seen him relax into the idea of a holiday. Walking Catriona to the river in the morning, watching television in the evening. He walked the town in loops after lunch, and came home from every stroll with word of some new friendship or acquaintance he'd struck up. Over dinner, he told us about Martin Stokes' daughter's upcoming wedding. About Orlagh Gibbons' dog and its litter of 12 pups. About the chef in the Royal, smoking treble what he did a month ago, run off his feet with all the guests and room service and the odd requests of the Americans – cheeseburgers and Cokes and eggs 'over easy'. He was loosening his tongue, readying for a run in '65. The weather helped his wandering, more sunshine than I could do with, as if my blood was on a constant simmer and brought to the boil in any bit of heat.

'There's a man like this Casey character in every town in Ireland,' he said. 'Sometimes more than one – and that's when things get interesting.'

'He won't let this go, I'm sure.'

Con shrugged. 'He can hold on as tight as he likes. He can take it to bed with him at night if that's what he wants, but you'd be mad not to run this up the ladder. He walked in to tell you himself that this mad lad said he'd shoot him. For the love of God, what does he expect you to do, wink and tell him he owes you, then send him off to Dunganstown?'

John put two pints on the table.

'Sláinte,' Con said, and drank. 'You don't look convinced?'

'When this is over, I'll be left to deal with a man who knows all the right ears to whisper in and all the right hands to shake, making a mission of seeing me blocked at sergeant. It's not just for me that I want to make Inspector, Con. There's Siobhán and Catriona to think about.'

He looked at his drink. 'This Hatten lad. You have to ask yourself honestly, Jim, black and white – is he capable of something like that, shooting a man?'

'He's most likely already shot a man.'

'But to kill a man?'

I thought about the last time I saw Patrick. When he helped me off the floor and I left him in that dusty room with a warning and advice. His dirty fingernails and the flowers on his windowsill. Of his itching and his tongue pressed into the gap in his teeth, and the impossibility of knowing what's going around in his head from one second to the next.

'Maybe,' I said and Con sat back and rolled his eyes.

'I asked for black and white. Grey is what got you into this mess in the first place according to Casey. Would you have been better off locking this lad up when you had a chance?'

'That wasn't grey. That was a decision I made. If you ever find yourself elected, Con, I'll make you promise to visit one of those places. I won't play any part in a man being thrown into Senan's without good reason. I've done it once and I'll never forget it.'

'We carry our mistakes until we atone, Jim. The best place to bury the past is in the future.'

'Well, I might never atone. But I learned from it. Casey should have listened to me. You take a youngfella and tell him he's no good and cut him off from the world and a chance of work, or any sort of purpose to get up in the morning, and what will he do? He'll find his own purpose. Even a dangerous purpose will be a damn sight more appealing than staring at a wall all day, waiting for the dole to come in.'

He nodded, no doubt imagining the same young men without work who sit in his bar while he plays witness to their passing lives.

'It's certainly a mess, Jim. If he does plan on hurting Casey, why would it be Thursday? Why doesn't he just go knock on his front door and shoot him as soon as he opens it?'

'Because it's not just about Casey anymore, that's what I'm saying. This town treated him like a leper since he was a boy. An ugly, wild thing in dirty clothes was all anybody needed to see. They pretend fine little boys who say their prayers and help the teacher after school, and who come from wealthy families are born good at heart. Lads like Casey's eldest, a spoiled and arrogant lad, with young women lining up to link his arm and their mothers and fathers all but praying that he chooses to marry their daughter.'

'You think Hatten wants to ruin the big occasion? Some sort of revenge.'

'I do.'

'Well, there's your answer – case closed. Call whoever it is you have to call to make sure Peter Casey's name isn't on any list that puts him anywhere near Kennedy. Or I'll do it myself. God above, could you imagine it? Making us look like savages. You see the Germans on the news today. Impeccable, not even two decades after the mess they made. And there we'll be, Paddy Irishman, shooting each other in the street over a miserable few acres.'

I drank and he raised a hand towards two men who came in the door behind me.

'Tell me,' he said, considering the Casey issue resolved. 'What do you aim to do with those rockets?'

'How do you mean?'

'Don't get me wrong, I understand the fascination. But when you're finished with them, do they just stay on the shelf?'

'They used to. But I'm going to take them in to the school, once it starts again. Let the children see them.'

'Well, I'll drink to that.'

'What about you, you're walking around these days like a man imagining that anything is possible.'

He grinned. 'You never know how much you need a break until you take one. I was thinking of Catriona in behind my bar, locals already knowing her by name. We've been in that community a long time.'

'Will you go for it again in '65?'

'Ah, I'm getting too old. Too tired. I was thinking of younger blood. There's a lot to be said for a strong family name in a community like ours.'

'One of the lads?'

'No, no. They're great sons, and have their own skills, but they wouldn't be cut out for it.' He drank, then looked at me. 'Not the way Siobhán would be.'

'Siobhán?'

'Aye, Siobhán. Why not?'

'Apart from us living here? There isn't a long line of women in the Dáil, Con.'

'Where did I just tell you to bury the past?'

'In the future.'

'That's right. Anyway, I'm only daydreaming. But there'll come a time when people want something new. Just look at Kennedy.'

We sat and didn't say much else and more than once I resisted the urge to ask him when he thought Siobhán would be back.

I waited outside while he spoke to John for a few minutes – about running a pub and their shared challenges and the price of kegs and spirits and import tax. We walked home as the sun set and he stopped at the top of the hill to turn around and face it. He took in a lungful of evening air. On the way into the house, he put his hand on my back, then went into the room and turned on the television. I lay awake despite the tiredness, thinking of what he had said about Siobhán, listening to the sound through the floor until the programmes stopped.

# 40

He felt his way from the wood, palms pressed against barks and branches, sometimes with his eyes closed and the sound of twigs snapping underfoot, moving like a blind man through surrounds he knows well, until he emerged in weak moonlight.

The walk was short compared to the miles he'd been putting in. The fields around Casey's stud were enclosed by a mix of dense hedgerow and high fencing. His camouflage rustled with every step. He could have walked through the broken wall outside his old home and crossed the field without trouble, but didn't want to see what state it was reduced to.

He walked through Casey's front gate. A dog tethered to the pole of the washing line failed to bark, curled up and dreaming. There were lights on above the front and back doors, and Patrick smiled at the thought of Casey sitting up in bed or his kitchen, twitching at every noise. He saw nothing at Rose's window beyond the memory of how she'd looked at him like a stranger, and he knew that his Rose was gone, if she'd ever existed.

He rounded the house and crouched in the rear field, the rifle standing on end and taller than him, his hands gripping the barrel. He thought about knocking on the door, knowing Casey would answer. Of saying nothing, just shooting him between the eyes. A cold wind came over the field and Patrick balled his hands against it, letting the rifle lean onto his shoulder. He imagined Casey's sons awake with weapons too, ambushing him from a top window or the side of the house.

He continued across the field and climbed a gate. His shoes dug into the earth on a slight descent and he walked carefully over the hardened divots left by cattle and horses.

The stables were silhouetted by the moon, like some king's house under construction. There were no lights on in the house or the yard. There was an empty bucket hooked over a tap against a shed wall, rattling lightly. Cars and Land Rovers bordered a tarmacked yard and a water tank dripped next to a round pen to the left. The home he left was somewhere in the darkness, across the paddocks and downhill.

He ran his hand over the stable door, then gripped a padlock as thick as his fist. He went to the side of the stables and took a couple of stones from the ground and threw the first stone high, thudding against the centre of the stable's wooden wall and falling into the grass. He waited a short time, then threw another stone, harder, then whistled once. He waited for a minute and nobody appeared.

The huge rear door of the stables was similarly padlocked. He took Rose's purse from his pocket and unzipped it, then took out the single key and put it in the lock. He smiled. He opened the door a foot and stepped inside and shut it, then took a torch from his belt and held it at shoulder height, the rifle in his other hand.

It felt like standing in a nave, with a high cathedral roof arching above him. He walked with the soft footsteps of somebody walking to the confessional, between empty stalls until he came to the final one. He raised the lamp and the horse was looking at him, as if he'd been expecting him. It made no protest against his appearance and Patrick wondered what it thought it was seeing. A living tree, holding a ball of light. He put the lamp down and set the rifle against the stall. He walked to the horse, then reached through the bars and rubbed the bridge of its nose, then brought both hands to its jaws and massaged them gently, whispering reassuring sounds. The nostrils and ears moved and Patrick rubbed down its neck and circled his palms around muscular shoulders.

'You really are something else.'

He remembered Bullet. Sitting next to him, whispering while burning chains of lightning whipped down the length of the sky as they sheltered in the cold and damp shed, and felt guilt for admitting to himself that Bullet was like a similar species, but certainly not of the same species as this horse. He read the name carved next to the gate and didn't know what it meant. Altair.

He stepped back and lifted the rifle, then aimed its long barrel at the horse, who shied to the back of the stall. He shut one eye and took sight at a target impossible to miss. He counted his breaths in a long and slow one, two, three.

'Bang,' he said, at the end of the final exhalation.

# 41

Catriona was at the table with Con and Margaret when I came down. They stared at the front page of the paper as if it might come to life. I looked over Con's shoulder and read the headline. *'Ireland Ready to Welcome Kennedy.'* There was a picture of JFK, standing in an open top car in Berlin. He was due in Dublin in the evening, with Lemass and Dev to greet him, alongside a small army of guards and security.

'I never thought I'd see the day,' Margaret said, breaking the spell cast by the smiling man on the front page.

I poured some tea and went to Catriona, rubbing her head then wiping her chin with my hand. 'Did you put sugar on them Corn Flakes? You don't want another bad tooth, do you?' She looked to her grandfather.

'Ah, we let her put sugar all over them for the day that's in it, Jim. The homecoming.'

'We'll have another homecoming today, won't we? An even more important one.' I drank my tea and raised my eyebrows. Catriona looked to Margaret and Con, wide-eyed, and they looked at each other, confused.

'Oh, Siobhán,' Con said. 'Right. I have you. She'd want to be getting a move on.'

'She didn't tell ye when exactly?'

Margaret offered a sympathetic smile. Con pulled the newspaper closer and turned the front page. Some moments are supposed to be shared. Standing in the kitchen on the morning of the arrival, I wished she was with us.

'Be good,' I said and hugged Catriona.

'Is that all you're having, a sup of tea?' Margaret said and I told her I'd get something in town once I'd finished signing the dole cards. She followed me to the door. 'If she gets in, I'll send her round to you straight away.'

'Thanks, Margaret.' I gave my best smile and she watched me go.

Cyril and Aidan Fay waved from the dole queue as I walked up the steps to the station. I started with a call to Kerins, explaining the Casey situation. He let me ramble on and then made little of it, seeming surprised that I called at all and saying that anybody who wasn't approved already wasn't going to be approved at this stage.

'Whoever was promising him a front row seat must have been leading him on,' he said. 'Men like Peter Casey are so used to playing the game that they don't realise when they're being played.'

'Thanks, Super,' I said, before a bit of back and forth about loose ends and best feet being put forward.

It would do no good trying to explain to Casey that I had no role in his exclusion, but still it eased my conscience a little, knowing all too well how much people wanted to see Kennedy up close, hardly believing I was only a day from it myself. I looked to his words on the wall.

The phone rang almost as soon as I had recited the last few paragraphs.

'Jim Field,' I said, expecting Casey or some intermediary to be on the other end of the line.

'You're busy, I take it?'

'Nollaig. What can I help you with?'

'It might be me that's helping you. Or it might be nothing. Meet me at the top of the turn for Raheen.'

'Are we going sightseeing?'

'You said to call you if I had anything strange. Well, this is certainly that.'

'I'll be twenty minutes.'

'Grand job.'

On my way out of the station, Flood was at the hatch, signing dole cards. He didn't even raise his head.

I saw Nollaig through his windscreen. He saluted, then started his engine and pointed to the road to the east. I followed his fumes for a few minutes of winding road and trail, with Carrickbyrne looming to my right, then my left, then my right again. I slowed to a stop behind him, between empty fields that looked ruined or cursed. He stood from his car, hiking up his trousers. He wore a long coat over his uniform and had his hat tucked under his arm.

'Jim,' he said, as I stood out, brittle as dry clay.

'Lovely spot for a picnic, Nollaig.'

He didn't smile. 'We've to walk in the rest of the way.'

He climbed over a stile with the lingering agility of a former sportsman, and in pained pursuit, I felt like the older man. He wordlessly led me down a tree-lined trail, sunlight flickering through branches, flies criss-crossing our path, the shadows of tall trees darkening the heather all around, while stray branches snapped back after him and bit at me.

We came to a clearing and he stopped about twenty yards shy of an old cottage, its thatch sinking inwards, its walls dark, like they were painted with muck from the yard. The dwelling was surrounded by rocky fields and built in a hollow, being claimed by the earth.

'Now,' Nollaig said, putting his hands on his hips and catching his breath. 'A man came to me this morning, to tell me he was delivering fish to the owner of this fine building. A man by the name of Roche.'

He turned to me with a question in his eyes, and though there were more Roches in Wexford than I had relatives, none that I knew had any connection to the little hovel in front of us.

He went on. 'I hope you had a light breakfast, because what's inside isn't for weak stomachs. The fish man lives out my way. That's why he came to me. Somebody has been living here more recently than the poor bastard that's dead inside. I'm going to sit on that wall over there and remind myself what fresh air smells like. Go in for a look, see if it there's any trace of your wild boy. I don't need to tell you to not touch anything.'

While he was talking, clouds came to give the scene a more solemn feel, as if sunshine was somehow inappropriate. I walked towards the cottage. There was a three-sided shed to the left, some wood stacked around an axing stump, with an axe lying across it.

'Jim,' Nollaig called after me and I turned. 'The body is in the byre, and the way it is, is how I found it.'

I walked in the door of the cottage and caught a frame of a dark living space through the spy window. The door to the byre was open to the left and I covered my nose and mouth before I went in.

A cool, grey space, with strands of rotting straw along the dirt floor and a white sheet over a human shape in the corner. The sheet was folded back from the head as if the man was tucked in and sleeping. The smell came through my hand and when I pulled it away to draw breath, I could taste it – raw chicken, turned cream, the brown rot of apples. I left Sean's handkerchief in my pocket. The extent of decay meant that there was nothing to learn beyond the fact of the man's death. I pulled back the sheet and the corpse looked like it had suffered through some inexpert autopsy. The man's hands were folded over his chest, bone showing through in parts, his ribs like a crude xylophone, parts of flesh pulsing as if blood was still moving through him.

I went outside to swallow as much air as I could before going back to the main room. Nollaig was still on the wall, facing away.

The room was tidy. A brush in the corner next to a pile of dirt, the table arranged with the debris of the dead man's life. I looked at the arrangement of his accumulated bits and pieces and tried to see some message or meaning to the way it was all laid out. I looked at what little the life had amounted to for a long time.

There were two chairs next to a fireplace, with a scalded kettle on a crane above a bed of ash. I walked the room, swatting at flies. There were some leaves that the brush had missed, scattered around the floor and more of them in the pile, all fresher than the man in the byre. I lifted a few inches of fishing line from the pile, then put it back.

I went to one of the chairs and sat, relieved that it didn't collapse under me. I closed my eyes and tried to imagine Patrick in this place and was reminded of a visit to his house months back, when the door was open and I didn't go in, but felt sure he could see me from some hiding place.

When I stood, something fell from the chair and I bent to it. I lifted it, knowing when and where I'd seen something near identical. A small rectangular patch of wool, just like those I'd seen scattered on the Hatten grave.

Outside, the sun was still hiding, maybe even scared off for the day. I rounded the cottage and walked through the barn. Behind a pair of decaying bales, a piebald cat was lying on her side with a troop of kittens feeding from her. I left them to it.

Nollaig heard my footsteps and stood and turned in a slow arc. He shook his head. 'That's how we all end up.'

'Best not to think about it. Who was he?'

He put his hands in his pockets and shrugged. 'Even the fish man only knew him as Roche. What do you think, any sign of your youngfella?'

I looked through the thicket of trees across from us, then at the sky, feeling all the better for its endless expanse after the confines of the cottage. 'I think so.'

'Good thing or bad thing?'

'Well, it means there's some reason he's staying local. I can't think of many good ones. What sort of person can live in there, with that?'

Nollaig didn't answer. Couldn't answer. I wondered again if I had it wrong all along. If I'd allowed my guilt to colour my judgement of Patrick. If Casey was closer to the truth of him – a lad damaged beyond repair.

I followed Nollaig back the way we came, glancing over my shoulder after a short distance. The cottage was already hidden from sight. I imagined walkers stumbling on it years from now, wondering how people ever lived that way.

Colfer followed me to my office and Flood watched him all the way. I sat and drank, the cold water floating all the painkillers and antibiotics in my stomach.

'Did you find him?' Colfer said and sat.

I shook my head. 'No. Nollaig Quinn found something much worse. A man who'd been living like a hermit out near Carrickbyrne. All but rotten.'

'God above. What has he to do with Hatten?'

'I'm near certain Patrick was there. Maybe he knew him. But it means he's still around. I'll need you to go to Peter Casey and get whatever contact he has for Colm Hatten – a number or address or the name of his pubs. See if he knows a man by the name of Roche.'

'Where was the house? I talked to plenty of people out that way.'

I took a road map from my top drawer and spread it across the desk.

'The little trail into it wouldn't be on any maps, that's for sure.' I pressed my finger to where the tomb was. 'Here.'

Colfer scanned the map and pointed out patches of land. 'That would be Fanning. Walsh. Fagan.' He moved his fingers over the green of the map. 'None of them saw anything.'

'Peter Casey won't thank us for it, but all we can do now is keep him out of harm's way. Get in touch with Colm as soon as you can.'

He turned and got as far as the door. 'Sergeant?' I met his eye. 'Jim. Are you feeling alright yourself?'

'Tip-top, Colfer.'

When I got in, Con and Margaret were watching the news, with Catriona colouring at their feet, crayons scattered on the floor. No sign of Siobhán. They didn't turn. Their eyes were fixed on yesterday's images of Kennedy in Germany. I stood behind Margaret's chair and watched the clip. Kennedy behind four microphones, a Berlin crowd roaring on every sentence, captivated by his repeated calls to *Let them come to Berlin*. Speaking in German and the reaction from the crowd sounding like a hundred jets landing. I envied the audience, a sort of pathetic jealousy, like a boy seeing his love with another. Then I realised that Kennedy was on his way here, likely at the very minute we were watching him on screen. That Nuala and her crew were on their way to the airport to join the crowds to welcome him.

Margaret had a feast of mash and lamb chops and gravy made with a recipe she said she'd take to her grave. It was a near perfect meal. My ears twitched at any sound outside, thinking it might be either Siobhán or Colfer. There was no doubt that Con and Margaret expected Siobhán to be back. Their concern was voiced in every silence, in every laugh stopped a beat too early.

Catriona sensed it and pushed her food on her plate. 'I don't feel well,' she cried.

'What's wrong love? Is it your tummy?' I looked for her eyes but she stared at her plate.

'I miss mammy.'

'I know you do, love. I know you do.'

I brought her to bed and kissed her head and told her that tomorrow, she'd see the President of America in her own town and that it would be something she'd remember for the rest of her life. She reminded me that it was my birthday tomorrow too.

I switched off her light and went to my room. I'd grown used to the sound of Con and Margaret downstairs, the drone of their few words, the ease of their quiet.

Kennedy would be come and gone by the same time tomorrow. About ninety minutes is all he'd spend around New Ross. Ninety minutes that people would talk about forever. The window was open and it felt as if I could hear the tossing and turning of every person in town, the air charged and humming, and I thought of Siobhán and wondered if Colfer had gotten anywhere, and still my body was too tired to do anything but sleep.

*

I woke to the sound of the door downstairs and investigated the dark, taking a few seconds to realise where I was, too tired to even sit up. There were footsteps on the landing, then our door opened. I had my eyes closed, turned away, but still I could see her, every inch of her, coming in the door, putting her case at the end of the bed, slipping out of her shoes and cardigan and pulling her dress over her head.

She climbed in next to me, the length of her body cold, her hand reaching over and finding mine, her kiss on my ear before she'd said a word, then her whisper into it.

'Happy birthday, love,' she said. I kissed her hand and held it tight and in those few seconds before we both fell asleep, everything was exactly as it should be.

# 42

Patrick looked east towards town, then to the route he'd planned through the fields. The night was silent. He was tired and hungry and the road to town promised an easier walk and a final look at the place – something he wanted, but didn't know why. He thought about being caught, or simply walking through town in his camouflage with a stolen rifle, and being thrown into the small cell after presenting himself at the Garda station – earning a bed and blanket, and a plate of food. He could hear Field's voice, plotting his best way out of trouble. All he'd done so far was steal a gun that he could make disappear. He'd shot a man with it, but that could never be proven.

He carried the thought with him as he walked in an almost dazed state, like a shellshocked soldier looking to the sky and the road, his footsteps and the leaves rustling on his suit the only sounds. The town looked as if some disaster had wiped out the population while he sheltered in the woods. There were flags and banners moving lightly as if raised by survivors in an attempt at resilience or surrender. There were a couple of lights on in the windows of the Royal. McCrann's window was patched with wood. Ann Nolan had taken her American flag from her window and he wondered if she planned on wearing it, wrapping it around her shoulders while she stood among the thousands. He looked at the shape of black bags bundled on benches and against walls, then stepped back into the shadow of the lane when he realised that it was people. A handful waiting through the night so they might get a spot up close to the platform. He walked on.

On the far side of the bridge, he turned and took a final look at the black blur of buildings and the few glinting lights strung along the dock.

He thought about Kennedy. Landed and asleep in some fancy Dublin hotel, or maybe awake and talking on the phone over some trouble back home, or in the Congo, or with the Soviets. The Barrow never slept. He followed it south, against a breeze that cooled and calmed his skin, and trudged on until he came to the little ruined gatehouse at the entrance to the long abandoned Stokestown Castle. A weathervane squeaked on the roof and he kicked his way through panels of rotten timber that were covering the doorway. Inside, the small space was in absolute darkness and when he sat, he sensed something else in there with him. He heard movement in the ceiling and across the floor and made a silent pact that he wouldn't stay long. He moved to the corner and put his head against the wall. He slept with his legs extended and the rifle lying between them.

When he woke, a panel of light fell over his feet. He looked around the room and saw the empty space for the first time. Some scattered grain and screws and empty feed bags, the wooden handles of headless tools in the opposite corner. Damp and rotten rafters that wouldn't survive another storm. Whatever he heard moving in the night had left before him.

He climbed through the space he'd kicked in the entrance and replaced the wood as best he could. It was the earliest light of day. He went to a tree and pulled down the front of his trousers and tried to piss but nothing came. His mouth was dry and his head was sore, his body aching after a restless sleep against the stone wall.

He kept to the fields on the final stretch. When he arrived at the sycamore, it looked as if it was waiting for him, its enormous arms extended in greeting, huge and dense with enough room for twelve men to live in it. Far enough from the road to make it a poor choice for anybody looking to see Kennedy from a high vantage, close enough that he could hit Casey as easily as seeds fall from the branches.

He knew nothing other than what Rose had told him. That Casey would make the journey to Dunganstown sometime this morning, and it made no sense that he'd arrive after Kennedy. All he had to do was wait.

# 43

When I woke, Siobhán was taking my uniform from the wardrobe. I sat up and watched her.

'Look who it is,' I said and she turned. I could see that she'd been crying. Her smile was full of sadness. She held the uniform in the light and examined it.

'This is looking well.'

'I was doing laundry long before I met you. What's wrong, love? Come here to me. Let me see you properly.' I reached out a hand and she lay the uniform at the end of the bed and sat next to me.

She put her hand on my face. 'You don't look well, love,' she said, fresh tears in her eyes as if she was somehow responsible for the state I was in, or cruel for pointing it out.

'I know, pet. But I think I'm near over whatever it is. I got a bad dose of something, that's all.'

'You need time off.'

'I know that. But it certainly won't be today.'

She clasped my hand in both of hers. 'Are you excited?'

'I can't believe it's happening. Do you know when ye'll go in? It'll be special to share it with your parents and Catriona.'

'We'll probably join the crowds in town nice and early. I saw people waiting out last night when I was coming in. Do you know what you'll say to him if you get a chance?' She wiped her nose with the back of her hand.

'I won't get a chance. Seeing him up close will be enough. Now, enough of your worrying. Tell me how you got on. Up North.' I did my best to disguise any reproach in my voice.

She looked to the window. 'They're great women. Brave.'

'You loved it.'

'I did. Being part of something instead of just talking about it. You know why I didn't say it to you?' She wiped her eyes and looked at me.

'I'd have worried too much? Or I'd have charmed you into staying?'

She laughed. 'I needed you to see me come back in one piece. To see you'd have been worrying for nothing.'

I rubbed my hand along the back of her neck, where the sunburn had faded to a few new freckles. 'What's next? Because I know this wasn't a once-off.'

'Organising. Structure. I met some great people the last few days. This country can be a terrible place. And still full of great people.'

I turned from bed and went to the window. Town was shining with anticipation. I thought of the old man dead in his cottage and wondered how long he'd been there.

'Jim, what is that?'

I turned and saw fear on her face. 'What's what?'

'On your back.' She leaned forward, wincing.

I went to the mirror in the wardrobe door and looked over my shoulder at a bright red rash on my lower back, to the right of my spine. 'It almost looks like a target. A bite or a sting I suppose, love. I was out yesterday in a part of this county wilder than I knew still existed.'

She looked unconvinced. 'Let me put something on it before you put on your shirt. Then I'll make you a proper breakfast. For your birthday. Forty years young.'

'Don't remind me.'

She kissed me, her hands on my face. 'You have me to keep you young, don't worry. We'll eat together, before Mammy and Daddy are up with Catriona. Don't forget she has a present that she wants to give you later.'

I walked into the kitchen, looking as well as I was going to, and she couldn't disguise her pity. There was porridge and a vat of black tea on the table, alongside a little row of tablets and tinctures.

She put her hand on my head when I sat. 'You're very warm.'

'I feel it.' I drank the tea and spooned the porridge, hardly tasting it, knowing it might be a long time until my next meal. When I stood it was as if the effort of eating had used my last drop of energy and every fibre of my body wanted to go back to bed. Sweat held my shirt against clammy skin, my chest and back breathing heat.

She came to the door and the breeze offered some relief, then blew too cold and I shivered. The sky threatened rain, defying months of people's imaginings, where they stood cheering in sunshine.

'One more day,' she said. 'I don't care what happens tomorrow, but you won't be working. And I'm taking you to a proper doctor.'

'Did you ever think it?' I said and wiped my forehead, my hat tucked inside my elbow. I turned to look downhill towards town. 'The President. In New Ross.'

Mrs Rattigan's door opened and her walking stick came out first, nosing the ground for solid footing, and she followed a couple of seconds later. She turned to us and smiled, stooped and in a light headscarf and her best coat and dress. A faint smell of meadow, some perfume she'd probably had for decades, waiting like wine in a cellar for an occasion worth surfacing for.

'Good morning, Irene,' Siobhán said.

'Good morning, love. Sergeant,' she said and smiled, gum and spaces and the odd slanting tooth.

'Are you walking down?' I asked her.

'I am. I want to find a place to sit if I'm going to be waiting a while.'

'Well, in that case, let me walk down with you.'

I kissed Siobhán's cheek and held her eye. 'Enjoy it all, love. It's a day Catriona won't forget.'

'Say hello to Kennedy for me,' she smiled.

I laughed. 'I hope he doesn't lay his eyes on you.'

I linked my arm inside Mrs Rattigan's, while her thin hand gripped the walking stick on the opposite side.

'So, what do you make of it all, Irene?' I said, as we started our uneasy descent.

'Oh,' she said, as if embarrassed to be asked her opinion. 'I think it's a special day. A very special day.'

'That it is.'

We walked slowly and she took a moment to get her breath when we were on level ground. I led her across the road and the Barrow glittered behind the platform, rolling on heedless of the day or the occasion. Green, white, gold, red and blue everywhere. Camera crews, guards I recognised and guards I didn't, lined up in navy-blue. A thick crowd already. She spotted a bench and decided that it would do her just fine. I walked her to it, weaving carefully through the bodies, not sure if it was me holding her up, or her holding me.

I don't know why I expected the station to be buzzing like a changing room before a match, with men laughing and slapping backs, getting ready to do battle. It was all but empty. Old Mal Clerkin manned the hatch, brought in from God knows where, the radio next to him on low. Most guards were already at their posting. I was due to leave for Dunganstown at half ten with a group coming back to the station from O'Kennedy Park.

'Anything happening, Mal?'

He cupped his ear, before realising that he had heard me. 'Have a man in the cell, but that's all. Brought in drunk last night.'

I looked in at Frank Sheflin, lying on his back, his hands on the dome of his stomach. The lock cranked open and he sat up.

'Are you bringing me a double, Sergeant?'

'If I let you out, will you behave yourself? You don't want to miss today.'

He stood and took a second to recalibrate. 'Did I ever tell you you're a good man, Jim Field?' He passed me and patted my shoulder, the smell of his breath turning my stomach.

I went to the toilet and splashed water on my face and the back of my neck and it dried like a drop on a hot skillet.

My office was used as a meeting room by the morning crew, and was full of the static energy of guards brought from all over. I could imagine their chatter and jokes, lads who hadn't seen each other in years catching up, and I envied them. Cups left all over the place, chairs dragged in from other rooms, the browned cores of apples in the bin beside my desk, a forgotten ham sandwich, squashed and wrapped, Siobhán's picture moved, having no doubt been admired and commented on. My notebooks stacked to the side, a folded newspaper at the centre. Kennedy's top half-visible, next to Dev at Dublin airport – like men from different centuries. Kennedy's speech askew on the wall. I recited it, thinking of seeing him up close.

I stood behind my desk and the room shifted. I pressed my palms into the desktop for support and something sounded in my brain like a distant alarm, straining to be heard over a roaring headache. It looked as if the clutter on the desk had arranged itself into a sort of anagram for me to unpuzzle. I sat and unfolded the paper and scanned the front page before putting it in the top drawer, thinking I'd keep it forever. I moved the cups and a couple of stained saucers. The road map was still there, open to where I'd circled it for Colfer. I had a sense that I had done this before – looked down on a map part covered by mess. I lifted a loose rubber band and remembered the bundle of them on Roche's table. I saw it when I closed my eyes, the faded lines of a map, drawn on plywood, the Barrow twisting like a long rope to Dunganstown.

Mal interrupted my thinking and the rubber band snapped against my fingers. He leaned against the doorframe.

'There was a woman here earlier, Jim. Asking to see you.'

'Who was it?'

'Rita Kirwan?'

I remembered telling Rita I could arrange a lift for her if needed. Another person I'd let down. 'What did she want?'

'Ah, you know what some of them are like. She said she started out early this morning, walked all the way to town from Ballybough.

She said that down near Stokestown, she saw somebody coming out of the little ruin by the gate. Said he was wearing a coat of leaves and had his face blackened. Said she knew trouble when she saw it.'

'Jesus, Mal, have you told anybody else?'

'Tell who what? That some auld one didn't like the look of a fella who's going round dressed as a shrub?'

Next thing I was running past him, racing for my Zephyr, knowing there were no cars at the station, every Garda vehicle put to use. My body protested like a horse refusing a stall, and I slowed and went on through waves of heat, through the flow of people outside the station, bumping my way through the throng by the quay with flags fluttering against my face, the uphill run to the car like a mountain.

I turned north out of town, knowing what roads were blocked, speeding east, blowing the horn at people stepping into the road. Hundreds of them, walking along the ditches, headed for town. When the crowds thinned, I floored it, the tyres lifting on bumps and hills, racing through Y junctions and crossroads, praying that there'd be nobody hidden around a bend. I had my window down and the air circled around me. The sound of the air and the road beneath the wheels was drowned out by a monstrous roar, as if the sky had shattered. I looked out the passenger window and saw three helicopters, like a military invasion, and I almost lost control of the car, slowing as I couldn't keep my eyes on the road, watching in the rear-view where they looked like three enormous birds swooping towards town.

# 44

He sat on the thickest branch with his back against the trunk. Since he had taken up his position, only a van had passed, with bundles of turf in the back. His body was tight and tense and more than once he was tempted to climb down to loosen it. The day was warming up but the sun kept itself hidden. He didn't know what time it was and it didn't matter. He imagined himself so well concealed that some small bird might come to rest on him. He looked right, to where the narrow road emerged from trees, then left to where the bend was swallowed by more of them.

He watched people gather on the roadside, through the scope of the rifle. A trio of young girls in their best dresses, lifted to the top of a fence by their father. An old woman in a shawl, sitting on a low wall. Men shaking hands and talking, women holding babies to their shoulders. They could have been a crowd gathered outside mass in their most presentable clothes. Others joined, some looking breathless as if they'd ran all the way from town or cycled as far as they could manage and abandoned their bikes in fields.

He fixed the sight on a young boy who was looking directly at him. In navy shorts and a matching jacket, the boy pushed away from the fence he was leaning against and looked harder. Patrick didn't move. He had the rifle aimed directly at the boy's head, for no reason other than visibility. He slowed his breathing. The boy turned and tapped his father on the elbow, a short-sleeved man who was talking to another man and ignored his son's summons. He tapped again and the man turned and leaned to hear the boy, who was pointing now. The man bent forward with his hands on his knees and his gaze followed his son's finger to Patrick, then he put a hand over his eyes.

Patrick considered jumping. He watched the man and boy, then glanced to the ground to gauge what damage a jump might cause and decided that he could land it. Their heads turned, following something's flight. Patrick kept the gun still and flicked his eyes to his right and saw a bird racing for a distant field. A falcon. He remembered his father telling him that pesticides were killing the falcons off and that there might come a time when there were none of them to be seen at all.

He looked through the scope in time to see the man rub his son's head, before turning his attention back to the other man, and he wished that he was a decade younger, standing on the roadside with his father, waiting for the cars to come.

# 45

Two young guards I didn't know waved me through a checkpoint, my uniform and badge compensating for my sweating, sickly, panicked face. The roads beyond them were all but empty and I drove as fast as I'd ever driven, as if the world was racing through me. The part of my brain that was telling me to hurry didn't fully silence the part that told me I might have it all wrong and that if I did, I might just about make it to Dunganstown to see Kennedy in person.

Farmhouses and sheds blurred in my side window. I checked my watch and knew that Kennedy would be well on the road, making his short journey south while thousands in town broke off into groups to compare what they'd seen. I thought of Siobhán and Catriona and how they might have felt among it all.

I left the car in the road and climbed a fence, stumbling through a field of cattle, chewing idly, unbothered by all that was happening around them. I stepped over a wall, into the final field before the road, and the thought crossed my mind that with my car idling and the shape of me coming through the field I'd make a fine target for a Secret Service man on the lookout for anything suspect. I stood near the centre of the field, struggling for breath, scanning the tree-line and just about making out the shapes of people lining the road beyond the hedges. I felt as if the field was on fire, heat wrapping around me in endless layers. I turned in a slow half-circle, eyeing the trees from the near corner, to the far right, then along the road, none of them giving me any clue as to why I was standing there, other than it being the nearest field to Stokestown.

On the bend to the north-west was a huge sycamore, nearly twice as big as any other tree I could see. I followed some primitive instinct towards it, my heart beating a band of pain across my chest, my joints aching and my breath struggling to catch up.

When I got closer, I thought I saw an unnatural shape on a high branch, then heard cheering and screaming, and a line of American flags were raised above the hedgerow – flapping like the wings of tropical birds.

# 46

On the road and through fields people were running, schoolboys in their white uniforms, women holding their shoes in their hands, racing barefoot across fields. From somewhere unseen, there was cheering and a surge ran through the line of people on the roadside as surely as the electricity running through the wires above them.

The first car rounded the bend and Patrick lay forward, the rifle like an extra limb, under his full control, his finger resting against the curve of the trigger. He sighted the driver and the passengers. Guards and men in black suits, and still no sign of Peter Casey. He knew from the cheering and roaring travelling the road that the next car would be the President's and that if Casey was in Dunganstown he'd gone some other way. He looked through the scope and nothing seemed real. It felt like a performance, a game, a hunt of just another deer. Colours intensified. A nest of rooks squawked high above him. He felt the coarseness of the branch through his suit, smelled the early death of the leaves that he'd sewn together.

Then it came. A long, black, open-topped sedan. There could have been ten people in it or there could have been only two and nobody in the crowd would have been able to answer – every eye was drawn, as if by some magnetic force, to the tanned and glowing figure – a person who didn't seem real. A person who slowed down time and carried the future with him. A person who had stepped out of television screens and from newspaper pages, this man, who raised one hand to wave and touched his tie with the other and smiled broad and bright. Patrick's eyes filled as the car neared, so close he could see Kennedy's hair moving in the breeze – lighter than it looked in pictures. His finger tensed on the trigger, his breath was drawn deeply, and the weight of every hurt and loss and sorrow he'd ever known came pouring over him as he exhaled, long and slow, and a terrible immortality called to him. He thought of his father and nothing else, and wished he was there to stop him.

'Patrick,' the voice called.

He looked down at some ghost-like version of Field, standing in the long grass below, like a rotten stalk looking up at him.

# 47

I called as loud as I could and wasn't sure I made any sound at all. My body was surrendering, as if it had chosen the shade of that great tree as its place to give up. The shape on the branch turned to me and I saw Patrick's eyes, looking out from his ragged and netted green disguise, a figure from a nightmare. I was almost sure he was crying. Leaves shrouded his head and it was hard to distinguish any human form below the neck.

He fell then, arms wide, a near-shapeless mass of leaves, as if the canopy had collapsed, and the long grass swallowed him.

I stepped towards where he landed and reached to my inside pocket for Sean's handkerchief, a sort of peace offering. My chest expanded, something pushing hard and trying to break the bars of my ribcage – sweat in my eyes, hands and handkerchief trembling. I turned and leaned against the trunk, taking rapid shallow breaths as the car passed. The couple of seconds it must have taken, slowed to a held breath of time. The back of Kennedy's head, his white collar and tanned neck, his hand raised like a print in a limitless sky. It was the last thing I saw, but not the last thing I thought of. I slid down the trunk and rolled over in the grass and she was there, behind the darkness of my closed eyes, turning and smiling at me over her freckled shoulder.

When I woke, Siobhán was there for real, smiling from the foot of the bed. I had recollections of people lifting me, an ambulance. Giving my name to a doctor. Asking about my car. An injection, and ceiling lights moving and the sound of other people on the ward. A radio playing somewhere and women laughing in the corridor.

'How are you feeling?' she said, her cool hand pressed on my forehead.

'Never better.' The words hurt. 'What happened?'

'They found you in a field by Stokestown. They thought you were gone. You were very lucky.' Her eyes were red.

'The luckiest man alive.' I reached for her hand.

'You were in long grass. Everybody was watching Kennedy or gone off walking the roads as soon as he passed. You could have lain there all night.' She cried and turned away then raised her hand to stop herself.

'Who found me?'

'One of the ambulance crews. They were a couple of miles along the road. They said some young lad came to them, his face all made up with paint, like he'd come from underground. He told them there was a garda lying in a field by Stokestown.'

I wondered where Patrick was. Wondered what he'd have done if I hadn't been there. Would anything have changed, or would the entire world have changed?

'How was Kennedy?' I asked her.

She smiled her fullest smile, and looked at me with wet eyes, shaking her head. 'Like a lightning storm.' She took my hands in hers, then pressed them to her face where her tears ran along my fingers.

She sat a while, telling me about Catriona on Con's shoulders and how Con cried, then denied it. She told me what Kennedy said on the quay and how the whole place was charged and electric and the crowd cheered like thunder. That he'd lit up the town for what seemed like no time at all. She kissed my head and told me she'd be back in the morning with Catriona.

'Oh,' she said, reaching for something on the shelf behind my head. 'This rag was folded in your pocket. I thought you might want it.'

She handed me Sean's handkerchief and I remembered taking it out, raising it towards Patrick before I fell.

*

A nurse woke me later, taking away my bedpan, and I thanked whoever there was to thank that there was no snorer on the ward as I fell back to sleep. When I woke again, it was to a touch on the shoulder and I opened my eyes, expecting to see my girls. But there was Colfer.

'How are you feeling?' he asked.

'Foolish. I don't know if it was anything more than a faint, nobody has told me anything. How did it all go?'

'Perfect. Not a foot out of place. Apart from yours.'

'There's something though?' I sat up, surprised by how much effort it took. 'What happened?'

He looked over his shoulder, afraid that a nurse would come in and scold him for bringing work to an unwell man. 'It's Casey.'

'Christ,' I said, imagining Casey pulling into his yard after leaving the crowds. Stepping from his car, then turning to a voice as he reached his front door. I thought that I had made a terrible mistake by not telling anybody about Patrick. 'What happened?'

'His horse is missing.'

'His horse?'

'Altair. He's raising hell over it.'

'But Casey is okay?'

'Oh, I wouldn't say that. Seems to think the country should shut down until his horse rears its head. He was in the crowd on the quay yesterday, and there in Ryan's last night, talking as if he'd shown Kennedy to the door himself. Went out this morning to an empty stable.'

'The horse. How exactly is something that size gone missing?'

'He hasn't replaced his security man yet. The stable was just there, waiting to be walked into. There's no sign of a break-in, so either it was left unlocked or somebody had a key. Drummond might be worth a look, he knew the run of the place and the worth of that horse. Once the door is open, all you need is a horsebox waiting out on the road. Every guard in the county too busy with the crowds to notice. Why were you where they found you? Was it Hatten?'

I looked out the small rectangle of window, at steam rising from the chimneys of the hospital laundry.

'You'd best get to work, Colfer. I'm on my holidays.'

A pair of doctors came in while Siobhán and Catriona were at my bedside. I'd managed some water and a sliver of birthday cake and was sitting up, watching Catriona playing with a perfectly scaled and painted Mercury-Atlas 6, with 40 carved on the side in neat calligraphy. Siobhán said she insisted on bringing it for me to unwrap, their work putting mine to shame. She took the plans from a magazine that she had Gleeson order from America.

The older doctor was bald and wore glasses too far down his nose to be comfortable. He stuck a baby finger in his ear then inspected it, before putting his hands in his pockets.

'And here's the good Sergeant Field, forty years and a day,' he said to the young doctor. 'Sergeant, I'm Dr Roberts, this is Dr Enright.' He carried on talking like a tour guide, looking at me like some artefact in a museum. 'Sergeant Field came to us with headache, fever, confusion, and a history of sore joints as well as a nasty-looking rash on his lower back. We've given him a hefty old blast of antibiotics, and will continue to – I can see that he's already improving.' He looked at me and smiled as he said it. 'Because of the response to the antibiotics it's fair to say this meningitis was bacterial, rather than viral, even if the Sergeant had some atypical symptoms and test results. It can, as we know, be a sophisticated germ. Hard to pin down, like a good criminal.'

He smiled and I registered the look on the young doctor's face, while he read my chart and then laughed dutifully at his superior's joke.

'You're feeling well?' Roberts said.

'I am. Improving.'

'Just the way we want it,' he said and slapped the end of my bed, then winked at Catriona. He was in full command of his stage, the white coat his costume, a detail to enhance his performance while he delivered his lines with the certainty of a man who'd done it thousands of times before.

They moved across the room to the foot of the bed of a man with a head injury and a pair of bloodshot eyes. Catriona was standing, poking at the thin mattress, then resting her head on her small arm, near my side.

'When will you be home, Daddy?'

'As soon as possible, love, don't you worry.'

'I'm going to bring her for a little walk. I think she's getting bored.' Siobhán moved the rocket from Catriona's seat to the shelf behind my head.

'How could you be bored in a place as fun as this?' I said to Catriona, pulling a face and she smiled and took Siobhán's hand.

'I want to take the rocket out,' she said.

'Go see if it will fly. Bye, loves.'

I watched them go, followed by Roberts, his white cape flowing. Enright was talking to the man with the head bandages, then patted him on the chest and went to leave, meeting my eye as he walked out.

'Sorry,' I called out to him.

He stopped and raised his eyebrows, then looked to the doorway before coming to my bed.

'You don't agree with the man in charge,' I said.

'Pardon me?'

'Part of my job is hearing what people are saying when they aren't saying anything. It makes no odds to me, I'm starting to feel better regardless. Why don't you think it's meningitis?'

He looked to the door again, then coughed drily into his fist and scratched his chin. 'I don't think anything for sure. The test we did wasn't positive and you've some symptoms that don't tally exactly. Pain for a couple of weeks prior, temperature up and down, tiredness in the extremities. You must understand that when we're dealing with things we can't even see, the science is always evolving.'

'I understand it well enough. All part of progress.'

'Exactly. The main thing is you're feeling better. We'll keep a good eye on you.'

'If you had to stab at it though. For my ears only, not the good doctor's.' I cupped my ears and smiled. 'Whisper it and I'll still hear you.'

He chewed his lip and bobbed his head from side to side. 'I don't like the look of the rash. There's plenty of new research around tick bites. People have been getting them since humans and animals existed together. Are you a hunter, by any chance?'

'I'm not,' I said and he lifted his hands in a humble admission of his uncertainty.

'Like I said, I'm not certain. See you again, Sergeant,' he said, hurrying to catch up with his senior.

Ticks. Animals and hunters. I stared at the ceiling and remembered the walk to Roche's, then remembered the day in the meadow in Cork, barely dressed and rolling with Siobhán until the deer interrupted us. I waved at the man across the way, who managed the most subtle tilt of his chin.

'Did you see Kennedy?' he groaned.

'I did. I certainly did.'

# 48

The horse's ears were pinned back as they rode on, still learning to trust one another. It took a couple of days to get used to the animal's height and breadth. Twenty miles at least before he settled, terrified and realising it was nothing like those young years on Bullet's back. The horse was so beautiful he couldn't bring himself to harm as much as its tail. Seeing it in the torchlight that night, trapped in Casey's stall, staring into the barrel of his rifle, he could do nothing only lower the gun and admire it.

In a little timber ruin, somewhere near the gently flowing Suir, he found a half-bag of lime, and coarsely painted the side of the horse, transforming it to a piebald. They sheltered and slept beside each other for five nights, in sheds and outbuildings, keeping to tracks and trails and paths walked only by them, sometimes forging new passages in thickets and fields. The occasional quiet road or towpath.

He opened his eyes in the darkness sometimes in the night, and made out the still and calm shape of the horse nearby, its huge bulk and the curve of its back, its head held high, a scatter of stars around it. He thought of those nights with Bullet, the storm and quiet lightning, nothing existing but the pair of them. Casey's horse was the perfectly realised ideal of an animal that humans managed to tame into compliance thousands of years ago. Bred and trained for all acts of servitude and sport. They'd stop using them soon. Replace them with cars and tractors and all sorts of machines conjured in great minds and built in factories by more machines. They could try for another few thousand years and still not even come close to creating something as perfect. He told the horse about Field, and his father's handkerchief, carried like a token of remembrance.

They cut across the country, aiming nowhere but west, past monuments to the civil war and the graveyards where so many men and women from that time were buried. Passing hollowed-out cottages from a century before, ruined outcrops from a land that had failed their owners. Stone towers built by monks, raided and burned and still standing. Past standing stones and stone circles. Through small villages, where the people who offered a bit of food and water for both him and the horse, did so *as Gaeilge*. They rode on, travelling back in time, until he smelled the Atlantic.

When he saw it first, raging against the edge of the country, as grey and endless as the sky, he felt that he had seen it before and knew that it must have been in dreams. He patted the horse's shoulder and stopped him, then climbed down and led him to the edge of the cliffs, where the animal shied away from the white and frayed waves appearing and disappearing on the blanket of ocean. Patrick opened his mouth to taste the air.

He walked the horse along the coast and it managed sections of stony descent like an animal born to do it. He encouraged it all the way, then climbed on as they entered a tiny port village and men in doorways and people on the road stopped to look at the horse as if it was part of a funeral procession, or a parade of one.

At the end of a dock, a small ferry was being loaded with crates and pallets and a few sorry-looking passengers stood on the deck, braced against the spitting rain and wind that had picked up cold on its journey across the sea.

He climbed down and walked the horse to where a redheaded and bearded man was shouting instructions at the men loading cargo. The man glanced at him, then stopped talking mid-shout and looked back again, this time at the horse.

'*Mo Dhia*,' the man said, sizing up the horse as if offended by its immensity, the whitewash fading like chalk on a blackboard.

'Where's that boat going?' Patrick asked, rubbing the horse's damp coat.

The man was confused by the question. 'The islands, obviously.'

'Any work out there?'

'That depends on what you can do,' the man said, keeping an eye on the workmen.

'I can do all sorts. Shoot. Farm. Whitewash. Fish. Dig.' The man put his hands on his hips, looking at the men carrying another crate, braced for them to drop it. 'Knit.'

'Knit?' the man said, turning back to Patrick.

'Knit and sew. I can do plenty.'

The man thought for a minute, then looked at Patrick and the horse. 'You'd be taking that creature with you?'

'I would.'

'Does it have a name?'

Patrick rubbed the horse's chin. 'Bullet.'

'You'd be the first youngster to move to that island in a long time. It's the other way they're going. My boys included.'

'I've no interest in the other way.'

The man scratched his chin. 'Well, listen. And I'm not saying anything for certain. I could do with an extra pair of hands. I've to spend too much time away with the ferry, just to make a living. My youngest built a little place a couple of years ago. Finished it just in time to leave it. It's a rough little spot, a roof and four walls, and not much more. I can't pay you. But whatever you grow in the ground is yours to keep.'

'What about the horse?'

'We split him evenly. He can stand in the field between us, but I'll use him as I need him.'

'He'll need a couple of weeks' rest.'

'That sounds fair.'

'How do I get across?'

The man looked around, then out to sea and scratched his beard. 'You wait here until I say so. And only when I say so, lead him on where those fools are loading up. If he pisses and shits all over the place, you muck it out on the far side. Alright?'

'Alright,' Patrick said and the man spat in his hand and offered it. Patrick did the same and they shook.

The man walked away and returned to shouting orders, while Patrick wiped the spit of the deal on the horse's neck. When they'd finished loading, he took money from his pocket and handed the workers notes, and Patrick watched them walk back to the village.

The rain fell hard, as if it had been waiting for the loading to finish. Sheets of it, coming in ordered rows, scouring them. When Patrick rubbed the horse's flank, his hand came away white. The bearded man was on deck at the stern, and Patrick looked up at him. He waved and Patrick gave the rope a tug and the horse followed.

It slowed as it crossed over the metre of water, hooves drumming on the steel walkway. Patrick led it between the boxes and crates and shushed it. He rubbed it endlessly, while motors turned and water responded, and the animal was comforting him as much as he was comforting it. The mouth of the boat closed slowly, and Patrick and the horse were swallowed in its dark belly. He laughed once when he felt the boat moving, and the sound echoed in the hold.

# 49

Con shook my hand then stepped back from the doorstep and looked at the house like a painter sizing it up. 'It's been a grand home for ye.'

'It has,' Siobhán said, putting her hand on my shoulder.

'Onwards and upwards,' Con said.

Mrs Rattigan came to see them off, returned to her plain clothes. Catriona had been kissed goodbye and was next to Margaret on the back seat, my model V-2 on her legs, every suitcase and bag we own packed and stacked around them. A letter from above met me from the hospital, telling me that I had failed the promotion exam and that I was being transferred to west Cork. Superintendent Kerins told me that Casey wanted me in a dole queue, and he had to fight his superiors to even make Cork possible, especially if I wasn't going to make sense of why I wasn't where I was needed on that day of all days.

Con climbed into the passenger seat, checking his watch, then glanced over his shoulder at me and Siobhán. What he was checking the time for I don't know, since Siobhán was driving them home, sparing him the train journey he'd despaired over.

'Drive carefully, I know what you're like on the roads.'

'I'll be careful. I don't need to tell you to sit and rest. And take your medicine, we'll be back tomorrow.'

Con leaned over and beeped the horn.

'He's in a hurry for you to start campaigning.'

She smiled. 'That comes later.'

'I look forward to it. No surprise stops on the way back to me this time.'

'I might visit Rita is all. She'll be glad to see Catriona, and there's people I want to put her in touch with.'

'Bye, love. See you tomorrow.'

I kissed her and watched as she got in and turned the key, then revved the engine long and loud. Con stirred in his seat and Margaret put her hands to her head. Siobhán smiled in the wing mirror as they pulled away.

I saluted Mrs Rattigan after they took the corner. She raised a hand before going inside. I checked that I had my keys, then pulled our front door shut. I walked to the bottom of the hill, and felt well enough to go on to the station. The platform was gone from the quay, the flag gone from the co-op.

Colfer was at the hatch.

'Jim, I wasn't expecting to see you. How are you keeping?' He looked to my office, waiting for Flood to come occupy it.

'Flying it. What about you? Are you looking forward to a new sergeant?'

'Ah, I know how to deal with Flood. Some dogs just need to bark themselves out. It's his master that's tough to manage. I won't thank you for leaving me with Casey in the state he's in. Aren't you supposed to be on sick leave?'

'Sick leave. A paid suspension is what it is. I'm taking the car for a while. Our secret.'

'Of course.' He rummaged in the desk drawer and handed over the keys to the patrol car, still in the yard but due back in Enniscorthy any day. 'Will you ever tell me what happened?'

'My secret.'

I took the long way through town, driving slowly, remnants of the 27th in the windows – flags and special offers and newspaper clippings. I turned on the wipers as soon as I hit open road, drizzle filling the windscreen seconds at a time, damp all over Wexford. Young lads were pucking in fields, farmers with minds returned to work, the radio talking of Kennedy and his meeting with the new

Pope. I switched it off and rolled down the window, the rain cooling me while I made my final pilgrimage.

Overgrown hedgerow scratched at the passenger window as I parked outside the gate. The Hatten land had become Casey land – the eastern wall knocked completely and the two old sheds at the end of the house gone with it. There was a digger standing idle in the yard, next to the two yellow tractors. Across the field, a couple of workmen sheltered under a tree, eating their lunches. I raised a hand, unsure if they could see me. Shovels, pickaxes, sledgehammers and crowbars lined the front wall of the house – all those things needed to knock the past and build the future.

Little had changed inside. There were three carboard boxes on the floor, filled with clothes and bedsheets, pots and empty containers, broken picture frames, and Maura Hatten's creams and ointments. I went further than I ever had, no longer feeling like a trespasser in his home.

Dust floated in the light through the window on the landing. Thousands of particles defying gravity, circling their own galaxy. I went into the first bedroom and knew it was his. The mattress was gone from the bed, a wooden frame with broken slats and patched-up legs. A couple of my old shirts bundled in the corner. There was a painting nailed to the far wall. Some local summer scene that looked unfinished. In the darkness of Patrick's room, the near-glowing turquoise sky drew me close enough to read the inscription in the bottom corner – *New Ross, County Wexford, June 1963*. I stood back and looked it over, this document of time, drawn by an unknown hand. The month was already the past. So soon would be the year, then the decade, then the century. In no time at all, there'd be no person left to tell the story of those bright hours that Kennedy came to town. I left the painting hanging there. The stairs creaked and the banister was smooth on my palm.

I lifted a dirt-caked shovel from among the tools outside the front door and weighed it in my thin arm. My strength was coming back. I took a few steps into the grass and broke the soil with the tip of the blade, then put a boot on the step of the shovel and dug a shallow hole. Across the field, the workmen were gone. The trees shed drops of rain, and cattle in the opposite field had no interest in my ceremony. I went to my haunches and reached into my left pocket. Sean's handkerchief was worse for wear. A rag really, as Siobhán called it. I traced the flowers with my fingers, admiring them a final time, then buried it in the cool, damp earth.

# Acknowledgements

With thanks:

To my father for sharing a love of words, and my mother, for making sure we learned to use them. To my siblings, especially my brother John for his advice. To the Brosnans. To Gerry Boland, Roscommon County Council and Ryan Dennis for early support. To Brian Kirk and Andrew Hughes for valuable readings.

To Donal Ryan, Sarah Moore, Joseph O'Connor, classmates and all at Creative Writing in UL. To my friend Bob McDonald for his constant encouragement.

To the Irish Writers Centre for introducing me to Niall Williams, whose wisdom made this book possible, and to Christine Breen for welcoming me in Kiltumper.

To Vanessa Fox O'Loughlin for support and generosity. To my agent, Simon Trewin for his belief, dedication and hard work that can't be repaid. To Georgina Dent for helping along the way.

To Deirdre Nolan, publishing director at Eriu, I will always have huge gratitude, also to Lisa Gilmour, assistant editor at Eriu. To Miriam Mulcahy, for 'nodding' me in the right direction. To all at Bonnier who turned this story into a book with their skill, talent and commitment to Irish writing, in particular: Sophie Raoufi, Clare Kelly, Kevin Hawkins and Emily Peyton. To Declan Heeney, Simon Hess and Helen McKean at the brilliant Gill Hess.

To anybody who reads this book.

And above all else, to Sinéad, for everything.

# ABOUT THE AUTHOR

Neil Tully lives in Cork. He has an MA in Creative Writing from the University of Limerick.

*The Visit* is his first book.